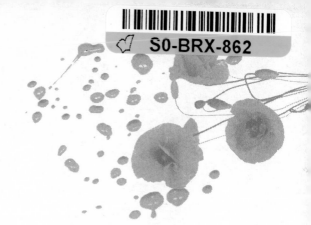

FUGUE STATE

M.C. ADAMS

Fugue State

Copyright © 2013 by M.C. Adams

Published by Cardinal Press

Cover Art: Rita Toews at Yourbookcover.com

Editor: Tamara Hart Heiner at TamaraHartHeiner.com

Visit the author at her website: mcadamsauthor.wix.com/authorpage

Join her mailing list at eepurl.com/boaY7X to receive updates on new releases!

To Will, because he supports all of my crazy ideas,
and I am forever grateful.

CHAPTER 1

Alexa DeBrow adjusted her black-and-gold brocade Valentino pencil skirt. It hung more loosely than she remembered. Easily ten pounds lighter today than she'd been nine months ago, she gathered the spare fabric in her fingers and counted down the dress sizes she had lost. *Two, one, zero.* She nodded in affirmation. *Zero seems fitting. Zero is nothing.*

The hollow words echoed in her empty head. For the first time in months, she examined the woman looking back at her in the mirror. "Hello, Alexa," she whispered aloud in an attempt to recognize her own reflection. Her cheeks had lost their fullness, yet she maintained her curves on her new slender frame.

She fastened the gold buttons on the sheer, black silk chiffon three-quarter sleeve blouse she wore over a fitted camisole. Long blonde locks contrasted with the dark chiffon. "Alexa Demure," she said, an ugly smirk marring the pretty face in the mirror. *Too attractive to be a doctor.* The words she had heard too many times to count crept into her brain. Demure was the goal. She clothed her barely bronzed skin from elbow to knee in an attempt to keep the unwanted glances at bay. Experience had taught her beauty didn't belong in medicine; it distracted intellect.

Her shoulders slumped. *Does it really matter anymore? Nothing I do will shield me from their judgment. I could attach a yellow star or a scarlet "A" to my chest and receive less public scrutiny. Everyone who watches the news or listens to gossip knows Dr. Alexa DeBrow, and their eyes follow me like shadows.* The publicity was wholly alienating. *I've lost everything that is important to me. Yes. Zero is fitting.* She took one last glance in the mirror. She tucked the loose fabric that hung around her waist into her skirt and pressed the front flat. *It's a good outfit to resign in.* She grabbed her sunglasses and headed to the car.

Exiting the driveway, her hand went to the stereo knob. She pulled away as if she'd stuck herself with a needle. *No radio. No need to catch the latest news on the Alexa DeBrow trial secondhand when I get the scoop before it hits the presses. I don't want to hear any housewives phoning in and telling disc jockeys their thoughts on why I should be tried for manslaughter or murder.* Her fingernails dug tiny crescents into the leather steering wheel. *Why listen to their mock sentencing? I'll have my verdict soon enough.*

She drove to her office at Community Northwest Hospital in silence, and in silence, the haphazard thoughts surfaced from her subconscious. She pushed the unwanted thoughts away, but it was like trying to dodge bullets. Inevitably, she took a direct hit.

She thought of Dawn and Stacey, her two closest friends in Austin for the past three years. *What are they doing now that we've lost touch? Have they moved on? Pushed my drama out of their lives? Is Dawn's divorce finalized? It was her divorce party that started everything.*

One night out with two close girlfriends turned her world upside down. She had relived the night time and again throughout the course of her trial. Now, her mind flipped through the pages of the worn memory without prompting by the police or prosecution.

Thursday, August seventeenth. The three girls went downtown to Costello's on Sixth Avenue for cocktails to celebrate Dawn's divorce. Alexa dressed as if she were in college again, clad in a scandalous, cleavage-bearing top and a mini skirt that Dawn insisted she wear. Alexa had laughed out loud at the ensemble, which was far from chic, and the girls celebrated as if it were a bachelorette party.

In hindsight, the outfit was a poor choice. Her attorney told her that a conservative jury would say she was "asking for it." She told him, "No one asks for *that.*" Too late, she realized how many of her decisions that night would be incriminating.

Alexa had two cocktails, a lemon drop, and a 007 martini. Not quite sober. Not intoxicated, either. She wasn't sure what difference it made, but the prosecutor seemed very interested in the quantity of alcohol she had consumed. She feared it was an attempt to better define her "poor character." The prosecution seemed to equate martinis with immorality.

After a few hours of dancing and karaoke, Alexa left the bar alone around 1:45 a.m. But she didn't feel alone. Music filled the air from the various bars around her, and the street still felt alive. She hummed the chorus of their finale song and pressed the unlock button on her car keypad. She heard the heavy breathing at her neck an instant before she felt the dull thud on the back of her head.

Damn, that hurt! Her small frame landed hard on the asphalt below, and she lay stunned for a moment, floating just above unconsciousness. A second, maybe two, passed before she could react. Her attacker grabbed an arm and a wad of blond hair and dragged her across the asphalt. Hairs uprooted from scalp, and skin scraped against pavement as he hauled her away from the echoes of the street.

Alexa tried to scream, but the fall had knocked the breath out of her, and the noise that came out sounded like the muffled cry of an alley cat. Strong hands grasped her shoulders and flung her body into a dark side alley. A pang of terror hit her chest as her senses returned, and a wave of nausea ran over her body as the sounds of other human beings faded away. The shadows of the alley swallowed her like a black hole, and while only a few yards from her car, the music evaporated. In another second, he flipped her thin frame over. Again, she tried to scream. The sound was the same. In response to her cry, large black hands slammed the back of her head into the ground. Her skull bounced with a thump against cobblestones. A steel-toed boot landed one swift kick to her gut, and again Alexa went breathless.

The attacker yanked her skirt up to her stomach. It was the first time she saw his face. His dark features melded into the blackness of the alley. All she could clearly make out was the glimmer of his eyes — dark brown pupils swimming in a sea of yellow. The smell of whiskey and tobacco emanated from him.

Something shiny and reflective cut through the black night. He straddled her with a knife in his hand. The blade pierced her skin in the center of her right thigh and carved up toward her hip, severing the elastic of her panties. Sharp pain swept over her like an electric shock. His hands went to his belt. While she heard his fingers work the buckle, Alexa scrambled to counterattack. Her keys remained clutched in her right hand. She adjusted the larger car key between her second and third fingers and gripped the remaining ones in her palm. The moment he looked up from his belt, Alexa jabbed the key into his left eye. She stabbed the key deep into his medial canthus, where his eye met the bridge of his nose. He let out a deep half moan.

The knife fell from his right hand and rattled on the bricks of the alley. *The knife! I must get that knife.* She scrambled to find it. Her nails scraped across the moist, muddy cobblestones, and her fingers found the cold metal blade. She wrapped her palm around the handle of her new weapon. Her attacker lunged for the knife at the same moment she attempted to strike him. He fumbled his aim. Alexa did not.

She thrust the knife into the right side of her attacker's neck. More than half of the three-inch blade was lodged in flesh. Warm, sticky blood oozed from the wound. *Venous blood.* She had plunged the knife into his right internal jugular vein. Her attacker jerked away, but Alexa reached up and gripped the handle with her other hand, strengthening her hold. She pulled the knife hard across his neck from right to left. It tore through the soft tissues of his neck, and blood began to pour out of the wound, pumping steadily. *Arterial blood.* She had severed his carotid artery. Her hands became gloved in his blood. The warm goo flowed over her body as she lay underneath him.

Unexpectedly, his fist knocked against her temple as he covered the wound on his neck with his other hand. The blow blurred her vision momentarily. His body collapsed onto hers. His face landed on her chest. Her sight cleared, and she looked into the eyes of her attacker. She saw hate in the yellow-tinged sclera of the man atop her. *Jaundice.* The tension in his brow and the twisted curl of his lips relaxed, and Alexa focused on the little brown orbs floating in yellow pools as she watched his life slip away. Then she turned her gaze away from him.

She writhed beneath him, struggling to roll the two hundred pound corpse off of her. The blood stopped oozing from his neck, and the liquid-iron odor filled her nostrils. Fighting fatigue, she staggered to her knees and pushed her skirt back into place. She felt woozy. Sick. The stench of his blood stifled her breath. The world spun, and she lurched for the building next to her.

Trembling steps led her out of the alley and into the light and liveliness of the street. She looked back at the body, but it was too dark to see him. She couldn't help but think if it were *her* body left in that alley, no one would discover it anytime soon.

Music flooded out of a nearby nightclub. She followed the sound and met a bouncer just inside the door. She peered over his shoulder and saw a dive bar with an odd crowd. People clad in all black with colored hair and multiple piercings shuffled toward the bar. Flamboyant tattoos covered the skin of dancing bodies, and there were a few twenty-somethings dressed as vampires sporting fangs.

The bouncer didn't seem startled by Alexa's blood-soaked appearance. Maybe he thought she was in costume and would be followed by a gray-skinned zombie date. Still heaving oxygen in gasps, she tried to yell, "Call the police!" But it came out breathy and indistinguishable. She pressed the palms of her hands to her ears and tried to speak over the loud music playing inside. The pale, heavyset man just stared at her, his expression behind the braided beard and pierced nasal septum conveying disinterest.

Breathe, Lex. "Call the police," she stated, her words clearer now.

His eyes softened. He blinked twice and leaned closer to Alexa, as if straining to hear her. "What did you say?" he asked. "I -I can't hear you."

Exasperated, she snapped. The unbearable music that drowned out her words was a song from a nineties band. Nine Inch Nails, "I Want to Fuck you Like an Animal." The irony of the lyrics sent her over the edge. Hot angry tears formed in her eyes and frustration ripped through her body. "Turn off the music!" she screamed at the bouncer, her face heaving toward his.

His brow furrowed, and for an instant his face looked like a fuming bull with that ring in his nose. Alexa cleared her throat and said, more calmly, "Call the police."

He nodded, then turned away from her, shaking his head side to side as if in a state of disbelief while reaching for the phone.

Alexa sank into the brick wall behind her. She couldn't

control her quivering body as she collapsed downward and crumpled to the floor. Her rear stung when it smacked against the cold concrete. She pulled her knees up to her chest and curled into a ball, careful to adjust her skirt and legs to cover her exposed crotch, painfully aware that her torn panties were still lying in the alley. She sat in a daze, head throbbing, trembling until the police arrived. Her mind raced and was blank at the same time, until reality slipped away from her.

Alexa failed to overhear the bouncer's conversation with the police dispatcher. But the recording played at her trial. The judgment in the bouncer's voice echoed in the courtroom, cold and real. "Yeah, I think I got a hooker here. She looks pretty beat up — like she's been in a fight or something. I don't know, maybe she pissed off her pimp."

When the audio paused, she didn't have to look at the jury's faces. She could feel their scornful glances burning into her skull. If only she had heard him speak with the police, she would have demanded a rebuttal. But it was too late. It was too late to undo any of the mistakes she had made regarding the incident.

CHAPTER 2

Alexa turned into the physician's parking garage, her left eye twitching from chronic sleep deprivation. She popped open a canned energy drink from the glove box and quickly slurped it down. *Don't look tired or depressed. Don't let them see the hurt. Remember, you're resigning, so they don't fire you from the career you've worked your life to achieve.*

As a neuroradiologist, Alexa interpreted advanced imaging studies of the brain and spine. She evaluated patients with neurological problems such as seizures, brain tumors, and trauma. She took pride in her expertise, which made quitting even more difficult. Her own lackluster attitude was more than she could tolerate. *Relax, Lex. It's just one more goodbye. Goodbyes are a cakewalk these days.*

Too-old-and-stubborn-to-ever-retire Norma Pate served as the garage attendant. Norma's eyebrows rose nearly up to her hairline when Alexa's Mercedes SLK pulled up next to her. "Dr. DeBrow," Norma said with a tone of condescension. "I didn't think you were with us anymore. I thought you were . . . locked up somewhere."

Ah, Norma, you old bat, you must be the welcome party. Alexa wiped the go-to-Hell look from her face and replaced it with a look of complacency, tightly pressed lips with upturned corners. "I'm afraid you're mistaken. I'm out on bail," Alexa said, handing out her parking pass.

The old bat frowned so heavily her seventy-two-year-old face could have passed for the remnants of an Egyptian mummy. "Humph," she fumed. Her eyes scanned the permit through her developing cataract clouds, and she thrust it back in Alexa's direction. Alexa's eyes met the old woman's testy glance, and she fought the urge to speed away in contempt.

Now at the height of her trial, the public appearance made her stomach flip-flop. As she pulled into an empty space, she used the last swallow of the highly caffeinated beverage to wash down a double dose of antacids. She addressed the rumbling in her midsection. *Sorry, can't avoid the hospital today.* She'd tried to avoid the leering glances of her peers since the trial began. Five months ago, she emptied her office and lived as a recluse, interpreting the overnight emergency department studies from a computer system she had set up in her home. But the stress of the trial had corrupted her abilities, and she was no longer fit to read anyone's MRI.

She refrained from removing her Burberry aviator sunglasses as she walked through the shadows of the parking garage. *Maybe I should leave them on. Why not shield myself from their scrutiny?* She hesitated when she got to the revolving door and slowly pushed the aviators to the top of her head. *Always a martyr. Let them look.*

She squared her chin and entered the hospital corridors with a glassy glare as patients, employees, and visitors stared her down. Eyes rose from all directions and followed her intently when they met her face. People whispered. Someone pointed. One man chuckled. She blinked and bore her look of complacency and hoped her face didn't show the pain she carried with her every step. She made her way to the radiology department, and to Dr. Jimmy Thornton's door. Jimmy, the youngest senior partner in her radiology practice, served as her immediate supervisor. Although they spoke often over the years, she never really understood his character. At times, the arrogance he displayed was intolerable. His ego dominated both his short stature and his mid-gut paunch. He seemed to have a need to belittle those around him in order to feel less mediocre.

Jimmy's self-centered nature stopped with Alexa. He seemed to have a genuine interest in her. He asked questions about her personal life and listened carefully to her stories. He always left a simple, tasteful card — nothing lewd or disgraceful — on her desk on her birthday. She tried to forgive his many faults for that reason. But in the end, she didn't like him.

Jimmy had left his door open. *He's expecting me.* The click-clack of her heels on the linoleum must have stirred him. Jimmy's head popped out of the doorway, and he invited her in. "Ah, Alexa. It's good to see you."

She winced at the trepidation in his voice and found the lighthearted façade reproachable. Everyone at the office must have known this day was coming. She'd asked to meet with him at the lunch hour, knowing the ancillary staff would be gossiping in the break room and swapping their desserts, so she wouldn't have to face them when she walked in. They were her coworkers, people she'd known well and whose eyes she couldn't bear.

"How are you holding up?" Jimmy asked, taking a seat. It felt good to think for a moment that someone still cared about her well-being, even if his words were merely a polite banality.

"I'm fine, Jimmy. Thanks for asking," she lied. She wasn't fine, and they both knew it. If she were fine, she would be working her usual daytime hours, not spending her days in a courtroom while struggling to interpret a few MRIs at night.

"How's the trial going?" Thornton asked and motioned toward another chair. The words fell from his lips slowly, as if treading lightly on the subject.

She hesitated before she sat. Today was the only day all week she wasn't scheduled to be in the courtroom. *Please don't make me talk about the trial.*

"Everything's fine."

"Good, very good. We look forward to having you back full-time again. Isn't that why you wanted to meet with me? That voicemail sounded urgent." His cheery expression faded and little frown lines settled in around his mouth.

She raised an eyebrow, and a small sigh escaped. *Why make this difficult? You know why I'm here.* He knew the stress was getting to her, and her work was suffering. *The urgent voicemail.* She scolded herself. *I'm going to spare you the details of that night. The night I let that word slip out.* She shuddered. Two nights ago, after a long day in court, Alexa tried to get some work done reading MRIs at home. With the help of speech recognition software, the word she'd spoken into the microphone instantly appeared on her computer monitor. She stared at the word in incredulity. She had meant to say the word *myelogram*, a follow-up procedure she was recommending on a postoperative spine patient. Instead, the word she saw on the computer screen was *murder*. The horror.

She wanted to blame it on the late night, the stress of the trial, the combination of alternating sleeping pills with caffeine pills and the other stimulants on which she relied in an attempt to maintain a steady balance of sleep and wakefulness. No. She had cracked under the pressure. After deleting the word one letter at a time, she called Jimmy and left a message requesting that he meet with her.

"You know I'm not coming back, Jimmy. You know that's why I'm here."

"Alexa, you just need more time. You...You'll be able to come back. Perhaps after the trial is over. You can still make partner next year. You need more time, that's all."

Don't fight me, Jimmy. "I can't do it anymore." She tried to sound strong and unwavering, but the abrupt change in the pitch of her voice conveyed her apprehension.

"Is it the nightmares?" he pressed.

Damn. My loose lips have said too much. The vivid nightmares she'd been having since the incident were so frequent, so commonplace in her daily routine — occurring nearly every time she closed her eyes — that sometimes she doubted she was ever asleep to begin with. It slipped out once to Jimmy in passing. She had mentioned them indifferently, as if they were discussing the weather, and hadn't expected him to remember it. But of course, Jimmy Thornton would remember that moment.

"You're still having the nightmares?" He stood abruptly, his questions becoming louder and more assertive.

Are you actually concerned?

He paced beside her now, his words and footsteps quickening. Her hand covered the queasy sensation developing in her stomach. Having put on such a strong front for so long, it pained her to acknowledge the nightmares to others.

Every night, when she drifted into sleep, the dark man with the yellow eyes crept into her dreams. Every slumber, he attacked. Sometimes he raped her. Sometimes he maimed her. Sometimes he killed her. Although unsuccessful in life, he had great success in the afterlife. *He* was the victor now.

"Yes, Jimmy. I'm still having the nightmares." Her voice quivered. The nightmares became insomnia and spurred the sleeping pills. Alexa quickly tallied last night's concoction — one-hundred milligrams Benadryl, twenty-five milligrams Phenergan, and a shot of NyQuil for good measure. She experimented with a variety of mild sedatives, hoping not to become addicted to any one substance.

Jimmy stood behind her now, his hand dropping onto her shoulder like so many times before. He'd done this frequently in the three years they worked together. She hated that it had taken her nearly a year to realize his predominant goal was to place himself above and behind her so he could gaze down her shirt. He paused in that location, and she felt his eyes drift to her neckline. But there was nothing for him to see from his familiar vantage point. *You pervert.* She seethed. *I've buttoned my blouse clear to the chin today.*

His hand fell to his side, and his words turned firm. "What you need, Alexa, is a gun. Get yourself a handgun, and learn how to use it. Go to a shooting range and shoot it often." His advice turned fatherly now. "A gun buys you peace of mind. Buy a gun. Love your gun, use your gun, and you won't be scared of that son-of-a-bitch anymore."

She nodded, but his words were slow to sink in. In spite of the antacids, the sour burn in her belly progressed, and she pushed her fist into her midsection, trying to force it away.

There were other things Jimmy Thornton said. She didn't absorb them all. When it was clear that their conversation was coming to a close, Alexa stood. She reached out to shake his hand, but he stepped in for a hug. It was awkward, but it felt good to feel the arms of a man — even this man. The embrace lasted too long, and she squirmed away from his grasp. His eyes met hers; there was longing in them. *Maybe that look is more than lust. Maybe a part of him is in love with me.* With that thought, she told him goodbye.

Her meeting had lasted longer than she expected, and the ancillary staff was trickling in from their lunch breaks. She avoided their glances and hurried out the door, leaving the Radiology department for good.

CHAPTER 3

On her way out of the hospital, Alexa paused outside of the emergency department while a young man in his twenties lying on a gurney rolled by. The man wore a c-collar, and his face was speckled with blood. Two uniformed male police officers accompanied him; a red-headed officer with a face like a horse and a tall, thin, slightly balding man. These were the same officers dispatched the night of the incident. The horse-faced man had talked with the bouncer that night, and they both thought Alexa was a prostitute. He'd seemed amused by her story, treating her situation with a subtle sense of humor rather than the gravity she demanded. *An ass with an ass' face, how fitting.* She cast a steaming glare at the men, and then turned her head before they could notice her.

The horse-faced man's questions had only stopped when the detective arrived. Her thoughts went to Detective Kevin Marcum, the slightly overweight and average-height man in his early forties, who began interrogating her that night after a brief introduction. She began telling him her story, but he didn't want a narrative, only the answers to his questions. "Where were you leaving? Where were you headed?" He wanted to know the timing of the night's events. He asked specifics about the attack. "Where did the knife come from? Who stabbed first? When and how did you gain control of the knife? How were you able to stab your attacker?" He seemed particularly intrigued by Alexa's ability to slit Jamar's throat.

"Miss DeBrow, most victims aren't capable of making such calculated moves when facing an attacker. The fact that you were able to cut through your attacker's carotid artery with such precision speaks volumes. I can't help but think that you are either well-trained with a knife, or you've done this before." She shrugged at what seemed like an empty comment. But his words would come back to haunt her. Now she realized it was an accusation rather than an intrigue.

Her knowledge of anatomy directed her aim that night. Perhaps she should have been clearer about that to begin with. Instead, her precision with the knife led Marcum to think that Alexa was not the victim she claimed to be, and that she killed on purpose. He indicted her on multiple weak charges of criminal homicide against her attacker, Jamar Reading, a forty-year-old African American who worked at a fish market for the four months preceding his death.

Travis County police, led by Marcum's investigation, deemed Jamar's death an unreasonable use of force following his attempt of forcible rape. Detective Marcum assumed the media spotlight and worked closely with the prosecution. He seemed determined to hold her accountable.

Alexa hurried past the ER before the horse-faced man

could recognize her, although it seemed very unlikely he would find any resemblance between the polished young lady before him and the blood-covered *hooker* he met on the street that fateful night.

She stopped off at the lab just down the hall to pick up her second set of blood work. Alexa glanced at the paperwork. *Hepatitis C: Negative.*

Jamar's blood was tainted with hepatitis C, a consequence of a lifetime of dabbling in IV drug usage that produced his jaundice eyes. His blood had mingled with hers via the cut on her thigh. She exhaled; relieved she wouldn't acquire his yellow-tinged sclera.

Exiting the garage, Alexa passed by Norma Pate once more. Nastiness still lurked in the old woman's eyes when she grasped Alexa's hand along with the parking pass she held. "Hand is looking bare without that rock on it." Norma smiled to herself.

Alexa winced at the cutting words and tugged her fingers away. She glanced at her bare left hand, and her heart yearned for Britt. She would never be Mrs. Britt Anderson. She had given back the engagement ring of her estranged fiancée a few months into the trial.

Alexa flashed a wicked smirk at Norma and forced a quick lie. "I'll be back by next week, Norma. See. You. Next. Tuesday." She formed the last four words individually, hoping her listener would spell out their clandestine meaning. With a sly wave, Alexa drove away. The gawking face in the rearview mirror didn't appear to catch the dig. *Damn.*

Pulling out of the garage, she received a text message

from her attorney updating her on tomorrow's court time. She would meet with her lawyer, Jacob Appleby, at seven-forty a.m. with an eight-fifteen a.m. court time. A second text immediately followed.

"Get some sleep. Don't look so tired."

Alexa frowned. *Sounds like a vodka martini with a double dose of Unisom kind of night.* She drove past a sign on an unfamiliar building that read "Otter Creek Shooting Range." Without even realizing she was changing her plans, Alexa turned off the street and pulled into the barren gravel parking lot.

She didn't know why she stopped. She'd been living in a daze for the past few months — a side effect of chronic sleep deprivation. The decision seemed hidden within her subconscious. Then Jimmy Thornton's words flooded her head. *A gun buys peace of mind.* She looked again at the sign on the building, reading the words slowly and out loud this time. "Otter Creek Shooting Range." *I'm at a shooting range. Yes. I'm going to buy a gun.*

The dimly lit building took Alexa by surprise. *Shooting firearms in here can't be safe.* The gray-haired man who sat behind the counter bore a *Semper Fi* tattoo on his left forearm that peeked from beneath the rolled sleeves of his plaid button-up. A half-snuffed cigar bobbed in his mouth.

Alexa eyed the gruff salesman with a moment of hesitation. He pulled the unlit cigar from his mouth and stood up straight.

"Can I help you, Miss? This here's my place. Joe Reynolds at your service. Most folks just call me Smokey Joe, suits me fine."

Alexa approached the counter. An array of handguns filled the glass case under the man's resting elbow. Her gaze scanned the case slowly, and then moved to the rifles on the wall behind Smokey Joe. Her eyes finally met his. "I want a gun."

"A gun to shoot, or a gun to buy?" asked Joe, his bright eyes beaming now. He motioned to the double doors with plexiglass inserts behind him, and she peered at the indoor shooting range in the adjacent room.

"Both," she replied.

Joe took her small hands in his and examined them. His gentle touch relieved the lasting sting of Norma's grasp. Within moments, he had a selection of half a dozen handguns for her to try.

Joe gave her a forty-five-minute lecture about the six guns he had selected for her before he escorted her into the shooting range in the back. He briefed her on his extensive military training. She took comfort in his expertise. The more he explained, the more she wanted to know. *Who'd have thought there was so much to learn about a handgun?*

Alexa's shooting lesson took another hour and a half, and most of that time, Joe left the front counter unmanned.

He picked out a simple target for her — the silhouette of a human figure. There was a bull's-eye on the chest over the heart, and another in the center of the head. She aimed for the target on the head. She concentrated on her aim and the stillness of her hands, and strove for both accuracy and precision with each squeeze of the trigger. Precision came first, which Joe applauded. She managed to hit the target just a few inches to the left of center every time. He said precision was much more difficult to learn, and a careful adjustment in her technique would easily improve her accuracy. Joe was right. She had made several perfect shots by the time she finished her first lesson.

"You've got a knack for weaponry, pretty lady," he complimented and stretched out his hand.

"Thank you." Alexa blushed. "Truly, thank you." She reached out to shake his hand, taking his hand in both of hers. "Call me Alexa, Please."

She took an instant liking to Joe, and she happily accepted his invite to meet again for another lesson at the end of the week. Texas didn't require a waiting period, and Alexa left with a .38 caliber snub-nosed revolver with a two-inch barrel. A common choice of handgun for a female; it wasn't too bulky to fit in her Fendi handbag.

The door chimed as Alexa walked out, leaving Smokey Joe alone behind the counter to straighten up and lock the door. He licked his lips. He liked the look of his young female client — long lean legs and perfectly manicured hands; it was a nice change of scenery. He wished he'd bothered to wash the tobacco spit from his shirt collar before they'd met. Her determination was striking; her face memorable. He had recognized that pretty face from the television at first glance, but there was something more. The thought rolled around in his head the way an empty beer can would in the back of his truck. The trepidation in her voice. The way she hesitated. *She's afraid. Somebody hurt that girl. She let her guard down when she thought I wasn't looking, and I saw her fear.*

She had the same wide-eyed stare Laura Beth had the night I hit her. The face that haunted him flashed in his mind, and he recalled the slap that caused her head to spin all the way around before her body hit the ground. A chill ran over him that left his hand shaky, so he reached for the flask he kept under the counter. The doctor called it post-traumatic stress disorder due to the war that led him to hit his wife. Joe called the monster inside his soul Hyde. *Good thing she left me. I'm afraid I'd have killed her.* Joe reached for the remote to turn off the muted television monitor that hung high on the wall in the corner of the shop. Channel five news mentioned updates on Alexa's case, and her picture appeared on the screen. Joe nodded to himself. *Yep that's the one.* He muttered aloud to the reporter covering the story. "Somebody hurt that girl." He flicked the television off and spit tobacco into the trashcan, with another stray drop landing on his shirt collar.

CHAPTER 4

After leaving Smokey Joe, Alexa still managed an hour of kickboxing before night fell. Physical exhaustion helped her sleep. She followed the workout with a combination of sleeping aids, which included Benadryl, propanolol, and an Ambien. After a couple of restless hours, she slept.

That night, the yellow-eyed man crept into her dreams. He entered through her bedroom window, breaking the glass with an axe. Alexa instinctively rolled underneath the bed and lay there, paralyzed. Her heart beat rhythmically, fast and hard, while the axe hacked away at the bed sheets and the bed frame overhead until she could see the glow of his yellow eyes through the gaping hole above. Then he reached underneath and yanked her from her hiding place by her ankles. With the axe, he hacked at her extremities, beginning distally with her fingers and toes, and moving proximally toward her shoulders and thighs.

She awoke with tightness in her throat, and her hand reached for the source of the pain. *My screams woke me.*

The clock read 4:09 a.m. *Too close to court time for any*

more meds. She rolled out of the covers, laced up her running shoes, and ran in the cold night air until the sun rose. The coolness of the air felt good on her tight throat, but she worked to breathe. Her chest moved in spasms as she gasped for breath. She returned to her apartment in a cold sweat, trembling from her lack of sleep. After a hot shower, she prepared for her trial. She stepped into a navy skirt and cream-colored silk button-up blouse. Both colors conveyed innocence, according to Appleby. She wrapped herself in that small bit of hope, while her insides felt numb. Concealer and a brightening serum under her eyes helped relieve the discoloration of chronic fatigue. Eyeliner and mascara wakened her tired eyes, and a pink-hued blush returned life to her hollow cheeks. The makeup helped, but it couldn't stop her constant eye twitching. Alexa sighed as she walked to Appleby's private car outside.

Jacob Appleby's initial words were uplifting. "The prosecution's attempt to brand you a serial killer won't pan out."

Pictures of a dead nineteen-year-old male, gagged with wrists bound, naked in a ditch by the railroad tracks flooded her mind. His throat had also been slit with a knife ten months earlier, and the prosecution tried to link Alexa to the murder. The allegation seemed fueled by Marcum's insight on Alexa's knife skills. He had an astounding influence on the prosecution. Using various tactics to describe Alexa as a doctor by day, streetwalker by night, the prosecution accused her of living a double life, similar to the "Craigslist Killer." They presented her as a woman veiled in a respectable and personable professional front, who secretly perused the streets of Austin after hours looking for lone men to target for acts of sex and violence. *Absurd*. But once the seed was planted in the minds of the doe-eyed jury, convincing them otherwise proved difficult.

"There's no supporting evidence to tie you to the murder of anyone other than Jamar. I had the accusation stricken from the court's record. Not only is that homicide a separate charge, those allegations are purely circumstantial."

Her shoulders slumped. "But the prosecution's speculation left quite an impact in the courtroom." Not only did the slander ignite curiosity in the jurors' golf-ball-sized eyes, the media clung to the accusations. A local newspaper labeled Alexa a "Female Physician Femme Fatale." The questions and comments from friends and family that followed the allegations were heart wrenching. She shuddered.

Appleby raised an eyebrow and pushed forward. "Your character witnesses have helped. I don't think the jury is convinced you set out that night with the intent to slay anyone."

Yes. The character witnesses. The friends and family who took the stand on my behalf, and the stress of the media spotlight that severed the ties between us. Her eyebrows rumpled in frustration. *They gave their testimonies. Then they disappeared from the courtroom.* Her stomach churned thinking of the row that would be left empty behind her today. Could she blame them? The trial was dreadful. Even her Texas-native parents stopped going to the courthouse after receiving death threats that her mother couldn't handle. Alexa would skip her own trial if it were possible. Yet, she did blame them.

He continued, "I think murder is off the plate." His words jarred her back to reality. "There are still charges of manslaughter and criminally negligent homicide to deal with."

"Yes. We still have those." Sarcasm seeped from her pores. *Why must there be so many different words for kill?* Much of the publicity the trial generated revolved around the definition of homicide in the Texas legal system, with variations spanning from capital murder to forms of imperfect self-defense, with or without adequate provocation. She frowned at the ugly words she heard so regularly and wondered how such terms came about.

Alexa rolled her shoulders in tight circles in an attempt to break the mounting tension. Although Appleby touted good news, she still feared the jury's critique of her character. *I've seen enough scowls in that pulpit to know that the saints think I'm a sinner.* Her eyes flashed at Appleby.

"I'm relying on you to create *a shadow of a doubt* in the jurors' minds. Convince them it wasn't unnecessary force." It had seemed like a daunting task for so long, but Appleby had made serious ground recently.

"Relax. It'll all be over soon enough." His lips pressed into a tight line, and he turned his glance to the window.

Walking into the courtroom, Alexa's eyes scanned the audience. Her eyes glided across a haggard middle-aged woman with stringy black and gray hairs. She recognized this woman as the mother of Jamar's youngest child. According to Appleby, Jamar had fathered two children with different mothers. One child was ten years old and shuffled between the mother and other family members. The older child was an adult son serving time in prison. Jamar also had a soft criminal record, in and out of jail since he was twenty. He had two counts of rape against him — but the most recent was over a decade ago. He had a few arrests for various drug charges, and one count of child molestation. Jamar had lived alone and never married. The woman didn't seem to notice Alexa walk in.

Alexa bit the inside of her lip as she took her seat in the front. She stole a glance at the jury, trying not to stare; she yearned to know their thoughts. Appleby had warned her not to make too much eye contact with them. He wanted the facts to speak for themselves. He was afraid they would be distracted by her looks and develop their own preconceived notions about her character. She had involuntarily made so many mistakes throughout the process. She turned away from the jury and considered adding "too much eye-contact" to her list of faults.

She went over the list of errors she had created in her mind. *That scandalous outfit that led both the bouncer and the police to think me a prostitute — bad idea.* She winced. *Don't forget the cocktails that left my blood alcohol level at point oh-six, not far below the legal driving limit of point oh-eight.* She rolled her eyes to herself as the voice in her head mocked the legal limit. *I'm a whore and a lush. Check. Next? Oh, yes. Too deliberate with the knife when I turned on Jamar.* According to the prosecution and Detective Marcum, a victim is typically much more precarious with their counter attack, stabbing away haphazardly without thought or recourse. They deemed her use of the knife "an unjustified use of force" in comparison to the superficial cut Jamar had made on her thigh. *Finally, the first words the bouncer heard from her were, "Turn off the music."* The grimaces on the juror's faces revealed their dismay. She didn't sound like a victim to them, and Alexa didn't know how to convey innocence. She behaved defensively and sometimes defiantly; Appleby kept her off the stand whenever possible.

She wanted to tell them how painful the song lyrics were in her head, how those words tortured her even after her attacker lay dead. She wanted to remind them Jamar would have left her dead body in that alley. She fidgeted in her seat with frustration. *Who knows what other mistakes I've made?*

The prosecutor stood. "I call Alexa DeBrow to the stand."

Her toes curled in her designer heels. She was expecting deliberations, not more questioning. *Whatever is coming, I'm not ready for it.* Reluctant to stand, she turned to Appleby in desperation. He held a blank expression. Having faltered time and again on the stand, she relied heavily on his coaching. With unexpected questioning, she feared another failure. Her nervousness could be misconstrued as guilt, while her attempt to defend herself came off as arrogance. She also feared the judge didn't like her. He told her she had "an authoritative attitude that would not be tolerated in his courtroom" when she challenged the prosecutions questions. *Challenged the questions? She twists my words in a manner that changes their meaning.* Alexa had argued over the prosecutor's use of the word drunk.

"How drunk were you that night, Miss DeBrow?"

"I wasn't drunk."

"So you didn't have anything to drink?"

"I had two martinis."

"If you had two martinis, you weren't sober. Agreed?"

"I had two martinis." She said each word more firmly than before.

"Were you sober? Yes or no?"

"I had two martinis. That is the only answer you get." She had raised her voice.

The judge banged her gavel and scolded Alexa's behavior.

His reproach sparked a silent fury.

Alexa's feet marched toward the stand, tension mounting within her subconscious. *How am I supposed to behave? The fact that I am on trial for killing my attacker is ludicrous!*

As she took her seat at the front of the courtroom, she flattened the front of her Emilio Pucci skirt.

"Dr. DeBrow, I'd like to remind you that you are under oath," the prosecutor stated.

Alexa's eyelids fluttered in a state of disbelief. *She said Dr. DeBrow — not Miss DeBrow, like every other day in court.* She was startled to hear her own professional title, but only for a moment before she felt more at ease. *Perhaps this new gesture is a sign of good faith that they are preparing to admit defeat?* She'd wanted to request the judge that she be addressed as Dr. DeBrow because she thought her title would help to portray her as a more debonair and intellectual persona, further separating her from the role of a prostitute that the prosecution had contrived. However, when the judge stated Alexa conveyed an air of authority, she had decided not to ask. She adjusted her posture and sat more upright as the prosecutor began.

The prosecutor was a dark-haired, older lady with oversized glasses. She shuffled through her paperwork as she addressed Alexa. "Your title as neuroradiologist has required extensive training, Doctor. Four years of college — at Dartmouth, nonetheless, followed by four years of medical school — where, I see you graduated at the top of your class." The woman forged a counterfeit smile, before her eyes returned to the paper. "Then a year of internship in general surgery at the University of Texas, Southwestern, followed by four additional years of radiology residency there. You also completed a year of subspecialty training with a neuroradiology fellowship at Vanderbilt. Very impressive, Dr. DeBrow."

Alexa's face grew warm. It felt good to have her positive attributes publicly acknowledged after all the negativity. The words created hope that the charges might be dropped, and she could return to being a respectable citizen again.

But something in that woman's eyes said otherwise. Something about the prosecutor's sharp features and pursed lips said she was hiding something up her sleeve. Alexa's optimism wilted beneath the woman's gaze. How *could* she trust someone named Janice Finkle? How could she trust a woman with scattered gray hairs that she left uncolored, and scuffed up shoes that were obviously too big? No. She would not trust the prosecution. *Janice Finkle would probably ask for me to be stoned to death if it were legal.*

Ms. Finkle went on to list a series of medical board examinations that Alexa had passed, and additional training with competency exams and continuing medical education requirements. Finally, she mentioned more simple hospital training requirements, including basic life support and advanced cardiac life support, both of which required yearly certification, for which Alexa had been certified for over a decade.

Finkle concentrated on Alexa's brief surgical training. "Dr. DeBrow, I think we should all take comfort knowing someone with such vast medical training was present for Jamar Reading the night of August seventeenth. Dr. DeBrow, with a year of general surgery experience, can you tell us what a physician should do when they encounter a rapid arterial bleed?" The words exited her lips with a hiss.

The question was as pointed as Finkle's chin, and Alexa stole a quick glance at the jury. A dozen eyes stared at her quizzically.

Finkle continued, quoting an excerpt from Alexa's initial police statement. "'The blood spurted rapidly from his carotid, and he bled to death on top of me.'" Finkle repeated her question. "Now, Dr. DeBrow, given your medical expertise, I would like your *medical* opinion. Can you tell the court what a physician *should* do when they encounter an arterial bleed?"

A gasp slipped past her lips. *They expected me to save that brute!* Anger surged through her veins. Her jaw locked tight, afraid her words would incriminate herself. *I killed that monster!* she screamed in her head. *My victory should be applauded! I was supposed to die that night!* How she longed for someone to tell her they were glad that she killed him — glad because it meant she was the one who got to walk away that night. Glad that Jamar Reading had one less victim.

She would have to keep waiting to hear those words. No one had spoken them yet, and she doubted she would hear them today. She clenched her jaw, fearing her lips would incriminate her.

The prosecutor pushed forward with her attempt to crack Alexa. She referenced portions of the modern-day Hippocratic Oath that Alexa had sworn out loud as a medical student over decade ago, along with several statements issued by the hospital where she had been employed until yesterday that discussed the character and expectations of their physicians.

Alexa's hands balled into fists. *How can they do this to me? How can they hold my medical training against me? Did they really expect me save that bastard?* She glared at Appleby in a state of fury. They weren't ready for this. She wasn't prepared for this line of questioning. They needed a plan. She needed coaching. She needed to vomit. Her mind swam, her thoughts racing.

Appleby's eyes rested on his Blackberry, apparently lost in some other project.

The prosecutor asked more deliberately now. "You were taught to heal the sick and save lives. Dr. DeBrow, why should we expect any less of you when Jamar Reading's life was at stake?" Her condemnatory tone made the veins in Alexa's throat throb. "Was it because he was a *black man?* Is that why you chose to let him bleed to death in the alley?"

Now you're calling me a racist? The media will love this. News reporters had successfully twisted her story into a racial conflict that highlighted the disparities between upper- and lower-class Americans. Both issues had gained attention of left-wing radicals who criticized Alexa under the spotlight of the television cameras.

"What's the first rule when dealing with an arterial bleed, Dr. DeBrow?"

Hold pressure. The words echoed in her head.

Finkle continued through narrowed eyes. "How is it that someone with such advanced training and education is incapable of carrying out the most basic medical treatment strategies? Why didn't you hold pressure on Jamar's gaping wound, Doctor? It's your responsibility as a physician, Dr. DeBrow. Why did you let Jamar die when you alone were capable of saving him?" Her accusatory voice echoed through the courtroom.

Alexa sat, silently appalled.

Why is Appleby still enthralled with his Blackberry? She really needed him now. She stared him down while screaming *Jacob!* in her head over and over.

"Dr. DeBrow?" asked the prosecution.

She froze.

"Miss DeBrow, answer Ms. Finkle's question." It was the judge now.

But Alexa wouldn't answer. She gritted her teeth and shook her head slightly back and forth. *No. Not going to hang myself on your questions.* She needed coaching. *They shouldn't be asking this of me. Why would I save him? Don't they know I wanted him dead?*

Appleby's head bobbed up from the Blackberry, and he seemed aware of what was happening in the courtroom. "I'd like to call for a recess in regards to the new line of questioning on my client."

Finally!

Nods exchanged between the judge and prosecution. The judge banged the gavel. Alexa was afraid to move. Appleby had to walk to the front of the room and take her by the arm to coax her from her chair.

CHAPTER 5

Hold pressure. Hold pressure.

The words echoed in her brain. Of course Alexa would hold pressure if a patient's life were at stake. If it had been a family member, a friend, a stranger in distress, she would have stepped up to help them. But it wasn't a patient that she found in the alley that night; it wasn't even a human being she'd encountered. It was a monster. Jamar Reading was a monster. As he smashed her head against the alley cobblestones, Alexa had only one thought on her mind — not to escape, but to *kill* the man who hurt her. She was afraid to speak on the stand, fearing those words might escape her lips, and she would condemn herself.

The idea that she would ever try to save him was outlandish. *Why would anyone try to save a monster?* She left the courtroom disheartened and disheveled.

Appleby escorted her into the hallway. She caught Jimmy Thornton's glance as she exited the courtroom. She hadn't noticed him in the audience. She turned away from him trying to avoid his questioning stare. Thankfully,

Appleby tugged her aside.

"Try to relax, Miss DeBrow. This is her attempt to try you for criminally negligent homicide; it's a step down from manslaughter. Take comfort in that." He sat her on a bench far away from the crowd while he paced a few steps away and made calls on his Blackberry.

Too flustered to relax, her mind raced. *Why is Jimmy here?* Jimmy Thornton was more intimately involved in the ordeal than Alexa cared to admit. He had been there the night of the incident. After she had spoken with the police that night and given her statement to detective Marcum, the detective had accompanied Alexa in the ambulance to the hospital so she could have her injuries evaluated. She hadn't known which hospital to choose. She wanted to go somewhere where no one would know her, but she had so many connections in the medical field that any decision risked stumbling into someone she knew. She chose St. Joseph's Hospital on the east side of town. It was a small private hospital near the Country Club, and the farthest option she knew from Community Northwest.

Nonetheless, when a physician arrived at the hospital emergency room in the middle of the night covered in blood, it made quite an impression, and word got around. One doc called another, and it wasn't long before Jimmy Thornton showed up at the hospital.

So much for HIPAA, Alexa thought when she saw him. The Health Insurance Portability and Accountability Act legally required confidentiality between a patient and their healthcare provider. It had been thrown out the window in her case.

Seeing Jimmy outside the courtroom brought on another

flashback of the night's events. She relived the moment he had walked into her hospital room. She was alone. No family. No friends. No one to comfort her during her time of distress. She cringed with embarrassment, knowing how it must have looked to Jimmy. She hadn't called anyone because she wasn't ready to explain the situation.

Jimmy scanned her up and down, fumbling for an explanation for his arrival. "Jeb Gunderson, one of the ER docs, told me you were pretty banged up and a-a-lone. I, um, I wasn't sure if you needed something." He didn't ask her what happened. *Yes, word got around, indeed.*

"I have some stitches in my left thigh, and in the back of my head. I'll be fine, Jimmy."

He frowned as if unsatisfied with her response.

She continued, "They made me get a head CT." He raised a questioning eyebrow. Alexa shrugged. "They said if I had the CT, they would let me sleep." She had initially declined the head CT, deciding for herself she had suffered a concussion, and doubting she had suffered any treatable head injury. She had not wanted the unnecessary radiation that accompanied the scan, but the neurologist who examined her required continuous, in-hospital monitoring for forty-eight hours if she refused the study. That meant no sleep, and Alexa's tired body begged for rest.

"Can I see your CT?" Jimmy asked. He shared her background in neuroradiology.

She nodded and waved him out of the room. Her head ached, and she rolled over on her side and closed her eyes in an attempt to shut out the pain. She thought about what her head CT might reveal, carefully weighing the possibilities.

She stretched out the hand tethered to the IV, and her fingers moved over the focus of pain in the back of her head. *I could have a skull fracture — perhaps one of the parietal or occipital bones.* She ran her hand over a tender lump near her hairline, a hematoma. She felt the prickly sutures the ER doc used to unite the scalp laceration. *The bones don't feel displaced.*

She contemplated the intracranial injuries she could have sustained. *I could have a head bleed.* She scrutinized her risks for an intracranial hemorrhage. An epidural bleed occurred just deep to the skull and above the thick meningeal covering that surrounded the brain. But epidural blood most commonly accompanied skull fractures on the side of the head where the middle meningeal artery lived, not the back of the head where her injury lay. She could have subdural blood trapped beneath the thicker dura and the more delicate meninges that covered brain. But subdural bleeds arose more commonly in the elderly due to a combination of stretching veins and atrophic brains. Both scenarios could require surgery, but neither fit her mechanism of injury.

She could have subarachnoid blood forming along the surface of her brain, pooling within the sulcal grooves that gave the brain its lobulated configuration, or even intraparenchymal blood trapped within the brain itself. Small amounts of either of those two forms of blood were generally monitored, but left untreated. Although initially confused, she felt more oriented now, and she sensed her neurologic status had improved. *I doubt I have a head bleed that would need intervention*, she thought with a groan.

When Jimmy walked back into the hospital room, Alexa rolled her face toward him. The minute movement produced earth-shattering pain in the back of her head and twinkling lights in her vision.

"Just a scalp hematoma. You'll be fine."

She repeated his words in her head with skepticism: *You'll be fine.* When the nurse came in to discharge her, handing her a slip of paper with a follow-up neurology appointment, Thornton offered to take her home. Alexa agreed reluctantly. She wasn't ready to call anyone to get her. She didn't know what to say. Her story seemed surreal. She couldn't even recall what she had told the police or detective Marcum.

During the long car ride back to her condo, Alexa had started to doze when she heard Jimmy ask her, "Did he hurt you — you know, in another way?" His voice sounded troubled. "You don't have to tell me. I know it's not my place. It's just — I want you to take some extra time away if you need it."

Half-asleep, Alexa was slow to respond. But when she did, she chose a fierce tone. "No. Jimmy. He smashed my head against the ground. He cut my leg. He beat me. I killed him. That's the whole story." *Surreal.*

The car was otherwise silent until they arrived at the condo she shared with Britt. She stepped out without a word of thanks. Jimmy waited until she disappeared inside before driving away.

Alexa passed the security guard with her head down, wearing only a pair of borrowed scrubs and hospital socks without shoes. Her clothes had been bagged for the investigation. Although exhausted, she chose to walk up the eight flights of stairs. Her heart thumped in her ears with every step. She forced her numb mind to think. *Britt. What do I tell him?*

Britt was in Malibu, golfing and hobnobbing with the political elite in an effort to gain campaign support for an upcoming election, and wouldn't return until late Monday.

He's so optimistic about his budding career in politics. I won't mention it until he returns. His campaign for State Representative means the world to him, and I can't interrupt his networking opportunities. Besides, the attack was in the past; she was ready to put it behind her.

When her head hit the pillow, she failed to sleep. The nights' events replayed in fragments, with Nine Inch Nails providing the background music. It was the first moment she realized Jamar would continue to haunt her. How naïve she had been to believe her nightmare was over.

CHAPTER 6

The flashbacks were commonplace. They passed in and out of her reality, forever blurring the finite constraints that separated past and present. She feared she had lost a part of herself in the past, and that ghost of herself haunted her and kept her from moving forward.

Alexa sat on her bench outside the courtroom, watching Appleby's feet as he paced back and forth. Jimmy Thornton approached him, and the two began an intense discussion.

What are those two debating? Why must Jimmy always get involved?

Her glare burned through the back of Appleby's head. *We need a new strategy before I go back up there.* The last thing she needed was to make another critical mistake in the courtroom. Her biggest mistake of all was giving a statement to the police and the detective prior to consulting with her attorney. Appleby reminded her of that grave mistake time and time again. *How could I have known I would need an attorney after being attacked in an alley?*

She realized onlookers were staring at her, and she sat

up tall in attempt to look confident. She avoided making eye contact with the crowd. Appleby returned with good news. Given the new line of questioning, the defense was granted a recess until the following morning. Alexa sighed in relief.

"We're not out of the woods yet, sweetheart," he stated. Appleby reached for her arm and led her to the car. They sat next to another on the cold black leather bench seat.

Despite her better judgment, just once she needed to say aloud the real answer to Ms. Finkle's question. "Jacob, you know the reason I didn't try to save that man. I wanted him dead — for what he did to me."

Her confession cut through the silence of their typically solemn drive from the courthouse. He grabbed her wrist, and his nails pressed into her flesh. She'd opened Pandora's Box and released Hell's fury. Appleby's eyes became daggers, his words authoritative and severe. "You can't say that in the court room. I don't want to hear you say that again. Don't even think it. Not if you want to walk away from this." He turned away and muttered something into the air. She thought she could make out the word *fool* in his words, but she couldn't be sure.

She moped with watery eyes, surprised at how much his actions managed to hurt her. *So much for the truth. This is what the truth gets me. Back to hiding my feelings from the world and letting Appleby feed me lines in the courtroom.*

Jacob Appleby was an amazing attorney. But he wasn't nice to Alexa, or tactful. He strategized. He behaved methodically. But he lacked compassion. She doubted he believed in her at all. She wasn't sure anyone believed in her. Even her mother had asked, "Why did you have to *kill* that man?"

"So he wouldn't kill me," she responded, half angry, half pleading. She waited to see if her mother's eyes forgave her. Nope. Nothing.

They stopped talking. She was convinced her own mother would have convicted her. The ulcer forming in her stomach made her wonder if it would've been better if she had died that night. Friends and family would have swarmed the funeral. Her eulogy would have been filled with cherished memories and heartfelt praises. Maybe that ending would have been easier, but she wasn't ready to concede. Not yet. She had too much fight left inside her.

More than once, she'd wanted to replace Appleby with a lawyer she could get along with; but she needed to win. If he could win her case, it was enough. She accepted his patronizing reluctantly. They continued their drive in silence. Alexa didn't want to talk to anymore. Except, perhaps, Smokey Joe. She needed a distraction from the day's events. After parting ways with Appleby, she drove to the shooting range, Emilio Pucci skirt and all.

Alexa smiled at Joe's gruff "hello," her little handgun tucked neatly into her Chanel handbag. There was an ease to their acquaintanceship that made Alexa feel more herself than she had in months. Thornton was right; shooting the .38 caliber helped her regain her confidence. She could feel the tension dissipate with the squeeze of the trigger. *Four bull's-eyes in a row!* Her aim was impeccable.

Joe grinned. "Pretty shot for a pretty lady! Now let's mix things up a bit. I want you to learn to shoot with your left hand as easy as your right." He challenged her with basic military tactics that served as a much needed mental distraction. During the training, her mind felt sharp again. They worked on multiple targets that day. Alexa aimed and fired. One, two, three shots quickly and without hesitation. She preferred a two-handed stance, but Joe often pulled one hand away. Eventually, she even became comfortable using only her left hand.

They chatted after the lesson ended.

"Do you enjoy teaching me as much as I enjoy learning, Joe?" Her lips pressed into a faint smirk.

"Shooting was the one thing I wanted to take with me after Vietnam." He snorted. His eyes shuffled around on the floor, but they eventually rose and met hers. "War is insufferable. No man should see or do those things." He shuddered. "It messed with my head. Post-traumatic stress disorder, they called it." His eyebrows rose, and his words slowed. "Caused nightmares and such." Alexa broke away from his stare.

Although they never discussed her situation, both local media and a few select national news channels covered her trial. Joe had to be aware of her dilemma. Was this his attempt to empathize? She didn't care for his attempt to comfort her; she refused to discuss the matter. She liked her complacent experiences with Joe. He made her feel safe — a feeling she couldn't risk losing.

"Thanks, Joe. How can I repay you?"

"No need." He waved his hands in the shape of an X and shook his head. "Unless you cook?" He cocked his head slightly.

"I'm afraid not. But I know great take-out."

She indulged his appetite with a filet from Jupiter's off Pleasant Point, with asparagus, garlic mashed potatoes, and an apple crisp in return for the day's lesson.

Alexa followed her shooting session with two hours of sweaty kickboxing alone in her underwear. She found the solitude encompassing. In those silent moments of the night, she longed for Britt the most. The place she lived now was so different from the homey condo they had shared for the duration of their nine-month engagement. They had chosen to move in together before the wedding. In the media frenzy, conservatives ridiculed the decision. When Britt's candidacy fell under attack, she moved out, trying to separate him from the scrutiny.

She lost her ability to connect with him. She couldn't be passionate. She couldn't interact with him intellectually. The qualities that made them amazing together crumbled.

Alexa left the love of her life in the whirlwind of panic that followed the attack. Feeling as though her life had ended, she refused to take Britt down with her as she spiraled into Hell. The future politician deserved better. She left to protect him.

That night in her dreams, Alexa relived the day she ended her engagement. She picked Britt up from the airport after a business trip. It was a simple gesture, an expected gesture earlier in their relationship. They shared a lukewarm embrace, and then stopped for coffee outside their condo. Over coffee, Alexa slid her ring across the table, and she told him goodbye. Britt held the same blank expression he'd worn for months. He held her one last time. He held her tight, but his arms felt cold.

As in life, her dream was replaced by a nightmare. As she followed Britt out the door, she realized something was off. She only saw the back of his head, but he looked different. *Is that Britt?* She touched his shoulder, and he spun around. Some of the features resembled Britt; his lush brown hair, his square jaw, his high cheekbones.

Those aren't Britt's eyes. This man's eyes were dark as night with yellow sclera. She watched the man's features transform into those of Jamar Reading. To her horror, he rose in size and stature. Now towering in front of her, he grabbed her by the shoulders and dragged her over the ground into the park across the street. The park was surrounded by a black iron picket fence. Jamar threw Alexa's body onto the sharp tines at the top of the fence, piercing her back with the pointed metal and skewering her belly button. On cue, she screamed. The screams continued as she woke.

It was only midnight.

The satin sheets were damp with sweat. She grabbed a blanket and used it as a towel to soak up the moisture on her skin. She headed to the medicine cabinet and composed a concoction of sleep aids to get her through the night.

The musical tone of her cell phone startled her. His name didn't appear on the screen, but she knew that number by heart. As much as she had tried to erase him from her life, there he was, staring her in the face. *Britt Anderson.*

CHAPTER 7

"**B**ritt." She said the words out loud once to herself, and then once more into the phone.

"Alexa." She wanted to drown herself in the strong, pure sound of his voice. "How are you holding up, doll?"

His simple terms of endearment nearly melted her heart of stone. "I'm fine, Britt," she lied. She couldn't bear to ask how he was doing. She didn't want to know how he was getting along without her.

He digressed to happier times. "I was thinking today of that night we went to the Hope benefit together. It was the first time you met my father." He spoke with a slow, comforting drawl.

Yes. The night you announced you would run for State Representative.

"You were so beautiful that night, dressed in gold sequins. Every eye watched you from the moment you walked in. Every man wished you were his. I think even my father wanted to steal you away from me. That was the night I knew I wanted to marry you, so no other man could have you but me. I guess that was selfish of me."

She held the receiver in silence while she recalled the night. She had worn a champagne-colored Sue Wong cocktail dress, covered in intricate gold beading. Britt wooed her with Texan charm, telling her over and over how he would love her *forever*. He held her close and kissed her until she had to break away for air.

What would it have been like to be a politician's wife? Her heart winced at the thought. *How could such a happy memory harbor such pain?*

Yet, she couldn't help but indulge them both a little while longer. "I knew I wanted to be your wife the weekend we stayed at your parents' cabin. That Saturday morning we spent filling out a crossword puzzle together on the porch. We were wrapped up in blankets and immersed in our espresso. It was so perfect, sitting there next to you, watching the mist rise from the valley. I figured if that was the most exciting thing that ever happened in my life, I would be perfectly content." Her words trailed off. The magic of those moments had slipped away, exposing their harsh reality, and Alexa scolded herself for her indulgence.

"Are you content now, Alexa?" he pressed.

She instantly regretted her choice of words. "I'm fine, Britt," she lied again. The truth had become too much to bear.

"And the nightmares?" he continued.

"I'm getting used to them." She was a terrible liar.

"I've been thinking about this, and I want you to try something, doll. I think it will help you get over the nightmares."

Her free hand grasped a stray lock of hair that she spun

into a knot. She didn't want him to help her with this. She didn't want him to enter this world of pain, yet he continued.

"The next time you wake up, I want you to relive that nightmare, step by step. Only this time, I want you to change the details. Create your own ending. Make each nightmare end so that *you* win. Imagine yourself stronger than him, faster than him, smarter than him. Imagine that he is weak; imagine that he is afraid of you. Know that he can't hurt you anymore, Alexa. *You won.* Don't forget that."

Holding the receiver, rocking back and forth, with the blanket wrapped around her shoulders, she feared she resembled one of the psychiatric patients from the third floor of the hospital where she used to work. She'd acknowledged more than once that she might benefit from being committed. *Perhaps after the trial,* she thought.

She reached for another blonde lock to defile. She let Britt's words permeate her brain, one neuron at a time. *Damn, he's smart.* She wanted to tell him how smart he was and how much she respected him; how much she loved him and missed him. She missed his touch, his kiss. She missed the sex. She couldn't remember their last intimate moment, and she'd give her right arm to have one more night with him. Instead, she thanked him solemnly.

"You'll make a great politician." *I only hope I haven't ruined your chance in politics.*

"Promise, Lex, that you will think about our happier times together before drifting off to sleep," he begged.

"Of course, Britt."

"Good night, Lex."

"Good-bye, Britt." She hung up the phone and repressed

the finality of her closing words with a drawn out sigh.

She thought about the three weeks they spent together exploring Europe last year. Her thoughts settled on the little French café they visited in Paris for espresso at midnight. They had been arguing over something. Perhaps it was the time Britt had suggested they head off to the red light district in Amsterdam. Alexa had been appalled by the idea. She wasn't sure Britt had any real interest, or if he was just trying to rile her up. He seemed to enjoy trying to aggravate her.

Their discussion was interrupted by the Norwegian accent of their waiter. Alexa figured they must have been the only Americans to venture to Paris and be greeted by a Danish waiter. Alexa found the waiter's accent humorous, and the argument faded.

"I don't know any Danish words." She pointed to the small flame of the tea light on their table and asked, "What is the word for candlelight?"

The waiter replied, "*Levende lys.*"

Alexa repeated the words one syllable at a time. "*Levende lys.*" The lovely words sounded like a lullaby as they rolled off her tongue. She thought about them and stared into the little flame that sat in the middle of their table. The flame was a thing of beauty and power, yet it could be extinguished with a single breath. The perfect light shined bright and pure. Like a halo atop an angel's head, she equated that intangible purity with goodness. Her mind caressed the beautiful words and tucked them away in her memory.

That night, she and Britt returned to their French chateau and made love by *levende lys*. In the morning, Britt proposed over breakfast in bed with espresso. Yes. She missed Britt Anderson.

Alexa wiped away tears of remembrance from each eye. And after taking the proper combination of sleep aids, she dozed off again around four o'clock in the morning. She slept for three hours without a nightmare.

Alexa told Britt about the assault before any of her other loved ones, and she let him break the news to her family. She waited four days to tell him; she waited until he returned from Malibu. For four days, she tried to develop a plan that never materialized. She was showering when he returned home. He walked into the bathroom and saw the stitches in her thigh. He saw the bruises on her abdomen and her cheek. His cheeks flushed with rage.

"Who did this to you? Who did it, Alexa? I'll make him regret it."

"Don't worry, Britt. He regrets it." Her body became weak with emotion and she grasped the shower door to stay upright. She took a deep breath as her eyes welled with tears. "I killed him," she stammered, her mousy voice unfamiliar.

Deafening silence. She watched Britt's face twist from anger to a look of disgust. She feared his opinion of her changed in that moment, and she'd lost him. She didn't know how, but she knew that she'd failed him. Somehow, she hadn't lived up to his expectations.

Over the next few days, her fears cemented. He drifted further and further away from her, or maybe it was the other way around. It was hard to tell. The distance crept between them. When the nightmares started, Britt became visibly disturbed. Alexa thrashed the bed sheets. She woke screaming or crying or both. He seemed afraid to touch her;

afraid of the killer he shared his bed with. In time, he stopped trying to console her.

CHAPTER 8

She woke to the sound of her alarm and prepared for court. Gold Christian Louboutin heels and a white fitted dress with a square neck, and a thick layer of concealer beneath her eyes. Still groggy from the sleep aids, she forgot to eat breakfast. She didn't forget the coffee, though. She needed the caffeine to keep her eyes open.

Alexa met with Appleby at eight-thirty a.m. to discuss their plan.

"Good morning, Jacob." She tried to sound polished and assertive. She hoped he had forgotten chastising her the day before.

"Alexa, you look tired. Try not to fall asleep in front of the jury today. It's not very professional."

She rolled her eyes to herself and nodded to him. *Deliriously tired, but not more so than usual.*

"I'd like to keep you off the stand, but I need you to recite some lines today."

Her stomach let out a half growl, half moan.

"Relax. I just need you to read your deposition to the

jury." Appleby planned to strip her initial statement to Detective Marcum from the record, as that seemed to be the root of her self-incrimination, and replace it with the softer version she had given the prosecution early in the trial.

Alexa's initial statement to Detective Marcum had been too harsh. Her version of the events seemed overly strategic. It didn't sit well with the jury. Alexa had told Detective Marcum, "I aimed for his carotid and kept cutting until I saw arterial blood. When I knew he was dead, I rolled him off of me." But Appleby's version of her statement was the more sympathetic damsel in distress role. Alexa nodded. "Sure. I'll do whatever you need."

She walked into a flurry in the courtroom, with people scooting past one another trying to find their seats. The jury shuffled in. Alexa eyed the jury of her peers, skewed with minorities more so than the standard Austin population, and wondered if the decks were stacked against her.

"The court is now in session." The gavel banged, and the judge sat.

Surprisingly, Appleby began with his first witness. He called Dr. Phil Holston to the stand. Alexa's forehead rumpled in confusion. The name of the ER doctor wasn't immediately familiar to her. Dr. Holston testified to his name and his position, and that Alexa DeBrow was his patient the night of the incident. Appleby gave Dr. Holston Alexa's medical records from her hospital admission for him to read to the court.

"The patient, a thirty-two-year-old female, was attacked earlier tonight. Her attacker cut her left thigh, resulting in a seven-centimeter superficial laceration. She suffered small lacerations to her head/scalp posteriorly, with a large scalp hematoma, and there is concern for intracranial bleed. Patient has suffered a concussion and is disoriented to date. She also had difficulty with her contact information, including her phone number and zip code. Bruises to abdomen noted, without peritoneal signs. Assessment and plan: Head CT with neurology consult. Stitches for the thigh and scalp lacerations."

Appleby looked satisfied. "Thank you, Dr. Holston. That is all." Appleby now addressed the courtroom. "I ask the court, how can a woman who suffered a concussion, disoriented to most basic information, give an accurate account of the night's events to the police officers and detective who questioned her? She couldn't even remember her phone number. How can we expect her to have functioned in the capacity of tending her attacker's wounds? Due to the injuries she sustained, Dr. Alexa DeBrow functioned in a diminished capacity and lacked the ability to adhere to the typical medical standard of care."

Alexa watched one of the jurors' heads nod in agreement.

"I ask that my client's initial statement to police be stricken from the court's record, and that we rely solely on her deposition for all details of the assault."

Appleby had trained Alexa well prior to her giving her deposition to the prosecution. He knew which questions would be pertinent, and she had been prepared for everything the defense might ask. In fact, the majority of her answers were rehearsed lines given to her by Appleby. She hoped the court would accept Appleby's request. If so, she didn't think the prosecution would be able continue ranting about how the lady with the concussion should have saved her attacker.

"Miss DeBrow, please rise and read the lines from the court records and your deposition, highlighted for you in yellow."

Alexa stood and cleared her throat, then read aloud. "I stabbed at the neck of my attacker because it was right in front of me. The knife was stuck, and I tried to get it out, but I couldn't pull it straight out; I pulled it to the side. When the knife finally came free, there was blood everywhere. I was so scared. I was crying. I couldn't get away from the blood. I couldn't get him off of me. He was so heavy, and I was exhausted."

Her voice rang loud and clear, with just the right mousy undertone to sound vulnerable. Finally, she was someone the jury could sympathize with. Alexa considered this edited statement a "Hollywood version" of what really happened. The facts were the same, only the words were rearranged. Appleby had contrived a persona that was novice and naïve. Now he requested to replace one statement with the other. The judge called for a short recess to consider Appleby's appeal. It seemed promising.

She followed Appleby out of the courtroom during the recess, and her stomach groaned of emptiness. She had just stepped into the hallway when the room began turning dark, and sound faded away. Her body hit the floor hard.

She regained consciousness slowly. Her head throbbed as reality seeped back painfully. Alexa opened her eyes and was surprised to see Dale Anderson, Britt's father, kneeling beside her.

"Mr. Anderson! I didn't even know you were here . . . at the trial." She was too perplexed to move from her place on the linoleum.

He propped up her head. "I just wanted to make sure things were going okay. I was thinking of you the other day . . . and I find you like this — on the floor. You're not well, Alexa." He shook his head and frowned as if scolding her.

Appleby caught her eye. He made his way toward her cutting through the crowd. His scowl showed dismay. With Dale's help, Alexa scrambled to a bench nearly.

"I'm fine, Jacob," she said defensively as Appleby approached them. "I forgot breakfast, that's all."

Appleby nodded. "I'll get you something. I need you on your feet." He muttered to himself again when he left her with Britt's father.

"We've missed you," Mr. Anderson started. His worried eyes scanned her face.

Alexa smiled. He had always been a fan of hers. "Thanks, Dale. I've missed you — and Britt." Her lip quivered. She bit down hard to keep it still. She didn't have the strength to convey emotion.

"It's not too late for the two of you, you know. I know you kids still love each other. Your trial is almost over. I must confess, Alexa, this old man is hoping that you kids will reconcile." His warm, comforting words were too much of a fantasy for her to succumb to.

"Yes. I think we still love each other. But so much has changed. We were the perfect match. . ." Her words drifted off. She didn't know how to say it. Britt fell in love with the beautiful, successful, put-together and flawless Alexa

DeBrow. She was the Golden Girl, a nickname her classmates had given her as a symbol of perfection. And Britt deserved that perfection, someone who could complement his many attributes. Now that she had fallen from her pedestal, she no longer deserved him. Besides, he could never see her as he once did. She knew that. Britt knew that. His father had to realize it, as well.

He looked in her eyes as though he were trying to look into her soul and raised an eyebrow. "It's a damn shame, Alexa."

She forced another meager smile. "You don't have to worry about Britt, Dale. He has a bright future ahead of him." *Without me weighing him down.* "You don't have to worry about *me,* either." She feigned confidence.

"I just picked you up off the floor, Alexa. I have *every* reason in the world to worry about you."

She shunned the truth in his words. "I've dealt with a lot worse. I'm a survivor. More than that, I'm a fighter. I'll just keep fighting. Until the fight is *won.*" Warmth spread across her face as her color returned and thoughts of redemption flickered in the back of her mind.

He held Alexa's hands in his own and forced a smile through quivering lips. "I love you, Alexa, like you are my own. But you've changed so much. I hope the goodness inside you shines through when this is all over."

She'd heard similar words from her mother about how much she had changed. *Have I changed so much that the people I love don't recognize me?* He wrapped his arms around her, and it was like saying goodbye to Britt all over again.

Appleby arrived with a cream cheese bagel and an

orange juice. Dale left her side, and she ate her bagel while Appleby lectured her. "You can't do this. These fainting spells of yours have to stop." She'd fainted once before during the trial. That time she was in the courtroom. Everyone saw. "No one will believe this is real. They'll all think you're a bad actress trying to play them for a fool." Perceptions could change so easily with one wrong move. Appleby eyed the hallway. "Seems like few people took notice. For God's sake, if you can't walk, I'll hold you up. Just say something."

Alexa tuned out the rest of his speech. Instead, her attention fixed on a thin black lady at the end of the hall. The woman's eyes locked on Alexa. The woman wore orthopedic shoes that suggested she worked on her feet all day, and a sullen, plaid-printed button-up dress. She had a small black boy with a visible overbite clinging to her skirt. Alexa watched the woman step closer. The recess had ended, however, and Appleby motioned Alexa into the courtroom.

The judge accepted Appleby's request. Murmurs spread throughout the courtroom. Finkle suggested they proceed to closing arguments. The judge turned to Appleby, who requested to begin closing statements the following day. The judge banged his gavel once more, and the court day was over. Appleby wanted to meet once more with the prosecution, so Alexa left the courthouse alone.

CHAPTER 9

Her weary mind drifted to sleep around two in the morning, after popping a few Benadryl and a downing a large glass of red wine. She dreamed she was driving her Mercedes to the courthouse with the top down. She stopped at a red light when a man appeared in her driver's rear view mirror. Before she could react or respond, she felt his hands on her throat. She gasped for air, as her foot went to the gas pedal. The car sped away, but the hands never left her throat. She wrecked the car into a lamppost.

The man lifted her into the air and spun her around to face him.

She stared at Jamar. A knife appeared in his other hand. It wasn't the knife from *that* night, however; this was a larger knife with a sharp curved blade. He shoved the knife into her belly, and she watched her insides fall from her midsection.

Alexa awoke, heart pounding.

As her pulse began to slow, she recalled her plan — Britt's plan. She closed her eyes and made herself replay the nightmare. She imagined herself in her car at the stoplight.

She saw Jamar. She was ready when he reached for her. Foot pressed against the gas pedal, she sped away.

She'd driven halfway down the block when she realized she shouldn't run from him. *Kill him.* A quick U-turn back toward Jamar. She reached into her handbag and pulled out her gun and applied the gas. She targeted his yellow eyes and fired. He fell. She stopped the car next to the body. Two more shots fired into his skull. She saw the pool of blood form around him. She opened her eyes. She felt calmer.

She relived the nightmare over and over. Each time she became faster, her shots and movements more accurate, until her fear lessened, and she fell back asleep.

She woke for her last day of trial. She chose loose-fitting black trousers with a white, silk blouse that she tied carelessly low on her neck. She wanted an outfit that conveyed ease. She pulled her tousled hair to the side in an attempt to look relaxed, despite the gravity of the situation.

She slipped into her silver snakeskin Manolo heels as Appleby's private car pulled up, six-forty-five a.m. on the dot. She pulled open the door to find Appleby with the phone glued to his ear, as usual. After fifteen minutes of firm debate, he put down the phone and turned to Alexa. He shoved a brown paper bag that contained a blueberry bagel with cream cheese into her hand. Apparently, he didn't trust her after yesterday's episode. Alexa forced the food into her uneasy stomach.

Appleby divulged that he had met with the prosecution and the judge in the conference room yesterday after he left her. "The judge suggested that the charge of criminally negligent homicide be tried separately in an entirely new trial if the prosecution wished to pursue it, since the line of questioning has changed." Appleby stated in between sips of his latte. Alexa raised an eyebrow.

"I handed him this list of thirty physicians willing to testify that you were unable to perform standard medical duties after suffering a concussion, certain that it would clear you from the charge. The prosecution agreed, and they vowed not to pursue the charge any further." His drab voice affirmed his inability to convey joy despite the good news.

"But, that's great! They can't use my medical training against me," Alexa stammered, reaching for the paper in Appleby's hand. "Where did you get this?"

"Your pal Jimmy Thornton," he said with a curl of his lips.

"Really?" Alexa gasped, unable to hide her surprise. *Thanks, Jimmy.*

"The only viable charge that remains is manslaughter. Although it's nothing to be proud of, it won't get you life in prison, sweetheart," he mused. "I guess we'll find out today whether we convinced them you're not the she-devil they've made you out to be."

She ignored the sting of his words. *It's almost over.*

"There'll be a crowd today. Be ready for that. Reporters will want to interview you. I will shuffle you through the crowd and back into the private car. Understand? I will give a statement on your behalf. You are not to speak with the reporters," he hissed, and rolled his eyes away from her.

"What will you tell them?" she asked.

"Depends on the outcome. If you're innocent, we play

the role of gracious victor. If you're guilty, we simply state that we will continue to fight. There is another alternative, however. The prosecution may drop these charges in lieu of charging you in a civil trial. You're not out of this yet." He paused for another sip of his latte. "No comments to friends or family . . . if they come. Reporters will go to them for a story if they are willing to talk. We don't want any comments that may jeopardize our strategy."

Alexa nodded, not wholly understanding the strategy he spoke of. *Civil trial?* Her pulse quickened at the notion of enduring another trial. *No. It's almost over.*

Media groups with news cameras swarmed the courthouse. Alexa's confidence failed her. Appleby exited the car first. She waited while he spoke with the media. He didn't want to risk her doing something unwanted with the cameras on. She obeyed. He motioned for her; she followed, trying to appear as strong as possible.

The day began with the closing arguments of the prosecution. Janice Finkle walked to the center of the three-ring circus to perform for the spectators. Alexa quivered. A wave of despair washed over her, and she turned her gaze to the floor. *I can't listen to a word of this. I can't, and I won't. Think of something else. Anything else.* Her mind jumped around between fragments of thoughts. Memories of her mother, happy times with Britt, even Jimmy Thornton popped in and out. She couldn't focus. *I've gone crazy. My mind doesn't work the way it used to. I should have pled insanity.* She concentrated on Britt, trying to remember the last time they were intimate. *No sex after the incident.* Why hadn't she thought of this before? *No wonder we failed. I was too broken to tolerate his touch. He deserves better.* Her mind continued to search for their last night of lovemaking. But the memory was lost to her. Before she could mourn its loss, Appleby stood and stole her attention.

He took the place where Finkle stood and began his closing arguments. He worked to make Alexa appear vulnerable to further gain the jury's sympathies. "I need not remind the jury that my client, Dr. Alexa DeBrow, is a physician. More than that, Dr. DeBrow is a beautiful, single, thirty-three-year-old female who was attacked while walking alone on a dark night. She was victimized and assaulted by a man who tried to take advantage of her. He beat her, and she suffered injuries that required hospitalization and resulted in a concussion. Although she was injured and afraid, she was also strong. She overcame her attacker, in what can only be described as fate." He paused for a sip of water. Alexa stared in awe of Appleby's poise and charisma, and for a moment, she forgot how much she disliked him.

"Now, the prosecution wants to punish this young woman for unnecessary use of force. I tell you *force* was necessary in taking down a two-hundred pound assailant. It's a shame Jamar Reading did not survive Miss DeBrow's attempt to defend herself so that he could stand trial for the crimes he committed." All eyes were locked on Appleby. "Additionally, the prosecution wants to punish Miss DeBrow because she wasn't in the proper state of mind to provide medical assistance to her attacker." He shook his head, eyes on the ground, as he paced toward the jury. His eyes scanned the jury members as he pled with them. "I ask that the jury choose *not* to punish Miss DeBrow, because Alexa DeBrow has been punished enough. I'm sorry. She's sorry. We're all sorry that Jamar Reading didn't survive that night. But I'm also sorry that Jamar Reading attacked my client. She was his victim, and he was hers. It's an ugly situation that doesn't have a good answer, so I ask the jury to let it go. Let the events of that night end today. Don't punish Alexa DeBrow anymore."

Simple and direct, but will it work? The court fell into recess for the jury to decide on a verdict. Appleby said it should be quick. With nausea churning in her stomach, Alexa headed to the ladies' room. She hovered over the toilet while her stomach went into convulsions, and the blueberry bagel came back up in chunks. The vomit burned her throat. She soothed the burn with cool water from the faucet, scooping it by hand to drink, and then rinsed her mouth thoroughly. She had just stepped out of the restroom when she stumbled into the thin black lady from the day before. It was as if she had been waiting for Alexa.

The woman wore a similar outfit to the prior day, with the same orthopedic shoes. Her hair was pulled back neatly, and the boy with the overbite still clung to her side. "Miss DeBrow, I'm Kensie Phillips," the woman said quietly. There was something about the woman's timid nature that drew Alexa toward her.

"Yes," Alexa responded, stepping closer to the woman.

"I know that man you kilt."

A twinge of pain hit Alexa's stomach.

"He raped me outside the library on Third Street a few years back." The woman spoke with an odd little accent; although southern and sweet, it came out all wrong. Alexa's forehead wrinkled into a state of confusion. "He raped me a few times, that's how I know for sure it was him. He would wait for me to get done cleaning the library. I walk home about eight blocks after that. He found me a few times, beat me pretty good, too." Her voice turned quieter; it hovered just above a whisper. "He stopped the first time he saw my pregnant belly."

Alexa stared at the woman in disbelief then looked down at the little boy, wondering how his mother could speak so candidly about something so awful with him in earshot. Kensie must have known what Alexa was thinking, because at that moment she pulled her child in front of her and covered the boy's ears with her hands. "I just wanted you to know you weren't alone. I thought it might help you to know there were other women that he hurt, too." Kensie's lips formed a simpleton smile.

Alexa nodded and placed a hand on Kensie's shoulder, mumbling "thank you," as she turned away. She walked back into the courtroom while the woman's words sank in.

Anger. She felt the anger rise, but it took a moment to pinpoint the source. *Kensie's confession came too late.* She said that Jamar had raped her multiple times, yet she waited, almost strategically, until the point in the trial in which witnesses could no longer testify to admit that Jamar had other victims. Kensie could have been a key witness if she had only come forward sooner. If she had told the jury about her attack, it would have solidified the defense's theory that Jamar was a serial rapist — an abomination to society. Kensie Phillips held crucial information that could have helped clear Alexa's name; yet she never offered to take the stand. More than angry, Alexa felt defeated.

That boy clinging to her skirt. Could he be Jamar's child? Is that why Jamar stopped raping her, because he knew he'd knocked her up? Alexa shuddered at the thought. She couldn't imagine any product of Jamar remaining in this world.

Her mind raced now. *Kensie was raped repeatedly, yet she never fought back. She just let it happen. But she could have planned for the attack. She could have carried a gun, arranged for someone to walk with her, called the police, even.* Yet, she did nothing. The fury rose to unbearable levels. *If Kensie had bothered to call the police just once, maybe Jamar would never have attacked me.* Maybe he would have been in prison where he belonged. Alexa stewed on her rage while the court reconvened.

The jury had reached a decision. The anger blinded her nerves. *If Kensie had bothered to testify, I doubt I'd be standing trial right now.* Alexa stood to face the jury while they announced the verdict. *Chin up, buttercup. Here it comes.*

The clerk read the outcome aloud: "Superior court of Texas in the county of Travis, in the matter of the people of Texas against Dr. Alexa DeBrow, we the jury in the above entitled action find the defendant, Dr. Alexa DeBrow, in the charge of second-degree murder of Jamar Reading, section 19.02: Not guilty." The clerk then polled the twelve jurors. The same followed for the charges of manslaughter, section 19.04, and criminally negligent homicide, section 19.05. Not guilty on all accounts.

CHAPTER 10

The court dispersed in a frenzy of media and commotion. Appleby swept Alexa under his arm while microphones waved in her face. He quickly coaxed her out the door and into a private car so he could give a statement on her behalf.

Appleby stood on the steps of the courthouse addressing the many reporters who surrounded him when the private car started its way through the crowd. Through the heavy tint of the windows, Alexa knew no one could see her inside, but she still saw their faces, and most didn't look happy. *Why must they be upset?* She wanted to feel like she'd won, but tears formed in the corners of her eyes.

A familiar floral cardigan topped with a Jackie-O bob carved through the crowd. *Mom?* Alexa's heart heaved in her chest as the figure dissipated in the masses. *Real or hallucination?* she debated, her eyes scanning for the cardigan through the camera flashes as the car inched its way through the sea of people.

The passenger door opposite her swung open and quickly slammed shut as a new figure slid into the seat. Alexa stared into the teary eyes of her mother.

"Mom! I can't believe you're here. I didn't think you could handle the media or the crowds."

Tess DeBrow's hand nimbly flicked the door locked without losing her daughter's gaze. "Alexa," she said, her voice hovering just above a whisper. "I'm so glad this is all finally over for you. I know everything will be all right now, and you can get your life back on track after this horrible incident." Tess forced a prim little smile that Alexa knew was typically reserved for public speaking and social banalities.

The proper, well-kept, sensible attitude her mother maintained was too much for Alexa to bear, and she became painfully aware of the distance between them on the bench seat they shared. Both women clutched the door handles beside them as if their bodies were adhered to the doors.

"I'm not sure anything will be all right, Mom. I'm afraid I'll carry this stigma with me everywhere I go. Everything is different. I'm different." She begged her mother to allow her to fall apart just this once.

"These things happen in life, Alexa. Bad things happen. People can beat you, they can rape you, but you should never let them change you." She looked deep into Alexa's eyes. The pools of blue looking at Alexa were a reflection of her own.

I look so much like her. The prominent cheekbones, the slope of her nasal bones; only the dyed chestnut hair and the age separate us.

"You were such a good girl." She slid a hand across the seat toward her daughter.

Alexa frowned hard and pulled her own free hand away. *Yet, we are infinitely different. You work so hard to keep face while Camelot burns to the ground, and I run around screaming.* "Why must you look at me like that? You look at me like I'm a stranger."

"I'm looking for my daughter," Tess stated grimly. "I feel as though I've lost her completely. I'm trying to look past the anger on your face. Trying to see beyond the vengefulness you display. I don't know who you are anymore. I want my daughter back." Her mother's stare burned as if she were a priest trying to exorcise a demon from Alexa's soul. Tess retrieved her outstretched hand and wrung them together in her lap.

"Why do you keep judging me? You never did that before." Alexa resisted the urge to open up and succumbed to the defensiveness to which she had grown accustomed. Feeling the tension grow, she tried to think of a way to steer the conversation another direction. It seemed as if the same argument unveiled itself every time she hoped to make amends.

"I think you should see Father Andrew, Alexa."

Seriously? The priest from couples' counseling? Yes, she's planning an exorcism.

"He can help you forgive yourself and find peace with the situation."

"No. Not happening. I don't want or need forgiveness. I'm fine." *You shouldn't have come.* She hung on the thought for a moment and debated whether to unleash the wrath of her words. She paused, lowered the privacy screen, and muttered her parents' home address to the driver. Her rage refused to subside. She raised the screen, and her head snapped back toward her mom. She'd bottled up too much for too long. The cork popped off, and she overflowed.

"You show up for the finale, but you missed some really great stuff in the middle, Mom."

"You told me not to go to court anymore. It was such a cause of tension — for you, me, your father. All we did was fight. All we *do* is fight. You won't let me help you. You only push me away. You've become very good at pushing people away, Alexa. I can count them on both hands. . . ."

"You tell me what I should feel and should think and should do. But you're not me. If I push you away, it's because you're not willing to accept me." *I told you not to come to court if you were going to side against me.* She shoved her head back against the seat. "Were you planning to say goodbye today, Mom, thinking they were going to lock me away? Do you think I should be in prison?" Her lips spat bitter sarcasm.

"It's not like that —"

"You shouldn't have come." *There. Done. No more lectures.*

The silence that followed fractured the roots that bound them. Endless blocks passed before either spoke. Saltwater pools formed in Tess' eyes. "It's cruel the way you shut me out. My daughter would never shut me out like that," she whimpered.

Okay. Maybe I went too far, but her words cut deeper than Jamar's knife. Alexa refused to back down. "I am your daughter!" she half-shouted with an exaggerated eye-roll.

Tess sighed. "My daughter wanted to help people, not hurt them." Their conversation slowed, each remark separated by awkward pauses.

"Mom, let it go. So what if he's dead? I'm alive. Your daughter is alive."

Tess frowned. "Of course I'm glad you're alive. Don't act

like I don't care about you, Alexa. You're my blood, and I'll always love you. I just never thought you were capable of such hate, such violence." She shuddered. "You wanted to help people; it's why you became a doctor."

"Not anymore. I quit, Mom."

Tess turned her head from her daughter to look out the window.

"I see. What will you *do*?"

What a condescending tone!

"I don't know. I need to figure things out. It's complicated."

"You can come home."

Alexa searched for real sentiment in the offer. *Hmm. Sounds a little cold.*

"No. That won't work. Besides, the media isn't ready to let this die down. I need to get away from here."

The car stopped. Alexa recognized her parent's massive English Tudor home, and her inner child yearned to retreat to her safe place — curled in a blanket, sitting in her grandmother's rocking chair in her bedroom. A news crew perched on the front lawn where she used to play.

Alexa looked at her mother. She had nothing more to say. Tess reached over to hug her daughter. Numb after the day's events, the embrace seemed lifeless.

"Why does this feel like goodbye?" Tess pleaded.

Alexa shrugged.

"Give me some time, Mom. I'll let you know."

Tess nodded and turned away quickly, wiping away a tear as she exited the car.

CHAPTER 11

Appleby sent Alexa to the Four Seasons that night, knowing her residence would be swarmed with media. She checked in under a fake name and had her food sent to her via room service. Although not guilty, she hid from the world like a criminal. Her mind toiled while she sat there alone for over an hour. *I should feel relieved*, she told herself, trying to unwind. Her fidgeting fingers reached for the phone, and she called Smokey Joe. The sun had set, and she wasn't sure he would still be at the range. She waited three rings before the familiar gruff voice answered.

"Otter Creek Shooting Range and Gun Club."

"Joe!" she declared, ecstatic.

"Ma'am?"

"Joe, it's Alexa."

"Shoot, girl. I thought I'd lost you."

"Yeah, me too." Her voice turned shaky.

"You're lookin' for some target practice tonight, I reckon?"

"Yes, Joe. If you're up for it, that is. It's late, I know."

"All right. I figure you deserve it after the day you've been through."

He's alluding to the trial. Damn. Why must everyone watch the news? She had assumed as much.

"I'll be there in twenty minutes," Alexa stated, making mental notes of everything she would need to do to get there that quickly.

"Not this time. I've got a better idea for tonight."

Alexa jotted down directions to somewhere just outside of town. She hung up and called for a cab. She grabbed comfortable hospital scrubs and tennis shoes and tucked her hair under a ball cap pulled low over her face. She glanced at the silly disguise in the mirror and hoped it was enough to keep the attention away from her. *What a perfectly unattractive ensemble!*

She had the cab driver stop at a liquor store to get a gift for Joe. She bought him a bottle of Tennessee White Whiskey. It was one of his favorites.

The address Joe had given her was another twenty minutes beyond the edge of the city limits. Finally, the cab turned onto a long dirt driveway. Alexa saw Joe standing in front of a clearing lit by a few large spotlights. She thanked the cab driver with a generous tip before turning to Joe.

"Why did you want to meet here?"

Joe grinned. "This here is my private shooting range." He motioned to the lighted clearing surrounded by trees and pasture. "I've got something special for tonight, kinda celebratory, given the situation."

Joe's reference to the trial made Alexa uneasy. She handed him the whiskey in an attempt to change the subject.

Joe accepted the bottle and nodded his head in approval; gratitude sparkled in the old man's eyes.

"You ever tried this stuff?" he asked. Alexa shook her head.

"Give it a swig. Ladies first." Joe opened the bottle and passed it to her.

The liquor smelled strong and sweet. She took a long gulp and hoped the alcohol would wash away her memories. The whiskey burned the back of her throat, still sore from vomiting earlier. She forced a swallow and passed the bottle back to her friend.

Joe chuckled to himself. "Yeah, it's pretty strong stuff straight up. But you get used to it. Come on. We better get started. I've got a lot to show you."

Alexa followed Joe into the clearing, and she realized he had a small arsenal laid out on a bench before them. She viewed the array of handguns, small semi-automatics with sights, and rifles. Only one of the guns looked familiar. On the ground behind them were multiple two-liter and twenty-ounce plastic soda bottles. Some bottles were spray painted in neon green, others were clear with the labels stripped away.

Joe beamed. "Target practice. Time we bumped you up to some moving targets."

"Nice. I like a challenge."

Joe handed her a simple handgun. He grabbed a neon green two-liter and threw it high into the air and about twenty yards in front of them. Alexa hit it on the second shot.

"All right, you're gonna have to do better than that if this is gonna be any fun."

Alexa blushed. He threw another two-liter high into the

air. This time she only needed one shot.

"Better. Now close your eyes, and open them when you hear me say so."

She obeyed her instructor and opened her eyes at his command, quickly firing before the bottle landed. When the bullet hit the two-liter, it exploded into a small ball of fire. Her eyes widened in amazement.

Joe laughed heartily. "Good thing you hit that one. It would have been a shame to miss your response. Told you I had something special out here. You can't have fireballs indoors, you know. Don't worry. We've got more to come. Close your eyes. Face me. This time, I want you to hear me throw the bottle. Then turn, spot it, and fire."

Alexa nodded.

She listened for the sound and turned, too late. The bottle had already hit the ground.

"Again," said Joe.

She turned back to face him and closed her eyes. She didn't hit the bottle with this approach until the third try. Another fiery explosion confirmed the hit.

The game continued for a total of twelve bottles, the last six being the smaller twenty-ounce variety. Alexa hit only seven of them.

"Not bad, for a girl. Where'd you learn to shoot like that?"

Alexa flashed a mischievous grin. "Where'd you learn to throw like that? Don't tell me you were the high school quarterback."

"A long time ago, I was a lot of things — football, baseball, you name it, I did it. That was before the army." His eyes fell to the ground.

"It's impressive — your throwing, that is," she added.

Joe frowned.

You don't like compliments, Joe? Funny, how we're similar in that way.

Joe took another swig of whiskey and motioned back to the clearing. "You've got more work to do."

He grabbed one of the small, semi-automatic weapons and crouched down behind the bench where the remaining weapons lay. "Like this," he told her. "You don't fire until the bottle crosses below the top of that pole."

Alexa gazed into the distance. She saw a wooden pole with a light at the top about thirty yards in front of them. The pole stood about twenty feet tall.

"It's a good thing you didn't wear those fancy clothes of yours tonight. You're bound to get a little dirty down there."

The ground was covered with dew, and dirt and grass stuck to Alexa's scrubs. She shuffled into position. He threw a total of twelve bottles into the air, one after another. Some went to the left. Some went to the right. She aimed at neon-green bottles and clear ones. She hit five of twelve, and only one was a clear bottle.

"All right," Joe sighed. "You can get up now." He massaged his right shoulder before taking another swig of whiskey and walking out into the clearing. He set the remaining bottles upright in the field, spaced apart in a line that ran a good thirty yards. Nestled in the short grass, the bottles were visible targets from where Alexa had been shooting.

"This one was a military drill. It frustrated the hell out

of me, but it will be good for you."

"Okay," she agreed, wiping away the wet grass and dirt that clung to her clothes.

"You run parallel to the bottles and shoot as many of them as you can as you go." He gestured with his hand the path she would take. "At the end, turn, switch hands, and shoot the remaining bottles as you run back. Continue like that 'til they're all gone." Joe spat at the ground. "It's harder than it looks. Good thing you've got your running shoes on. I'd hate to see you have to do it barefoot."

Alexa readied her stance, groaning to herself as she placed the handgun in her non-dominant left hand. She ran and started firing. One, two, three, four shots before she hit a bottle. The fiery explosion that resulted caused her to shuffle her steps. She fired more shots, struggling to steady her hand. Another bottle went up in flames. Alexa stumbled and fell hard onto the moist ground.

Joe appeared at her side. "You all right? Lord, I didn't mean for that."

"I'm fine," Alexa spouted back, sucking the blood from her lip. Joe reached out to help her up. She shoved his hand away and stood. "I said I'm fine," she repeated with an air of defiance.

"Then start running," He remarked with authority.

She took out another bottle before she reached the end and turned around. With the gun now in her right hand, she felt more confident. She took out three bottles in a row. She still had several misses, however, and she had to turn again and shoot with the left hand. She hit another bottle before she had to turn around again.

Only one bottle remained. She aimed at the bottle and squeezed the trigger several times with no success. *Damn.* After she passed the bottle, she turned and fired while running backwards. The bottle finally exploded into a ball of flames as Alexa tripped and fell, bumping her head on the soft ground.

She lay there. Her chest heaved in spasms. Joe's face hovered above her; looking down, he laughed heartily. This time, Alexa didn't wait for him to offer assistance. She extended a hand. He grabbed it and hoisted her to a stand.

"How'd it feel?" he asked.

"I needed that," she replied, still catching her breath. The field seemed magical as the sun inched its way over the horizon.

Joe followed her gaze and nodded. "All right, girl. Let's get you home." He coaxed her into a worn-down, thirty-year-old Ford pickup truck so he could take her back to the Four Seasons.

Alexa drifted off to sleep in the truck. She dreamed she was walking by the library downtown on a beautiful sunny day, with birds chirping and flowers in bloom. But her surroundings turned dark and cold. The flowers withered, and the air turned quiet as death.

Jamar sprang out of a bush. Kensie appeared at his side. Before Alexa could react, a large piece of metal struck her left temple. Jamar and Kensie tied ropes around her neck and limbs. A switchblade knife appeared in Jamar's hand, and he began mutilating Alexa's pelvis.

Kensie cheered Jamar on from the sidelines. "Do it to her, Jamar. Make that skinny bitch bleed." Kensie's eyes burned yellow like Jamar's.

Alexa awoke with a jolt, startling Joe so that he swerved to the side of the road and hit the curb, hard.

"You okay?" he questioned.

"Yeah. I'm fine," she lied. Joe shook his head. She ignored what she feared was an attempt to talk about her feelings.

When they arrived at her hotel, instead of saying goodbye, Joe said, "Someday you'll learn to trust people again, Alexa." His words rang in her ears like a prophecy.

"I trust you, Joe." She flashed a mouthful of pearls and reached over and gave his hand a squeeze.

Joe watched her slip out of the truck and enter the hotel. He shook his head while continuing the discussion he wanted to have with her out loud. "Fine, my ass. Why walk around telling the world you're fine when you want to tell everyone to go to Hell? Fine means leave me alone and let me sulk in my misery. I've been there." His eyes focused on the revolving door she'd entered. "You must have pushed everyone who matters out your life if you're celebrating tonight with an old man like me. No use trying to talk sense into you. Lord." The sound of the stranger's name from his lips startled him. He thought about his word choice before he continued. "Lord, help that woman face her demons." Before he could utter an *Amen*, a large whiskey belch escaped his lips, and he drove away.

CHAPTER 12

Once upstairs in her hotel suite, Alexa plopped onto her king-size bed, spread her limbs across the bedding, and thought about her nightmare. Kensie had been one of Jamar's victims, same as her; yet, Alexa couldn't control the resentment she felt for Kensie. *That woman had so many opportunities to fight Jamar, kill Jamar, or have Jamar arrested; yet she did nothing.* Free on the streets, Jamar could hurt whomever he chose.

That coward. If only she'd acted differently, I never would have been attacked. Alexa's rage turned to hatred as her thoughts materialized into words. "That coward! She kept her pain hidden and secret, while I had mine splattered across newspapers nationwide." Alexa doubted Kensie's life fell apart the way hers had.

Then she realized — that was what everyone had wanted from her all along. Her friends and family wanted her to be more like Kensie Phillips. *They all wanted me to just let the rape happen. They wanted me to stay silent and be a victim, and accept my fate without fighting back. To say nothing, like it never happened.*

Alexa jolted upright and let the thought permeate her mind fully. *No.* She couldn't accept it. Every cell in her body rejected the notion that giving up was ever an option. In her mind, only fighting back made sense. There were no options. From the moment Jamar attacked her, she knew only one of them would walk away that night. The other would be dead. It didn't matter the consequences that followed.

"I'm glad I am the one who walked away," she whispered to herself. Then she downed her usual concoction of melatonin and Benadryl, and topped it off with a vodka soda. She slept for three hours before a nightmare disturbed her rest. It was another blur of the night of the incident. She did as Britt had advised and replayed the nightmare time and again, each time with herself as the victor. She did this until she was calm enough to drift back to sleep for three more peaceful hours.

The next time she opened her eyes, warm rays of the morning sun greeted her. *My first day of freedom.* After ordering a large glass of orange juice from room service, she celebrated with a twelve-mile run through downtown Austin. After nine miles of running in a daze, twinges of pain in her left knee slowed her pace to a walk.

She hadn't made it a block before her stomach growled from its longstanding emptiness. She clutched the credit card she had shoved into her sports bra and sat down on the patio of a nearly empty little breakfast bistro. The waitress greeted her and then brought her a whole-wheat bagel with strawberry cream cheese and an espresso.

The espresso had been an accident. She wanted to avoid

caffeine, given her ongoing insomnia, but after inhaling the aroma of the coffee sitting in front of her, she couldn't resist and slowly sipped the warm indulgence. She closed her eyes, deep in thought. *I'll have to leave the hotel soon. Back to the small apartment where my six-month lease is almost up.* With no job and no ties to Austin after the wake of the trial, she was free.

What now? I haven't a single plan or schedule or anything. . . . Her mind reached for answers while she blew across the froth swirling atop her espresso. In spite of the six-figure attorney fees she had accumulated, she had some savings. *My life is so screwed up. I'm screwed up. If only I could set the restart button. I could just go somewhere new and start over.*

Suddenly, two words struck Alexa with such magnitude and clarity that she dropped her coffee cup on the patio. She barely heard it shatter over her own thoughts.

Fugue state.

It was a psychological disorder that had fascinated Alexa while in medical school. The term described a rare condition in which an individual would abruptly leave their current situation, change their name, location, occupation, and assume a new identity. It had always seemed like such a romantic idea to Alexa, to forget the past and change the future by becoming a whole new person.

But no one plans for that. It just happens, like a coping mechanism for stress, for people who are broken. A sigh escaped her. *But I am broken!* her subconscious begged, as she eyed the pieces of her coffee cup scattered by her feet. *Fugue state is amnestic; you can't control it.* She toiled with her thoughts. *That's my biggest problem. I try to control everything. If only I could let myself lose control, my mind would be free to escape. Nope.*

I'm too decisive for that. If I'm going to start over, it will have to be a conscious decision. You deserve this. Embrace the idea of fugue state. Leave Austin and start anew. Okay, she conceded. *But where will I go?*

The glaring eyes of her waitress interrupted Alexa's pondering. The waitress carried a broom and dustpan. Her rumpled expression conveyed her annoyance at the mess Alexa had made with the coffee cup. Alexa forced an apologetic smile, and the waitress's demeanor softened. *"C'est la vie,"* the waitress said with a shrug.

The waitress answered Alexa's question with her quoted French. *I'll go to Paris.*

She bid ado to the young waitress and used the three-mile walk back to the Four Seasons to plan for her move. She had left most of her furniture with Britt when they split. Her apartment had few residual furnishings. Alexa could easily sell her car and condense her extensive closet of clothes into a few trunks to bring with her. It was settled; she would move to Paris.

When Alexa returned to the Four Seasons, a plain-looking man in a bad gray suit accosted her with a white envelope in his hand. His only words to her were, "Miss DeBrow, you've been served."

Alexa's heart sank as she pieced together the man's words. *Served? No. The trial is over!* Alexa couldn't free her vice grip on the white envelope, although her fury tempted her to rip it into confetti. With her pulse already racing, she walked all the way up fourteen flights to her penthouse suite on the top. She texted Appleby: "911." He called within minutes. Alexa blurted into the receiver, "I'm at the Four

Seasons. I need you over here."

Appleby arrived at Alexa's door within twenty minutes. Before he could utter a word, Alexa shoved the bent envelope into his hand.

"What's this?" he asked.

She shrugged, too cross to feign politeness. "Open it. I couldn't bare it." She sat, shaking; her head swam.

He tore open the envelope and rattled off portions of its contents. The name of the other party was Portia Willis — not the family of Jamar Reading. It was a medical malpractice lawsuit. Appleby turned to Alexa.

She remembered that name from years ago. "What? I'm being sued by Portia Willis?"

Memories from her surgical intern year at the children's hospital flooded her mind. She had accepted the care of Portia Willis, a two-year-old pediatric patient, described as a "train wreck" case by the intern that handed her off to Alexa.

Portia had presented for an acute asthma attack and received oxygen and IV steroids in the ER. After a brief stint in the pediatric ICU, where she was intubated for hypoxia, she was later transferred to the inpatient floor, where she developed fevers and pus drainage from her IV site. Alexa assumed care when she placed the child's central venous line and removed the peripheral IV. She placed the girl on IV antibiotics for sepsis and tapered her steroids.

Post-op day one, Alexa went to examine Portia, and the child's mother complained that her daughter wouldn't walk. The child screamed when Alexa touched her, so Alexa ordered an x-ray. Portia had a broken leg — a pathologic fracture secondary to an underlying osteomyelitis. The blood infection had spread to her bones. Alexa ordered consults from infectious disease and orthopedics. That afternoon the child had a seizure, and Alexa ordered a brain MRI and a neurology consult.

Every time devastation struck, she contacted Portia's mother. Alexa gave bad news over the phone and face to face, time and again. An epidural abscess overlying Portia's left frontal lobe, another result of the sepsis, had triggered the seizure. Alexa ordered a neurosurgery consult for the abscess. As the month progressed, Portia developed more complications. Her condition finally stabilized, and Alexa discharged the girl home.

Alexa single-handedly arranged a family conference with Portia's mother and all of the consult services that required follow-up appointments. She scheduled the follow-up appointments and wrote the necessary prescriptions. She set up home health for weekly dressing changes. Portia had nine follow-up appointments and eighteen prescriptions on her date of discharge. Alexa never saw the family again.

Yes, Portia Willis, the train wreck case. But why would she sue me for malpractice? I did nothing wrong and was only an intern when I treated her. Alexa gave a summary of the details regarding Portia's case to Appleby.

At the end of her synopsis, he said, "This kind of thing happens a lot. People see your name on television, and they come after you for money. I doubt this case has any merit, but I'll look into it for you."

That wasn't good enough. "Make it go away, Jacob. I am *not* going back to court." She turned away from him and expected him to leave her. Instead, he changed the subject.

"I need to talk to you about something."

She feared he was about to mention the potential civil trial with the Reading family and refused to face him. She blamed him, somehow, for the second subpoena. "I can't go to court again, Jacob."

"You should be thanking me, Alexa," Appleby proclaimed while examining the empty glasses that lined her hotel nightstand. He picked up an empty highball and put the rim to his nose. "Vodka? Not what I would have guessed from you." He put the glass back on the counter as Alexa rolled her eyes. He curled his lip in a mocking manner. "Thank me because there won't be a civil trial. As it turns out, there's no one to benefit from Jamar's death. I had a DNA test confirm that his ten-year-old son is *not his son*, after all. He has no living family that I can trace aside from the older son who is in prison, and he is not in a position to file suit."

Alexa blinked twice in disbelief. *Good news, indeed, almost too good.* She wondered if Appleby had somehow arranged the outcome of the DNA test. His reputation of manipulation was partly why she'd hired him. "Thanks," she mumbled, checking his demeanor for a flinch or tell that might insinuate he was lying to her. He remained as calm as ever. *If you're lying, Jacob, I wish I were as smooth with it as you are.*

"That's not the only thing. I was approached by some of the media. They want to interview you, now that the trial is over." His attention returned to the glass on the dresser. "They pay you, and they pay well, if you're interested. It's not the kind of thing they advertise."

Alexa fell deep into thought. She'd given Appleby most of her savings, and she would need money to get to Paris.

"Who pays? How much?"

"The major news networks. They pay anywhere up to twenty-five thousand for an interview, maybe more, depending on how much they want you."

You mean how much they want to torture me. What a difficult proposition to concede to, but she needed the money.

"Okay. You make the arrangements. I want to do all of the interviews next week. You prep me. You assign the questions. Everything will be staged and rehearsed. I'll give you ten percent of whatever I get."

"Make it twenty percent, and we have a deal."

"Fine, Jacob," she agreed with reluctance, and shook hands with the devil himself.

Appleby emailed Alexa her schedule. He crammed three interviews into one week. They traveled together. New York on Monday, Chicago on Wednesday, and San Francisco on Friday. They spent Sunday evening and Monday morning rehearsing. Appleby hashed out the details over breakfast.

"Show them your sweet and innocent side. Never speak of Jamar. Don't say his name. You are the young, scared, female victim. Don't forget it." She gave long and exaggerated head bobs of affirmation.

"Then I quote statistics on rape, specifically those involving college students. I rattle off national counseling programs for rape victims and spout out classes where women can learn self-defense. I got it."

"No audience questions. No talk of the trial."

Now, she nodded in relief.

During the interviews, trained professionals in padded suits taught self-defense techniques to audience members.

The interviews were kept as light-hearted as possible, and overall, were much less painful than the trial she had endured. No questions were taken from the audience, no specifics of the trial discussed.

At the end of the week, she and Appleby flew back to Austin together. After a few glasses of first-class wine, Jacob Appleby's loose lips confessed his surprise that she ever went to trial for Jamar's death.

"Yours was a clear case of justifiable homicide. Usually, in such cases, you are arrested, but the charges are dropped. I don't know why they felt a need to pursue the charges. Maybe it was that detective who wanted the charges to stick. Marcum handled the Kennedy case, too — that nineteen-year-old found dead. Maybe he was running out of time to close that case and hoped to get you wrapped up in it in a way that would work to his benefit." His words ran together in a mellow sort of harmony that only inebriation could compose.

Alexa hung on the words of his drunken melody. *Could my suffering really be due to Marcum's need for a scapegoat?*

Appleby continued, "Defending you should have been easy, but you made my job difficult. I had to make them believe you never intended to kill Jamar, that you were a victim of circumstance. The problem, Alexa, is that we all saw through you. I did. The jury did. Everyone saw through you." He reached over and clenched her thigh with his hand. "Christ, Alexa. That mightier-than-thou look you wore on your face told them you could bludgeon a baby seal to death without thinking twice. You were so proud you killed that man, without an ounce of remorse for what you did." His grip tightened. "Innocent and not guilty are not the same thing."

"You're drunk, Jacob." She struggled for a defense.

"I'm *drunk*, says the alcoholic prude?" he mocked. "Don't worry, I'll be sober in the morning." He tore his hand from her leg and shuffled his body to the side of the seat farthest from her.

And terribly hungover, I hope! She fell silent. *No. He can't be right. Is there some truth to his outburst? The tension that's developed with my family — is it because they see the darkness their golden girl is capable of? I took the life of another human being and didn't regret it for a moment.*

"Your actions helped get you to this point, Alexa. Think about that as you decide where to go from here." A limp handshake departing the plane sealed their goodbye.

Back in Austin, Alexa packed up her belongings, moved out of her apartment, and headed back to the Four Seasons. She sold her Mercedes at the local dealership and took a cab to say goodbye to Joe. She met him at the shooting range. Knowing Joe got a kick out of a woman all dressed up with a gun in her hand, she grabbed a pretty pale pink chiffon blouse with a silver leather pencil skirt and python T-strap stilettos.

"Hello, Joe."

"Hey, there. It's good to see you. I have something I want you to try. I think you'll like it."

"You do? I'm intrigued, Joe. Is it a handgun?"

"Yep. It's lighter than what you're used to. It fires faster than the one you have."

Alexa beamed. They both knew this was goodbye.

"Okay, Joe. Let's try it." She watched him pull a little silver handgun out of a drawer. It sparkled like bright chrome. Her smirk grew bigger.

"You done with all that TV stuff now?" he asked.

"Yes, Joe. No more trial talk for me." Alexa allowed a moment of reflection before revealing her plans. "I'm leaving for Paris tomorrow."

He loaded the gun and handed it to Alexa. "Isn't that the city of love?"

Alexa shuddered. She took the gun from Joe and aimed at the target. "I like to think of it as the city of lights." She whispered into the air, "*Levende lys*," and fired eight times with amazing accuracy. "I love the gun, Joe. Thank you for letting me try it out. I can't thank you enough for everything."

Joe shrugged. "It was just nice for an old man like me to have something in common with a pretty young lady like yourself." He put out his hand to shake hers. Alexa grasped Joe's hand tightly with both of hers and pulled him close for a heartfelt embrace. "I hope you find whatever it is that you are looking for," Joe stated, his expression serious.

Her arms fell to her sides. "Me, too," she said.

The next morning, Alexa boarded her plane for Paris.

CHAPTER 13

The fourteen-hour flight allowed plenty of time for meditation, and Alexa became lost in her own thoughts. She found excitement in her opportunity to escape her troubled past and looked forward to what a future in Paris might hold. *What is my plan for Paris? Start over? Find friendship? Find love? Find a purpose?* The vague ideas left much to the imagination.

After the long flight, Alexa settled into a cheap, quaint boutique hotel a few blocks away from the Paris nightlife. It was a good fit for her, given her financial situation.

She spent her first day indulging in espresso and French delicacies while perusing miles and miles of Parisian streets. That evening, she carved out an eight-mile running path that paralleled the north bank of the Seine. Alexa donned a swanky black leather shift dress with red heels for her Paris nightlife debut.

Another Thursday night. Lights and music made a spectacle of the streets. Couples sipped wine at outdoor cafés. Men and women danced on patios that flanked the street.

Alexa found a lively venue and ordered a glass of cabernet. She sat at a table by herself, watching the scene from afar.

Halfway through her glass of wine, the waitress unexpectedly brought another. The woman didn't seem to speak English, and when Alexa tried to hand the glass back, the woman simply pointed to a handsome man sitting at the bar. Alexa's glance fell on the young man with glossy dark hair and tanned skin. He waved at her as his provocative glance seemed to undress her slowly. He rose from his chair and headed in her direction. She blushed and fumbled with her napkin.

But his course changed, and he grabbed the hand of a red-headed girl a couple of tables away, and the two began dancing and laughing.

Alexa's blush turned to crimson jealousy. She wasn't used to vying for a man's attention. Her sips of wine turned to careless gulps. She wanted drunkenness to creep in and wash away the envy. She directed her attention to people-watching elsewhere, but she kept gravitating back to that handsome man. He had a sense of charisma and energy about him that enticed her.

Another forty-five minutes passed before he approached her. He knelt down at Alexa's side, grasped her hand, and pulled it close to his cheek.

"You're American," he stated with an alluring French accent.

"Yes. You speak English." She had finished her second glass of wine, and her head spun.

"You're exquisite," the Frenchman said. "Come. Let's dance."

Alexa followed her handsome suitor to the dance floor, where he twirled her around. She kicked and dipped and shimmied on the floor. They danced for nearly an hour. He danced with such passion and seduction. *Oh, to flirt again is amazing!* Lust burned through her veins. As the night came to a close and the music faded, the Frenchman pulled her close for a long, wet kiss. He kissed with his lips, his tongue, and his teeth. His teeth caressed her lips, and the stimulation coursed through her body all the way to her toes. She wanted him. She wanted to feel his hands on her breasts. She wanted to feel their limbs wrapped up in a steamy, knotted embrace.

He led her out of the bar, and they walked the cobblestone streets, kissing and touching until they stumbled upon Alexa's hotel, and she froze.

"This is you?" he asked, and placed his hands low on her hips.

"Yes," she whispered.

The Frenchman placed his lips close to her right ear. "Do you want me to make love to you tonight, *mon amour*." Then he kissed her ear and teased her by slowly nibbling on her lobe.

She wanted to give in. She wanted to say *yes* to the nameless French suitor, but she couldn't. In spite of the desire in her bosom, she reserved making love for when she was *in love*. She wouldn't let herself go around screwing men precariously. Her mind instantly went to Britt, the only man she had ever loved. The only man who had ever made love to her.

Alexa broke away from the man's embrace, and he laughed out loud. "Not tonight, *mon amour*. Give me your phone. We'll meet another night." Alexa handed her cell phone to him and watched him type the name *Serge* across the screen.

"Serge, I'm Alexa." She was embarrassed they hadn't introduced themselves before.

A wide grin spread across his warm wet lips. "We'll meet another night. We'll go dancing. I'll teach you to dance."

Alexa's dancing didn't compare to Serge's. He had moves she couldn't match. But she hadn't realized he was scrutinizing her abilities. She scolded herself, wholly embarrassed by so many of the night's events.

"Another night, Serge. I'd like that. I like dancing with you."

"Tomorrow night?"

He pulled her close for one last kiss. He almost made her give in to him.

"Tomorrow night." *Thank goodness he didn't pursue things further.* He let her go, winked, and walked away.

She crept up the stairs of her boutique hotel in a mild drunken daze. She slipped off her cocktail dress and wrapped her naked body in the bed sheets. Alexa couldn't get the thought of Serge's teeth nibbling on her lips out of her head. She yearned for a man's body. Her hands moved up and down her body, slowly caressing the sensitive parts. She massaged herself in slow little circles until waves of pleasure rippled down to her toes. Almost in unison with Alexa's rhythmic ecstasy came moans of pleasure from another couple in the adjacent room. Alexa couldn't help but laugh out loud over the coincidence. She drifted off to five blissful hours of uninterrupted sleep.

She woke to a perfect Parisian morning. After a quick breakfast, she decided to spend the day at the Louvre. Alexa jumped in a cab outside her hotel, and they headed toward the museum. The skinny, pale, dark-haired cab driver appeared in his fifties and smoked cigars while he chauffeured his clients around Paris. *What a horrid stench.* Alexa put her window down as far as it would go, but she couldn't get it to open all the way.

The man sped through the winding streets at a rate that wasn't safe by anyone's standards. Alexa searched the crevices of the bench seat for a seat belt. Her hands scavenged across the stained upholstery to no avail. The car raced past a teenage girl on a vintage red bicycle. The tires of the bicycle were only about a foot away from the tires of the car. Alexa scowled at the cigar smoker's carelessness and screamed, "Hey!" out loud.

The cabbie answered with a nasal grunt and a wave of his hand. In that moment, another car pulled out ahead of the taxi, making the cab swerve hard to the left. The cab veered off the road and smashed through the short brick wall separating the road from the bank of the Seine.

The accident happened quickly, but Alexa's hands were already clutching the car door for stabilization. The cab plunged into the water below. Alexa turned the handle hard and thrust her shoulder at the car door, but she couldn't get it to budge. The car sank rapidly, and water flooded through the open window. She scrambled to maneuver her arms and torso through the window opening, forcing one arm at a time through the small opening. When the second arm passed through the window, the glass gave way. It didn't break; the glass merely separated from the window frame of the door.

Alexa floated the rest of the way through the window and to the surface of the water. The rear of the car continued to sink slowly. Bubbles rose from where the front of the car was submerged. The front windshield shattered after the collision, and water covered both the hood and the driver-side window.

Among the bubbles in the water, the unconscious body of the obnoxious cab driver bobbed along in the river. Alexa eyed the body. She held nothing but dislike for him, but she had to help him. She judged the distance to the shore and the current of the water. *I'm an awful swimmer, but I should be able manage that despite the current.* She swam to the cabbie and tucked his neck and shoulders under her right arm. She made slow, gentle strokes until she reached the bank of the river.

A small crowd had formed along the shore. Onlookers helped Alexa pull the driver's body out of the water and onto the pavement. She shouted to the crowd, "Ambulance!" in the best French accent she could muster. The words came out breathy. She knelt by the cab driver. His chest didn't rise. She turned and surveyed the eyes of the French patrons, silently pleading with them. She wanted one of them to step up and take over. No one moved.

Alexa grunted in desperation. She worried about liability, malpractice, and lawsuits. Rule number one in medicine — a physician should never render services outside of work, especially in emergency situations. Unlike other individuals who are protected by Good Samaritan clauses in emergent cases, physicians can still be held liable. It was a similar type of loophole that the prosecution had tried to use to hold Alexa responsible for Jamar's death. Alexa remembered the bitter taste of Portia Willis' lawsuit and silently thanked Jacob Appleby for his ability to make the charge go away with a meager settlement.

This isn't the United States; this is Paris. The lawyers don't act as such vultures in France. That's an American thing. Her eyes made a final search for a hero in the audience before starting basic life support.

She pounded his back to try to clear some excess water from his lungs, and then she flipped him supine. She laid two fingers on the man's carotid artery and felt for a pulse. *Maybe. No. Nothing.* She placed one palm on top of the other on his chest and began heavy, rhythmic chest compressions at the standard rate. She knew CPR to two rhythms: "Staying Alive," by the Bee Gees, and "Another One Bites the Dust," by Queen. Her BLS instructor had mentioned that everyone held superstitions as to whether the song that was chosen could influence the outcome of the CPR attempt. She upheld the superstition and chose the Bee Gees.

She felt a snap once, twice as she compressed the man's chest. She winced as his ribs cracked under the force.

She looked down at the man's gaping mouth, full of stained yellow teeth and amalgam fillings and considered mouth-to-mouth. *No. Not yet.* She closed her eyes and continued with compressions, humming the beat to herself. When she reopened her eyes, she saw his blue tinged lips and had no choice but to proceed with a couple of rescue breaths. She pinched his nose, tilted his head back, and covered his mouth with hers. She exhaled two long deep breaths into the man's mouth and felt his chest rise. A small amount of residual river water seeped into her open mouth, and she could still smell the cigar when the air poured out of his lungs.

After a second breath, she felt for a pulse. Nothing definite. *Come on! Dammit!* She continued with compressions, but started to fatigue. Another rib snapped. *He's dead, Alexa,* a sour voice crept in from her subconscious. She cranked up the volume of the song lyrics playing in her head to drown out the voice. *Press harder. Your hands are becoming limp.*

In the distance, a siren rang out. It grew louder. Alexa continued compressions until the emergency medical technicians pushed her aside.

"I broke some ribs," she stated, and walked away. She spoke English and doubted they understood her. As she broke through the crowds, she overheard one of the medical aides.

"Je sens un battement de coeur."

They feel a heartbeat! Relief swept over her as she let out a meager laugh. *Perhaps saving this life can make up for one I took.*

A police officer came forward and questioned her briefly about the accident. It wasn't a very official investigation. He spoke to her mostly in English. He asked if she was American and if she had lost her passport and identification, and directed her to the American Embassy where she could get assistance. He handed her a piece of paper that would serve as documentation that her identification was lost in an accident. Then the officer left her.

A second man approached Alexa. She thought he was another cab driver. Perhaps a friend or colleague of the man she saved. He didn't seem that interested in the other cabbie, however, and he didn't look French. *Czech, maybe?*

"I saw it," the man said in broken English. "You save him. You did good. You American?" She nodded. "American with money, no?" She froze in the awkward moment. "You lose your things?" The man motioned to the water where the car sank.

"Yes. I lost my passport, my wallet, even my phone."

"You go to Embassy now?"

She nodded again.

"You have money. I have friend, cousin. Can get you passport easy. Fast." He managed a dull finger snap that sounded like a thud. "Not like Embassy. You can be — anyone you want." He made a motion with both hands to convey infinite possibilities. "His card." The man handed Alexa a piece of paper the size of a business card with hand written information on it. An address and a name. That was all.

Alexa accepted it. The man nodded and smiled. "You save him. Very good." He walked away.

She stood alone on the street in a small puddle where the water collected at her feet. The ambulance containing the cabbie drove away as the crowd thinned. She looked down at the card and knew what it offered her. His words repeated over and over again in her head. *You can be anyone you want.* She couldn't help but succumb to the irony of the proposition. She had left Austin to start a new life, in a new place, and become a new person. *Fugue state. I can change my identity and forget Dr. Alexa DeBrow forever.* The forever part seemed to echo in her mind. In order for this to work, she'd have to disassociate from her former life altogether.

CHAPTER 14

A lexa pocketed the business card and walked the Parisian streets back to her hotel. The desk clerk recognized her and gave her a new room key.

"Miss DeBrow." He passed her the key with a deep nod that turned into a half bow.

She accepted the key with a quick "Merci" and wondered whether or not she wanted to stay Miss DeBrow. She considered the possibilities, as well as the possible legal infractions. *Fraud. Unless I legally change my name, this is fraud. It's against the law. And I'd be living a lie.* Her moral compass worked to sway her toward the straight and narrow, while her heart heralded other fantasies. *Do I care if it's wrong? Do I really care? I deserve this. I deserve to start over, a second chance of happiness. I can be anyone I want. . . .* With her heart and her head pulling her in different directions, she came to a standstill. Yet something about the timing of the offer seemed too good to pass up. She thought about the debit card tucked away in her luggage. *I have access to cash withdrawals. I have time to decide whether or not to go to the embassy.*

She rinsed the Seine's stink from her hair and her skin and prepared for a night of dancing with Serge and a couple of his friends. She slipped on a red chiffon dress with a deep V-neck and a flowing skirt that opened wide for twirling. She completed the ensemble with gold heels. The light and energy that emanated from Serge warmed her insides like smoldering embers. A bright red lipstick served as a tangible reminder of the passion that Serge evoked and her longing for the touch of his lips. She yearned to seduce him, but she was secretly afraid to lure him in. A spritz of expensive French perfume, and she was out the door.

She met Serge and two of his male comrades at a restaurant that stayed open late into the night and featured a jazz band until five a.m. They danced and drank wine and danced some more. Alexa twirled, and her skirt flew high, teasing the onlookers enjoying their late night cocktails. Luscious long tanned legs and exposed thighs, Alexa watched with pleasure as the eyes of the male patrons widened. *I have never behaved this provocatively. It feels amazing!* She watched Serge's finesse on the dance floor and mimicked his encompassing rhythm. His hips vibrated with the music. He locked his hands on her hips, not at her waist in a gentlemanly fashion, but low on her iliac crests and pulled her pelvis close to his. He moved her body with his, as she grew accustomed to the choreography he possessed.

As she learned spins, lifts, and steps that worked together harmoniously, she learned to breathe in the music and open her heart to possibilities. *With so much energy pulsating through me, I feel alive again!* She embraced the feeling, and the dancing came naturally.

Serge dropped down to his knees and eased her leg over his shoulder; he stroked her thigh to the music. His hands fell to her lower back, and he scooped her body off the floor. Her other leg wrapped around Serge's other shoulder, her crotch hovering inches from his lips. Serge spun Alexa around in circles while her skirt fell loose and covered her face. Her entire lower body was exposed; her lace white panties became a spectacle for all to see. Goosebumps of excitement rippled across her skin. *To be in the center of such an erotic and provocative scene — how invigorating!* Serge swung her torso to the side, and within minutes, she was in his arms.

The song ended. The phenomenal applause turned Alexa's face crimson. So many eyes locked on her. Serge grabbed her hand and led Alexa outside into the street. She anticipated a late night make-out session in the alley, but she was mistaken.

"What happen to your leg?"

"Wh-a-at?" She stammered.

"You have scar. There on your thigh." Without hesitation, Serge lifted Alexa's dress and revealed the long scar across her left upper thigh.

The scar from Jamar's knife. "It's nothing. A scar. That's all."

"What happen to you?" he questioned in his imperfect English.

"An accident. A long time ago."

He furrowed his brow. "Does not look old." He traced the scar with his index finger, following it all the way up toward her crotch. *Even when he touches that painful place, I tingle down to my toes.* She couldn't resist the urge any longer.

She wanted to give in to Serge completely — let him seduce her. Let him caress her body and make love to her. She had only given in completely to one person, Britt Anderson. But she needed to be touched by a man again. She wanted it to be Serge. She wanted to somehow take his energy and passion for life from him as he took a piece of her innocence.

One of Serge's friends interrupted Alexa's moment of intimacy. His hand pulled away, and her dress dropped to her knees; the two men walked away from her. They spoke French together for a good five minutes before she marched over and grabbed Serge's arm from behind.

"Hey!" she remarked jokingly. "Forgetting someone?" She tried hard to sound coy. She wanted to remind him of the passion they shared.

But Serge's attention rested on the new male friend. The man casually slipped his hand into the side pocket of Serge's fitted white slacks. This man's attempt to seduce Serge appeared stronger than hers. She watched his fingers outline the contours of Serge's package. Her mouth gaped as she stared at the spectacle. Without missing a beat, Serge put his finger to her chin in an attempt to close her open mouth.

"Victor and I will go have some fun at my place. What you think? Want to have fun? You join us?" While Serge's questioning eyebrow intrigued her, Victor's stone face negated Serge's invitation. She tossed aside her desire for a romantic tryst with Serge, shook her head, and turned away.

"Another night, then?" he questioned from behind.

"Another night," she mumbled without turning to face him.

She sulked as she walked the few short blocks back to

her hotel. *How was I so misled? I don't understand Serge at all.* She dissected the events of the evening. The men in the café were fixated on Alexa's lace panties, except Serge, who eyed the scar on her thigh. Did Serge dance to gather the attention of the onlookers, rather than his partner? Was Serge's dance to seduce Victor, not Alexa? *Is Serge bi-sexual? He seems so comfortable with his sexuality, more than I could ever comprehend. It's the same energy that drew me to him.* She furrowed he brow with the new information, and realized she was completely out of her element.

She decided to vault her lustful thoughts somewhere deep in her heart, where they belonged. Her first and last sexual encounter was with her darling Britt Anderson. It would stay that way indefinitely. She put a hand to her chest in attempt to soothe the ache for Britt that lurked within.

When she reached her hotel room, she placed her room key on the nightstand next to the handwritten business card the Czech man had given her. A new identity was a way to move on from Britt Anderson, a way to put away the past and move toward a new future. Her eyes scrutinized the writing on the card. The tops of the letters angled to the left, a characteristic of penmanship of left-handed writers. *Britt was left-handed.* She clenched her teeth together tightly. *Stop it!* she scolded. She didn't want to forget him, but the memories hurt, so she tried to box him away somewhere in the back of her mind.

With the sun about to rise, she popped a couple of sleep aids and rolled into bed.

Her dreams were tormented by portions of the day's escapade entwined by guest appearances by Jamar and Portia.

She relived the cab crashing into the concrete guard and splashing into the water. She tried to escape the car. She felt a hand on her arm — Portia's hand. The child tried to keep Alexa in the car in order to drown them both. Alexa kicked. She screamed. She grabbed Portia's face, wrapped her fingers around the child's head, and knocked it against the other window until the water in the car turned red.

Jamar took over where Portia left off. He thrust her head underwater. His strong hands and arms kept her there. He was drowning her.

Alexa woke sputtering and gasping for air — as usual. Her anguish quickly turned to tears. "No! I won't lose to him!" she yelled. She fought back the tears and followed Britt's advice once more. She closed her eyes and visualized the dream taking a turn where she could again be the victor. She sat in the back of the cab. Jamar drove. The car swerved hard, and into the river they went. Bodies bounced around in the car, and they both found themselves in the water. Splashes came toward Alexa. It was Jamar. She swam to the bank first. He pursued her, but she beat him to the water's edge. *I'm faster than you, Jamar.*

He tried to emerge from the river, both of his hands on the concrete edge of the canal. He lifted his body from the water, his head even with the pavement. With both hands and all of her weight, she thrust Jamar's forehead into the concrete. *I'm stronger than you, Jamar.*

When his body started to slip back into the water, she grasped his head and thrust it hard into the concrete. She heard his skull break. His body turned limp, and an indentation formed in the front of his head.

Alexa lay in bed a while longer, still unable to sleep. This time she planned to kill him *before* he entered her nightmares. She envisioned the entire event. She waited for Jamar by the library where he stalked Kensie. She packed her handgun into a vintage black Chanel clutch and sat on a bus stop bench across the street.

The man with the yellow eyes smoked a cigarette and drank from a brown paper bag on the sidewalk next to the library. He didn't see her. He stooped down by a tall hedge and stowed the paper bag and its contents in the bushes.

Alexa stood and crossed the street. She drew her gun when twenty feet away. His eyes locked on hers, and he turned to run. She shot his right shoulder. He stumbled forward. She came after him and pushed him to the ground, landing on top of him. He rolled over to face her.

"Bitch!" he yelled, and spit at her.

Alexa thrust the barrel of the gun under Jamar's chin and pulled the trigger fast. *I'm the victor, Jamar.* Then she imagined the course of the bullet traveling through Jamar's submental region, severing his tongue base, passing through his oropharynx, filling his prevertebral space with blood, and shattering his odontoid — sending bone fragments and bullet fragments into his brainstem. She put two fingers to his carotid and waited for his pulse to stop. She imagined the events once more. It brought her a sense of strength and security. Finally, Alexa slept.

CHAPTER 15

She slept away the morning and woke in the early afternoon. She had agreed to meet Serge again that night. He invited her to be his plus one at a private party in Paris. Serge mingled in different social circles, including those of high society. Tonight's event was a birthday gala for some scandalous Parisian bureaucrat whose mistress was one of Serge's ex-lovers. Although she gave up on the idea of a romance between Serge and herself, she still enjoyed his company. She planned to treat herself with a spa day and shopping spree before meeting him.

She went to a fabulous designer boutique on the outskirts of the fashion district. "*Bonjour, chérie!*" exclaimed the store clerk as Alexa approached. The tall, skinny twenty-something had straight black hair and pale skin. "American?" she questioned with a look of mild disgust.

"*Oui,*" Alexa stammered with all the charisma she could muster. She hadn't yet grown accustomed to the cold shoulder she received from some Europeans. She often felt embarrassed to admit she was an American transplant, but she knew this woman would forgive her once she opened up her pocket book. The money Alexa planned to spend would be enough to make any contemptuous Parisian feign kindness. She glanced around the store as the black-haired woman eyed her up and down. Alexa spotted a silk, white evening gown with a low back and high slit on the thigh. She carefully examined the high slit. It was on the right side of the dress, which meant only her right leg would be wholly exposed, and the scar Jamar put on her left thigh would be carefully hidden.

"Ah, madam. I can help you. It looks your size. Come with me." The Parisian lady swooped up the white evening gown and motioned Alexa into a fitting room with a luxurious blue-velvet loveseat, floor to ceiling mirrors, and a crystal chandelier that was clearly too large for the space. The French lady disappeared momentarily and returned with a sparkling glass of mid-level French champagne.

"The dress is Claude Montana," the sales woman said with a forced smile. "He is genius." Her English was fair.

Alexa stripped down and grabbed the gown. The silky sheer left little to the imagination and left no room for undergarments. The cut was more seductive than most lingerie — *perfect for a scandalous political gala.* She couldn't help but stare at herself. The slit on the skirt neared the top of her right thigh. She pulled back the fabric to look at the scar on the other leg. She traced the scar up and down its length. It still had a pinkish-purple hue that showed its newness. Serge had recognized this. She'd spent so many months trying to ignore it or hide it; perhaps she'd have the scar removed altogether. Nonetheless, tonight it would be safely hidden beneath the fabric.

"Madam!" the French woman yelled in a singsong voice, and then threw back the heavy velvet curtains of the fitting room and burst in on Alexa just as she released the fabric covering her thigh. "I have shoes for you, *chérie!*"

A beautiful pair of Casadei gold crisscross platform pumps landed in Alexa's outstretched hands. Alexa enjoyed two more glasses of champagne before paying for her merchandise with a wad of cash she'd pulled from the ATM using her one remaining debit card.

Too tipsy from the champagne to sit still for the hair appointment she'd booked, she rode a cab back to her hotel and took a long hot bath and played rock music in the background. She slowly sobered up and managed a proper get-ready on her own. She slipped on the gold platform heels and paired them with tiered, gold chandelier earrings.

When Serge beckoned, she slid into a cab containing Serge and a friend around ten-thirty at night. Everything started late in Paris, and their destination was another hour away. A red headed voluptuous woman sat in the cab next to Serge. She looked a little older than Alexa, and acted much drunker than her. The woman toted a bottle of Russian vodka, and the cap served as a shot glass. They passed shots of vodka around the car and laughed out loud for reasons Alexa never really understood, but it all seemed hysterical.

The cab made two more stops along the way, picking up other members of Serge's entourage. A tall blond man with a square jaw that reminded Alexa of Britt scooted in beside her. He didn't speak much English, but he kept finding ways to touch Alexa on her back or leg that she found creepy. The other passenger was a blonde girl a few years younger than Alexa, who was short and skinny and wore a red sequined gown with a plunging neckline that went down to her navel. The group exchanged shots and sipped wine out of a bottle the man had brought.

They arrived at a large pier lined with several yachts. A long white carpet lined the walkway and the gangplank of the largest yacht. Strands of lights wrapped around the boat illuminated the blackness of the night. Music filled the air. Luxury cars dropped off passengers for the party. Alexa counted four Mercedes and two Bentleys, and her stomach churned of inadequacy when she exited the cab that dropped them off. The blond man paid the cab fare. Alexa followed Serge up the gangplank onto the ship.

She eyed the spectacle. She saw women dripping sequins and trimmed in fur and jewels. Men were clad mostly in tuxes without tails with a sprinkling of navy suits, some with open necks bearing chest hair. An ensemble of Arabian musicians filled the air with song, while belly dancers and fire-eaters covered the dance floor. Sushi and caviar floated around the room on little silver trays, along with glasses of champagne and vintage wine. Scantily clad women perused through the ballroom from time to time while marketing themselves to the men in the room.

Alexa ignored the sex-capades and had another glass of champagne. She mingled with cliques of mixed origins. She spoke with politicians and their wives or mistresses, as well as up-and-coming artists, musicians, and philanthropists. She even met a Parisian fashion designer who once worked under Alexander McQueen.

She found a dance partner in an English businessman who divided his time between Paris and London. The slightly older gentleman had a bit of a paunch and his skills were no match for Serge. She sighed relief when Serge grabbed her arm from behind and stole her for a dance.

He moved wildly, and her long blonde hair whipped around and hit his face. He pulled Alexa tight and kissed her up and down her neck, with long wet kisses where his tongue traveled deep into her cleavage.

When he spun her, she lost her balance and stumbled away from Serge. Another man grasped her from behind. She found herself laughing fervidly when she looked at the man's face. An Arab man in his forties or early fifties with a small mole under his right eye smiled back at her. A party of bodyguards with stern faces quickly surrounded them.

Two bodyguards escorted Alexa a safe distance away and returned her to Serge. He took her arm and guided her outside onto the deck.

"What the hell was that all about?" She sneered through clenched teeth, afraid someone might still be watching them.

Serge threw his head back and chuckled. "Don't worry, love. You stumbled into one deadly Arabian . . . how you say . . . *hit man*? Maybe that is the wrong word."

Alexa's jaw dropped. "What?" she demanded.

"You Americans, so high strung. Relax. This is party!" His hips swayed in time to the music inside, and he reached out for Alexa's hands.

"Hit man? What *are* you talking about? Is he some kind of Islamic fanatic who goes around blowing things up?"

Serge feigned seriousness now to match Alexa's tone.

119

"Perhaps, something of the sort. He is dangerous man. He bring death to many people — Americans, even. And you — you watch too much CNN, like all Americans. Do not worry about this man. He will not harm you. The way he stare at you tells me he likes you." Serge's face beamed with excitement.

"What? No," she said. "Islamic radicals *hate* Americans. They bomb our country and attack our people. Why would you say something like that?"

He snickered at Alexa's remark. "Political hate and political prejudice are not lust. He likes you."

Alexa recalled the lingering stare she'd received. Yep. This Arabian found her enticing. "Who is he, Serge?"

He shrugged. "They call him *Castro*. He likes party. I see him at these things. No big deal." He shrugged again.

"Castro? Like Fidel Castro? No. That doesn't make sense at all," she pondered out loud.

"No. It is nate name or something." His brow furrowed in confusion, but he continued to sway his hips to the music.

"You mean nickname?" she asked.

"Ha, ha. Yes. That one." He grabbed her arm. "Dance with me. Inside." He led her back to the dance floor.

Her head spun. She couldn't stop thinking of the man she'd seen. Afraid to look at him directly, she imagined his face when he grabbed her waist after falling into him. Something about that mole under his right eye seemed familiar. She recalled news broadcasts she had seen. She and Britt used to watch the news religiously. Once Alexa had started making news headlines herself, she couldn't bear to turn it on or pick up a paper.

It hit her suddenly; a CNN special report she'd watched with Britt some two years prior that highlighted various U.S. terrorists throughout the last decade. She'd seen the same man with the mole under his right eye on the news that night. The recollection brought on a wave of nausea. She recalled pictures of families who were killed due to random bombings initiated by that man. She tried to think of his name. "Castro" was an alias he went by.

Serge spun Alexa time and again. She struggled to keep up as her mind was elsewhere. She couldn't stop thinking about that face. The nameless man made the FBI's most wanted list at one point. *Mohammed. Mohammed Ahmed, perhaps.* He was responsible for everything from blowing up public transit buses, to illegal trafficking of captured American tourists, to piracy in the Mediterranean.

Now Alexa had crossed paths with him in this random aristocratic soirée in Paris. *Yes. Mohammed Ahmed. That is his name.* She abandoned Serge and headed to the ladies' room. She could no longer contain the nausea. She cleared her stomach of the rich hors d'oeuvres and vodka shots. Her skin looked pale and clammy in the bathroom mirror. She splashed cold water on her face, pinched her cheeks, and applied a veil of bronzer that highlighted her features and brought life back to her pallor. *Much better.*

She rejoined the party. Serge and his entourage were looking for her. The red headed girl had left their group to have sex with a Russian businessman. The blonde girl lay passed out in a chair in a drunken stupor. The blond man who had been making flirtatious advances toward Alexa earlier had found a skinny black-haired woman who resembled the sales clerk from the boutique store earlier that day to accompany him home. Her red lipstick was smeared across the man's lips and chin, and her silk blouse had been unbuttoned and then precariously re-buttoned so that the two sides were askew. The woman's mini skirt raised so high her crotch played peek-a-boo with every step she took. The man grasped his lady's hand and glanced over at Alexa with a look that said, *See what you're missing? This could have been you tonight.* Alexa smiled curtly and headed toward the bar.

"How about one more round of drinks for the survivors in our party tonight?" She glanced back at the girl passed out in the corner. She needed some alcohol back in her system in order to complete the thoughts that were brewing in her mind.

Serge laughed wholeheartedly. "I like the American woman! Let us drink shots!"

It was one round of vodka shots followed by another. The group sang some French tune that only Serge really knew.

Then Serge approached Alexa. "If you don't want a French lover tonight, how about an Arabian one?" He motioned to the Castro character with the mole under his eye. "They say powerful men make great lovers."

Alexa absorbed Serge's words with disgust, but turned up her lips politely nonetheless.

"No. Powerful men *take* great lovers." *It is a very different concept.*

"Ha, ha. Americans," he retorted. "Fine. We leave. If not tonight, perhaps another night, *chérie.* We see him next Friday, no doubt."

Her lids fluttered in confusion. "What's next Friday?"

Serge raised an eyebrow. "It is your soon-to-be new lover's birthday gala. We attend. No? It will be perfectly amazing time." Serge flashed his enticing smile.

Internally, Alexa winced. But she wouldn't let the emotion surface. *Am I ready for another fabulous French party?*

"Let us go, pet." They roused their crew and headed toward the exit.

"Your man is watching you." Serge whispered with anticipation.

An idea came into her mind. The crazy, wild, capricious idea turned her blood cold. Yet the timing seemed so unbelievably fitting that she couldn't shake the idea — so she succumbed to it. Moreover, she embraced it and acted upon it. She turned, looked the terrorist straight in the eye, and gave him her most provocative, come-hither, passionate, full-lipped smirk. *Yes. Castro, remember this face. Burn it into your memory. Lock your eyes on my lips and accept that you want to taste them. I want you, too, Castro. I want to kill you.*

Alexa held the man's gaze for two long seconds before pulling away from his glance. She watched his lips slowly part as his jaw inched lower. Then she casually reached out for Serge's arm, and their entourage departed. Even the blonde girl who had passed out in the chair woke to leave with her fellow partygoers.

CHAPTER 16

That night, Alexa dreamed of being back at the shooting range with Smokey Joe. She shot targets with the small handgun she had bought from Joe at their first meeting. She aimed at circles with bull's-eyes. Then Joe pulled out a target that was a picture of a man — a man that resembled Jamar.

She looked at Joe questioningly. He gave a stiff nod. She shot at the paper target, and the bullet pierced the forehead of the man pictured. A second bullet pierced through the paper where the man's heart would lie. She felt satisfied, yet she sensed something more. The door to the indoor shooting range creaked open. Alexa saw a black hand on the knob and Jamar's body followed. She shot him once in the forehead, and his body started to slump. She shot him in the chest, piercing his heart just like the target.

She woke calm and collected. Her heart didn't race. She wasn't screaming or sweating. *Maybe I've finally come to terms with Jamar's death. Maybe I can handle the death of Mohammed Ahmed. Maybe I'm ready to kill Mohammed.* She was tired of being the victim. "Maybe I'm ready to kill Mohammed," she whispered.

She couldn't explain why she wanted to kill him. But she wanted him dead. She wanted to know he wouldn't be around to hurt anyone else. She thought of the bus bombings and the night raids, and the deaths of all of those children. She needed him to be dead in order to feel safe. She also knew, with a little seduction, Castro would let her get close enough to him to carry it off successfully. What's more, she wasn't afraid to try. *Haven't I lost everything already? What's left to lose?*

The details of the project would be a difficult. She didn't know where to start. She tried to solidify what she did know. She knew she would see Castro again on Friday night. It would be at a party — *his* birthday party. His bodyguards would surround him, no doubt. He would be the host of the event, and, therefore, the center of attention.

Doubt crept into her mind like a fog. She pushed it aside and tried to focus. She knew she couldn't get Castro alone with her. She'd have to be subtle. Shooting him in public wasn't an option; therefore, she couldn't use a gun. *Kill him in public without harming others.* She found only one real option: poison.

Alexa knew little about poisons of any type, but she could research the matter. The first possibility that came to mind was cyanide. Flashbacks of Michael Marin's trial immediately filled her mind. She had learned from videos of the trial that the drug was lethal even in small 'doses, making it easier to administer discreetly. She needed to find out how to acquire it and how to convince Castro to willingly ingest it without detecting it.

Crushing the pill into a powder and mixing it with a stiff drink would be optimal. But will he taste it? She didn't know if cyanide had a taste, but the laws of nature implied anything deadly to humans would be noxious. She assumed the same for cyanide, but hoped the Internet would tell her otherwise.

Another thought weighed on Alexa's mind. She needed an escape plan. She would need to flee the scene immediately after watching Castro consume the poison. She imagined the fiasco his death would cause. If they suspected her, she might be pursued as she fled. *I'll carry a weapon to defend myself, if necessary.*

She considered a new possibility. *Even if I escape, if they suspect I did it, how long would they pursue me? I could be running indefinitely.* "Maybe a new identity would keep me safe." Alexa reached over to the nightstand where she kept the worn business card the cab driver had given her. She rubbed it between her thumb and forefinger. She decided she would visit this man and get a fake passport.

If Castro's comrades catch me, they'll kill me. Maybe even torture me first. She decided to keep an extra cyanide pill for herself, in case the alternative seemed intolerable.

Alexa pulled out her laptop to search for information regarding cyanide and how to obtain it. When she pulled up the search engine, however, her fingers had another idea. She searched for Mohammed Ahmed. She needed to be sure before she took this plan any further.

He is still on the FBI's most wanted list. The picture she saw definitely matched the man she'd met on the ship. The reassurance quickened her pulse, and her eyes scanned the text eagerly. The website mentioned a monetary reward for information on the man and/or his capture, *alive or dead.* She hesitated. She could receive one million dollars for the death of Mohammed Ahmed from the U.S. government, with dividends up to five million dollars for his capture *alive*.

Alive? But that would be nearly impossible, and even more dangerous than killing him. She contemplated merely giving his whereabouts to the FBI. That would be easy enough. She didn't see a set reward for information on the man, but it was a safe and easy alternative. *But he needs to die; he has to die.* The idea brought her a sense of relief. She found justice in ending the life of someone cruel. It had been the same with Jamar. *Doesn't ridding the world of someone terrible make the world a better place?*

She had to help a murderer once. She had a prisoner for a patient. Alexa vividly remembered the man she had known as "Hannibal the cannibal." The gray-haired middle-aged man transferred to her hospital from a nearby prison in order to have a swallow study to rule out aspiration after suffering an episode of pneumonia. Alexa was the radiologist performing the exam. A stern guard warned her that the convict had murdered his mother and ate her remains. His record of violence continued even in prison, where he allegedly bit the ears off two other prisoners and tried to strangle a prison guard.

Although cautious, she remained polite and kind, as with any patient, and pushed the judgment from her mind. "Hannibal" stumbled forward when he arose from his chair, and Alexa stepped in and let her body brake his fall. It was her duty as a physician, yet she couldn't help but think to herself: *please don't eat my face off.* She cringed at the thought. *That duty is gone. I won't help another monster!*

Yes. Alexa would continue with her original plan. She proceeded with her Internet search for cyanide. She concentrated on cyanide salts of sodium and potassium. These were the same crystalline solids consumed by Michael Marin, Eva Braun (Hitler's wife), and even consumed by Hitler himself just before he put a pistol to his head. It was the ultimate suicide pill utilized throughout history. It seemed a very humane way to die for such an inhumane man. The drug inhibited the enzyme cytochrome C oxidase in mitochondria, resulting in histotoxic hypoxia — essentially suffocating the cells in the human body.

Lethal doses of two-hundred milligrams resulted in lethargy that quickly progressed to a comatose state. The victim would suffer cardiac arrest within minutes of ingestion, and the body would develop a pink hue due to the build-up of methemoglobin. It would be the tale-tell sign that Castro had been poisoned. Alexa knew that this only gave her minutes to escape.

Conveniently, cyanide came with a medley of antidotes. The simplest of these was hydroxcobalamin, a form of vitamin B12, which combined with the cyanide to form an innate compound that would be eliminated in the urine. *Hmm, the antidote may prove handy if I keep the last pill for myself.*

Acquiring the toxin would be a dilemma. Certain clinics and physicians scattered throughout Europe participated in forms of euthanasia and assisted suicide in which cyanide might be utilized. Perhaps she could purchase the drug from a local apothecary or French pharmacist. Alexa would explore her options when she went to look for the man who could provide her with her new identity.

She grabbed the worn, handwritten business card. Fearing where she was heading may be a sketchy venue, she packed her small handgun in her Burberry handbag prior to hailing a cab. She gave the cab driver the address of a bakery a block away from the counterfeit passport maker. They arrived at the bakery within thirty-five minutes. It smelled of fresh bagels and sweet pastries. Alexa paused at the window front and gazed at the sugary delicacies until the cab drove away. She walked down the sidewalk and around the corner, heading to the address stated on the card. She read it to herself: 42 Rue Cardinet 75017. The name on the card was Vincent.

The address corresponded to a small gray stone shop flanked by a large vacant building on the left and a cigar shop on the right. Alexa tried the door; it was locked. She pressed a small buzzer next to it but didn't hear anything. She grabbed the card and rechecked the address. The number "42" was tacked on the door in metal numbers. She looked around. There were no windows facing the street to peer into. She groaned in frustration when she heard a voice next to her.

"Qui se trouve present?" The voice came from the intercom next to the buzzer she had pressed.

"Pardon? English?" She struggled for the right French words. *"Parlez-vous Anglais?"*

She grimaced at her lackluster accent and cleared her throat.

"Vincent?"

Silence. After a few seconds, the door eased opened, but only a few inches. A skinny, dark-haired man peppered with stray gray hairs peeked out. His worn oversized clothes hung on his bony frame.

"What do you want with Vincent?" he questioned with a harsh scowl. His shrewd eyes and long, pointy nose exemplified the sharp words that fell from his tongue.

Alexa displayed the card for him to view.

"I need papers," she stated, but it sounded more like a child's plea.

He gave the card a quick glance, then his gaze fixed on her. She could feel her pulse quivering in her temporal artery. Her tension mounted.

"Papers. Passport. American identification. Can you help me or not?"

"Try the Embassy. I cannot help you." He pushed the door closed. She stopped it with her boot.

"Can Vincent help?"

The door opened halfway. The man revealed a cigar that had been hidden in his right hand. He took a long puff. The wretched smoke filled Alexa's lungs.

"There is no Vincent. You stupid American." He paused and snarled his lips at her. She didn't waiver. She stared intently into the cold eyes of the Frenchman.

"You want me to go the Embassy because you don't want my stupid American money?" She raised an eyebrow. The man scoffed. She shrugged.

"All right, I'll go to the Embassy." She turned slowly, her steps deliberate. The air turned sweet as she walked away.

"Four thousand."

She paused and took a couple small steps back toward

the man cloaked in smoke.

"U.S.?"

His eyes rolled around in his head before responding.

"Fine," she stated, unsure if he'd given her a deal with dollars over Euros based on the exchange rate.

"What do I get for four thousand?"

He cocked his head to the side. "What do you want?"

Alexa paused as she took a mental inventory. She wanted a new identity, but she needed to preserve the old one — at least to be able to get the money out of her accounts. Two passports would probably do.

"Two passports." She said the words with trepidation.

The man, who Alexa could only assume was Vincent, nodded slowly.

"Fine," he answered.

Vincent stopped puffing on the remains of his cigar. He pulled it into his mouth with his tongue and began to chew the residual into a black mush that he intermittently spat out into the trash.

"Four thousand U.S." he repeated.

Alexa's heart raced. She fumbled for her bag, which was clutched close to her chest. She pulled out a crisp stack of hundreds carefully folded down the middle.

"Here's two thousand. I will give you the rest after I receive the passports."

He spat another mouthful of cigar mush. This time, he spat at the floor in front of her feet.

"All right, stupid American. I need two photos." He opened the door wide and motioned for her to enter. Alexa still shook a little, but she felt satisfied with her success. She hadn't realized she was going to need her picture taken. She thought fast. She wanted the two pictures to look very different, yet they both needed to look like her. For the first photo, she pulled her hair back and left her face bare. For the second photo, she wore her hair down and applied eye makeup and lipstick, then removed her jacket. She also altered her information on the two passports. She made the up-do passport her alias and the photo with her hair down her real name. She added five pounds and a half-inch to her height for the alias, and subtracted two years from her age.

He snapped the photos in front of a white sheet hanging like a curtain. Vincent's workstation consisted of a digital camera connected to a laptop computer and a large box printer/scanner. He had bits of passports hanging on a wall behind him. Perhaps they were his creations. Or they could have been stolen passports used as examples to construct the decoys. Many of the passports came from the United States.

After taking the photos, he jotted down Alexa's true and false identifiers with poor penmanship on a dirty napkin. He tapped the photo to be used as the alias.

"What name for this?" Alexa scrunched her nose and mouth together as she quickly conspired a false identity. "Elizabeth." She chose her grandmother's name — the woman she idolized most. "Elizabeth Fuguay." Fuguay seemed appropriate, as it was just a minor adjustment to the fugue state that fueled the false identity.

Vincent muttered something to himself while rummaging through the cash Alexa had given him. Much of the tension between the two of them had dissipated by this point. Vincent seemed too enthralled with his work to be annoyed by the *stupid American* in the room, and Alexa was fueled by too much adrenaline to concern herself with his former harshness. She was even brash enough to ask if he needed anything else from her. He let out a grunt and avoided her question. She chose a more deliberate approach.

"I will pay you the remainder of your fee when the passports are finished." She paused. "When should I return?"

The Frenchman looked up at her as if he'd forgotten she was in the room altogether. He raised an eyebrow in a confused expression. "Thursday?"

Although taken aback by his confused air, she nodded in agreement. "I will be back Thursday afternoon. The passports will be ready then?"

Vincent moved his head up and down, grunted, and resumed his work. Alexa saw herself to the door.

She felt energized in a way she didn't wholly understand. She found excitement in leaving her pain behind, embracing her romantic fantasy of fugue state, and moving toward a future in which her ideas made sense. She basked in her accomplishment and repressed the dark voice in her subconscious that whispered it was the veil of deceit that enticed her. Too giddy to walk, she skipped carelessly back toward her hotel.

CHAPTER 17

She skipped a few blocks when she realized she was both very far from her hotel and from her goal of killing Castro. She'd forgotten about obtaining the cyanide. That could possibly prove to be the biggest hurdle of all.

She had gone without her smartphone ever since the cab accident, and, given her desire to change her identity, she canceled the service. Alexa popped into an Internet café to borrow their search engine. She typed in the words *pharmacy* and *apothecary* and waited for the Internet to answer her questions. Her online search brought up a small French apothecary three short blocks away. She doubted whether the trip would prove fruitful. *They sell medicines, not poison. I doubt I can find cyanide. But maybe they sell the manufactured antidote kits I saw online.*

She tried to invent a believable lie to establish her need to buy a cyanide remedy, but nothing she rehearsed seemed plausible. She considered turning around and quitting the plan altogether. But she was already so close, and she figured the worst thing that would happen is she would be rejected. If the situation became difficult, she figured she could fall back on American ignorance. She headed to the apothecary.

The store was combined with an even smaller stationary shop. She was greeted by a white-haired woman who looked to be about seventy with an upbeat "Bonjour!" in a high-pitched voice from behind a long granite counter. The jingle of the little silver bell tied to the front door echoed the pitch of her voice. The woman peered at Alexa through thick-lensed glasses that magnified her pupils out of proportion to her other facial features.

"*Parlez-vous Anglais?*" Alexa asked in her broken French, and waited patiently as the old woman nodded repeatedly.

Alexa wasn't sure if the woman had heard her or not. She repeated the phrase louder and more clearly.

"Yes," the woman responded abruptly as her head continued to bob ever so slightly.

Alexa took a deep breath and let the words flow slowly. "Do you have a cyanide remedy kit?" She tried to sound nonchalant. The woman held a crooked smile without response. *Perhaps the woman isn't just hard of hearing — perhaps she isn't all there.* Alexa guessed the bell on the door was an attempt to alert the old lady that a customer had entered to store, but it seemed more than a bell was needed to bring this woman back to reality.

"Cyanide?" the old woman said suddenly, and with an air of excitement.

"Well, yes," she stated, without clearly knowing if the woman thought Alexa was asking for cyanide or the cyanide remedy kit. Either way, her answer was *yes*, so she went along.

The woman paused and raised her left index finger high in the air, like she had an idea. The wrinkled finger trembled. Then she turned and shuffled to the end of the counter and behind a curtain at the back of the apothecary, leaving Alexa standing alone.

Alexa glanced around the store. She looked at a shelf filled with tiny bottles of serums and eye creams. Next to this was a shelf filled with bags of clay powders used for facemasks. Plagued by a shelf filled with beauty products, she wondered if she were in the right place. Across the aisle she recognized anti-nausea concoctions and urinary tract infection remedies. The medical names were similar to the English derivatives even in French, due to their shared Latin roots. Another more risqué shelf contained French versions of the morning-after pill. As the minutes passed, Alexa became agitated. The white-haired woman peeked her head through the curtain.

"Cyanide?" she questioned again. Alexa nodded stiffly in frustration.

To her surprise, the woman returned with a handful of items, including a box that looked promising. She dumped the items onto the counter and separated them for Alexa to see. The box that caught Alexa's attention was, in fact, a cyanide remedy kit. It was slightly discolored, as if it had sat on the shelf a long time. Alexa couldn't figure out what was inside the unlabeled jar she saw. She pointed at it. "This one?"

"Arsenic," the woman responded with a smile. Alexa felt a twinge of guilt and disgust run through her. *This woman seems to know I have sinister intentions.* She tried to think of a way to dismiss any murderous thoughts in this woman's mind. She furrowed her brow at the woman and shook her head fervently.

"No. No. I don't want arsenic — not at all." She tried to think up a quick lie to cover her crazy request. "It's a project I'm working on — an experiment, really. I'm a scientist. I am testing out a variety of cyanide remedies in order to determine the most effective and affordable remedy for cyanide poisoning." Alexa paused, unsure of how much the woman understood. The woman grabbed the arsenic bottle and tucked it into her apron pocket, then pointed at two small boxes. "Also cyanide remedy," she explained.

Alexa examined the smaller boxes. They contained vials of liquid sodium thiosulfate, which Alexa considered as a backup plan. The dose of sodium thiosulfate was twelve point five grams IV diluted, for a total of fifty milliliters in a twenty-five percent solution.

She also examined the larger box labeled *Cyanide Remedy Kit.* It contained the hydroxycobalamin she desired. The manufactured kit contained two vials of two point five grams of hydroxycobalamin to be administered intravenously. The smaller volume seemed more feasible.

The woman had not brought Alexa any cyanide pills. She looked up at the woman, and before she could speak, the old woman asked, "You need cyanide?"

Alexa smiled weakly. "Yes."

The woman went to a stack of stationary on the counter and wrote a note on the pretty pink paper. She handed it to Alexa. She saw an address listed at the top, and a paragraph written in French on the bottom.

The address was in Barcelona, Spain. Instantly

dismayed, her shoulders sagged heavily. Before Alexa could interject, the woman interrupted her thoughts.

"Go here. Elena, my friend, will help. The note will get you what you need." The woman pointed to the address she had written. "Take the train." Alexa digested the information. "Tomorrow. Take the train." Her firm tone was convincing. *Maybe this will work.*

Alexa sifted through the remnants of her cash to pay the lady. She purchased two different cyanide remedy kits and one of the clay facemasks. She watched the bundle of Euros in her purse dwindle. She would need to withdraw more money from her account soon. She planned to transfer money into a second account under her alias so she could spend money under the new identity. She would go to the bank after stopping by Vincent's. The passport would be necessary to open the account under the new identity. After gathering her bags, she headed back to her hotel. She wanted to change clothes and go for a run before dusk fell.

A mere five miles into the run her left knee began to throb, and she decided to walk the last mile back to her hotel. She arrived just as the sun began to set.

Each time she ran down the Paris streets, she tried to find the French café she and Britt had entered the night of *levende lys* that lingered in her mind. Tonight was another failed attempt.

Following the run, she applied the clay mask to her face and plunged into a hot bath. She declined a night of dancing with Serge. She still had so much planning to do, and such a short time to accomplish it all. After the bath, she went back to her laptop, back to the FBI webpage. She needed some encouragement, and chose to read over Mohammed Ahmed's crimes. She read until she cried, until the horror of it all became real to her. She paused on the reward page again. She put the computer aside and mixed a vodka soda to ease her nerves.

She lay on the bed and thought about the reward. *Is this a bad idea? Should I call someone? Should I tell someone about my plans? Who can I call? Who would take me seriously?* Her mind drowned in a sea of questions and alcohol.

A name floated to the surface. Justin Hunter. Justin was a very old flame from college. They had parted on good terms and managed to keep in touch by pure coincidence. They had bumped into one another time and again in the last few years, always meeting in the most peculiar of places. She saw him once in an organic food store in Atlanta when he had just started working with the Navy Seals, and once more in the O'Hare airport on a layover just a year ago. It was on this layover that Justin admitted working with a branch of the FBI that dealt in international affairs. He gave her his card. She had saved his contact information on her laptop.

Alexa grabbed the hotel phone. Two o'clock in the morning in Paris meant seven o'clock in Washington D.C. With the cocktail in her hand, she figured she had just enough courage in her glass to dial his number. She called the number and waited for Justin to answer.

"Hello?"

"Hi, Justin. It's Alexa, Alexa DeBrow."

"Alexa? Hey, girl. It's been a while."

"Yes, Justin. I know it has."

"This is a surprise. I didn't recognize the number. Are

you in town or something? Are you looking to meet up? It's not a good time for me."

"Justin, I'm not in town. I need a favor. I need a name, a contact, really. Are you still working in the same place?"

"Uh, yeah, same place. Hey, Lex — I have a little girl now. She's with her mom tonight. We're, um — getting married soon."

Alexa blushed. *Wow. Does he think this is a booty call?*

"That's great, Justin." She tried her best to change the subject. "I'm really happy for you. Listen, I am kind of in a situation now. I need to talk to someone who can help. I'm thinking someone from the FBI can help me."

"Um. Okay. I wasn't expecting this. Hmm, what can I do?"

"I've run into someone. He's a criminal, actually. I need to let someone know about it. Whom should I speak with?"

"Wow. That's pretty heavy shit, Lex. Are you in trouble or something?" His tone changed abruptly.

"No. Not really. No trouble. I just know things, and I need to talk to someone." Alexa had no intention of telling Justin the whole story. She just wanted to tell him enough to be sure he would get the appropriate contact for her. She waited on the line in suspense.

"Okay. Well, there is this guy I know. We've bowled together once or twice. The guy's name is Charles MacDonald; he works for the state department in special investigations and foreign affairs. Cool guy. I just call him Charlie Mac. He can probably help." Justin rattled off the number. "If you want, I can let him know you're calling."

"Don't bother. I'll try the number first thing in the

morning. If I can't get ahold of him, I'll get back with you. Thanks, Justin."

"Shit, Alexa. When I gave you that card, I was hoping to meet for drinks, or sex, or something. You know — before my kid came. I never thought you would need something like this. Does it have anything to do with that trial I saw on T.V. a few months back?"

Alexa winced.

"No, Justin. I'm fine."

"You would tell me if you were in trouble, right?"

"Of course. I'm fine. Thanks for your help. Congratulations again. Take care."

She hung up the phone. She had forgotten that Justin spoke without a filter. *Why did he expect a booty call when our relationship was mostly platonic?* They had only dated for a month, and that time consisted mainly of a few outings with a couple of good make-out sessions. It didn't take long for the physical relationship to fizzle, and she became aware of the lack of an emotional connection between them.

Alexa admired the little note with her new contact's information on it. *Charlie Mac, we will speak tomorrow.* She set an alarm to wake her in time to catch the train and fell asleep within minutes.

This time, she dreamed of losing Britt. He was with her in the taxicab, and he drowned in spite of all of her efforts. She woke with a sense of loss that could only be matched by the reality of losing him in real life. For a moment, she wondered if she would ever get him back, but the notion was fleeting.

The alarm went off at four in the morning Paris time, which corresponded to ten o'clock at night D.C. time. She would have to wait to call Charles MacDonald. A new thought crossed her mind. She would call later in the day, from Barcelona, where she wouldn't have to worry about her call being traced to her hotel. *What will I say to him? He works for the government; I can't lie.* She had a train ride to contemplate which version of the truth she would disclose.

CHAPTER 18

Alexa prepared for the early morning train departure of five-twenty a.m. She arrived at the station by five o'clock. She boarded the train and slumped onto a bench seat, rested her head in folded arms propped against the window, and drifted in and out of sleep. She fantasized about her time with Britt. So much time had passed, the memories became mere fantasies.

She remembered the day they met. She was running in downtown Austin along a popular running path. Britt's chiseled build ran toward her from the opposite direction. The sidewalk narrowed, and they both neared a woman struggling between juggling her cocker spaniel and her double stroller. She blocked the path ahead of them. At the last minute, Alexa veered right, and Britt swerved left. Since they came from opposite directions, their bodies smacked into one another.

Jarred by the brute force of Britt's body against hers, she stumbled backwards after the impact. She would have fallen onto the pavement if he hadn't reached out for her. His arm wrapped around her waist, and he pulled her body toward his. Their torsos collided once more. Her eyes met his honey-almond eyes, dotted with little flecks of copper. Feeling safe in his grasp, she became lost in his stare. She stopped breathing. She wanted him from that moment. She knew that she would love him, if he would let her.

Their intimate embrace loosened, allowing for the exchange of apologies and awkward smiles. Brief introductions and casual small talk centered on their running habits followed.

Her cheeks reddened. "I'm only running five miles today, but sometimes I go farther. How about you?"

"I'm about eight miles into my fifteen-mile run. I like to run by the water, and sometimes I veer off downtown." His confident manner and soothing voice warmed her insides like comfort food. "This is my first collision. I didn't mean for it, but I'm glad I ran into you."

Overcome by his good looks, a flash of desire burned in her cheeks and she looked away for a moment. When she turned back, Britt's eyes were scanning her curves up and down. He lifted his eyes to her face. "I'd like to get to know you better."

She flicked her lids playfully. "What are you suggesting?"

"Well, how about some company on your run?"

"I was about to head home."

"Okay. That works for me. I'll escort you home."

"I won't slow you down?"

"You can set the pace. I'll follow your lead."

"All right, then."

The two ran toward Alexa's apartment. They talked about themselves, their families, and their aspirations. She examined their commonalities. He shared her curiosity for everything — travel, history, religion, and literature. Each yearning to broaden their horizons, they had a mutual passion for enlightenment. Britt came from a family of political power, his father a former senator, and he was carefully persuaded to follow his father's path. Yet Britt maintained a foothold in the business world, as well, graduating with an MBA from Duke. A natural capitalist, his forte was purchasing struggling companies for low prices, and tweaking them to make them profitable again. She could see he made brilliant business decisions quickly, without sacrificing the blue-collar class workers that were often disrespected by his counterparts. He told her that one of his key strategies for increasing productivity was to decrease the salary gap between blue-collar and white-collar positions, and to give production bonuses to everyone on staff for both individual and group successes. She admired his wit and determination.

She was roused back to reality when the train brakes squealed and her body jolted forward. The sun rays warmed her face through the glass. She had slept for hours. Frantic, she looked for her watch to check the time. *Nine-fifteen a.m. I won't arrive until afternoon.* Alexa eased back against the seat and glanced at the address the white-haired woman had written down for her. *I'm going all the way to Spain based on the whim of a half-crazed old lady. Hope this isn't a wild goose chase.* The idea suddenly seemed very silly, and she held back a giggle. A refreshment cart headed down the aisle. She ordered a hot tea and a bowl of oatmeal. Around noon, she managed a second hot tea and a ham sandwich before she finally reached Barcelona.

She hopped into a cab and handed the address to the driver. A few winding blocks later, she arrived at a small, one-story building surrounded by much taller shops and residential flats. She entered through a little red door flanked by small windows with planter boxes containing yellow and purple petunias.

Inside, a woman sat stooped over a bowl of soup behind a counter. It looked like another apothecary, and the inside of the store resembled the one Alexa had encountered in Paris. This woman was much younger than the white-haired old French lady, and she was dressed far more eccentric, with colorful make-up and bright colored flowing clothes and scarves.

"Bonjour!" Alexa exclaimed in a cheery voice to get the woman's attention. Her countenance shrank when she realized she was speaking French in Spain.

The woman acknowledged Alexa's greeting with a peculiar smile.

"You need help?" she prompted in English.

She must know I'm a tourist. "Yes. Please." Alexa fumbled in her pocket for the piece of stationary with the note. As her fingers wrapped around the paper, she realized she had no idea what the message said. *I guess I'm putting my faith in the old woman.* She sighed and handed the note to the eccentric storeowner, wondering if this entire trip was an old woman playing a prank on a foolish American. Alexa held her breath as the lady scanned the paper. The woman grabbed a pair of purple horn-rimmed glasses from the chain that dangled round her neck to better inspect the note. The infinitely long and awkward pause caused Alexa's heart to flutter.

Finally, the woman looked up at Alexa with a very serious demeanor. But then her expression changed, and she burst out laughing. Her head flew back, and the purple glasses swung violently on their chain as she let out a bellowing fit of cackles.

Alexa stopped cold. *Her laughter is worse than the silence!*

The Spanish woman grabbed Alexa tightly by the arm and rubbed her shoulder, as if to console her.

"*Querida, pobrecita.* He must do horrible thing." The woman glowed with excitement and energy. Her eyes became alive and moved rhythmically as she spoke. "But I help you, *querida.* We fix him good. We fix him *for good.* Do not worry, *querida.* I fix many men for good. Is easy." The Spanish woman led Alexa to the back of the store, behind a back door into a small kitchenette area. From behind a cupboard, the woman grabbed a plastic storage container full of little pills.

"Cyanide, *querida.* One is good, but two work also. You crush them, yes? Mix with water." The woman acted out the words as she spoke broken English. She continued, "They beat, they cheat — you poison. No?" She smiled another devilish grin.

Alexa tried hard not to look dumbfounded as she slowly put together the words she heard. She eyed the now crumpled note held in the smiling woman's hand. *Does that note say I need cyanide to kill a husband or lover who treated me badly? Wow. Okay. Play along, Lex; it seems to be working.*

"I can crush them and mix them in water?" she

questioned.

"Yes." The store clerk led her back to the cash register. "Must not get caught," she pleaded. "How many?"

Alexa held up three fingers.

"Is forty euros."

Alexa paid in cash. As she put out her hand, the woman grabbed it.

"No ring. You leave him?"

Alexa hesitated; she was unaware of the details of the lie to better explain it.

"No. But I told my family I left him." She said the words solemnly and put her head down at the end. The woman seemed to believe her. *Maybe I'm not such a bad liar after all.*

"Go, *querida*. Give the pills. It will be okay."

Alexa grabbed the little paper sack the woman had put three cyanide pills into and smiled weakly on her way out the door.

Alexa walked through the cobblestone streets heading back to the train station, when she realized she still needed to call Charlie Mac. She checked her watch. Her train departed at two-thirty p.m. She had close to two hours before she needed to be back at the station. She decided not to make the phone call too near the train station. She wanted him to think she was staying in Barcelona — just in case.

She turned away from the train station and headed in the opposite direction. She hustled through tourists, sightseeing groups, and pedestrians. Her pulse quickened at the new pace. She continued such for about forty minutes before she stumbled across a pay phone. She grabbed the receiver and dialed the number she'd been given. It was early office hours in D.C., and she got a recording that transferred the call to his cell. It rang twice before he answered.

"Hello?" a stern male voice questioned.

"Hello, Charles. This is Alexa DeBrow. Justin gave me your number, Justin Hunter. He thought you could help me — or, perhaps, I could help you."

The voice on the other end turned softer. "Justin, eh? All right. What can I do for you, Miss DeBrow? And what is it that you think you can do for me?"

She hesitated while trying to place his accent. *Sounds northeastern.*

"Your name sounds familiar to me, Miss DeBrow. Have we met before?"

"No. We haven't met. Perhaps you've heard of me." *I made so many news headlines. Jeez, if he recognizes my name, maybe I should hang up and move on.* She pressed forward regardless.

"I have met someone of interest to you," she continued. "Mohammed Ahmed. I know the FBI has a bounty on his head, alive or dead. I plan to accept the bounty for the latter."

"Alexa DeBrow. Yes, I'm sure I've heard that name. No worries, the reason will come to me. Now, what did you say? I'm not sure I heard correctly. You've come across one of my *most wanted* men? Hmm. I hope he didn't cause you harm in any way."

"No. He didn't hurt me." His questions were distracting.

"Where did you find him?"

"I can't answer that. I'm sorry."

"Then tell me why it is that you want him *dead*, exactly? As you said yourself, the bounty is dead or alive. Wouldn't alive be easier for everyone?"

"No. I don't think so." Her words flowed slowly, as if she was inebriated, and her thoughts began to muddle. "Capturing him alive is riskier. Giving you his whereabouts is also a little risky. I need to know for sure that he is dead. It's safer for everyone." *Why so many questions? He sounds just like Detective Marcum.* She fidgeted with the phone cord, feeling as if she had returned to the trial.

"Why do you say that it is *safer*?"

Alexa weighed the question carefully, afraid of hanging herself on the short rope he dangled in front of her.

"Because . . ." she took a deep breath, "letting a man like that run around freely puts the rest of us at risk. We're all in danger while he's still breathing."

"Danger?"

"Yes. Danger. You know better than I do about how many innocent lives he has taken." Not just words, but feelings were pouring out of her lips, and she put a hand to her mouth to try to stop the flood. *Don't get emotional, Lex.*

He paused. "It's Dr. DeBrow. Isn't it? That's why you sound familiar. I remember your story. Is that why you took *his* life — that man who attacked you? You were afraid *he* put the rest of us at risk?"

She couldn't stop the hot tears from collecting in her eyes. She had failed Charles MacDonald's interrogation. She didn't know how to defend herself anymore. Her courage abandoned her, and she was only left with anger.

"No," she hissed into the receiver, pounding her fist into the glass wall of the phone booth. "There was no time to think when I killed Jamar Reading. I stopped him from killing me. It was all I was capable of. But I am glad I killed him, because that means he's not around to hurt anyone else."

"When you kill Mohammed, how do you plan to do it?" Charles never lost his cool.

Alexa paused. "Machiavellian strategy."

"What?" MacDonald scoffed.

"I'm an opportunist, Mr. MacDonald. I plan to make use of the opportunity I'm given."

"Are you trying to woo him with your charms, Miss? As I recall, you're aesthetically pleasing, but I'm not sure that strategy suits you." He was flamboyant with mockery.

"No." She hesitated. "I plan to distract him with cunning manipulation, until I can get close enough . . . to poison him."

"Poison?"

"It's clean."

"You mean *cleaner than a knife to the neck*, Dr. DeBrow?"

His taunts gave her chills. Livid, she wanted to curse and scream.

"Jamar's death wasn't planned. Understand that."

"I do, Dr. DeBrow. I understand justice isn't always pretty. It's my job, and it certainly isn't a *pretty job*. All right, Miss, we'll play things your way. If you want to take out one of America's most wanted, I won't try to stop you. Are you expecting compensation for you efforts? Or is this an act of human decency?"

"It's why I called you, Charles."

"I suppose that's fair. If you carry out your end of the agreement, I can make sure you receive the appropriate compensation. I must warn you, however, Miss DeBrow. It isn't an easy task you are attempting, and I strongly recommend you reconsider. You are dealing with a murderer, and I guarantee you he has no concern for the loss of another life. He will kill you if he can, or he will have one of his employees kill you for him. Regardless, you should know your life is at stake. If you die in your attempts, our agreement will no longer exist. Understand that."

"Agreed," she murmured.

"You will need to contact me immediately if you are successful. We will speak of compensation if you survive. Tell me where you are."

"In time."

"All right. Have it your way, Miss DeBrow."

"Charlie?" Her voice turned small and childlike.

"Yes, Alexa." His words turned softer as well, to match her tone. He almost sounded parental.

"I will be successful. I'm sure of it."

"I hope so, for your sake, my dear. Enjoy Barcelona."

"Goodbye, Charlie."

She hung up the phone and contemplated their discussion. *He traced my call.* Despite MacDonald's jeering, she was glad she called him. She needed someone to confide in. The conversation had been emotionally taxing, however, and her anxiety materialized in the tears that fell from her eyes.

She wiped the salty liquid from her cheeks and checked the little gold Rolex on her wrist. She needed to hurry if she was going to make the train. She jogged back to the station in time to board as the final passenger. Another hot tea and a granola bar sustained her until she reached her hotel.

CHAPTER 19

Alexa lay in bed thinking of Charlie Mac. She wanted to like him; she wanted to trust him. But she feared him. *Who knows what he has in store for me? Perhaps he's on his way to find me now and arrest me.* Had she committed a crime? Not yet. *Perhaps my intentions are criminal.* She wasn't sure. She feared she had overstepped a boundary today, and she fell asleep disillusioned.

When she awakened, it was early morning and still dark outside. Restless, she went for a run before breakfast and an espresso. *Thursday. Time to pick up my new passports from Vincent.* She hoped he wouldn't be cross with her. After suffering Charlie Mac's questioning, she didn't want to deal with Vincent's sarcasm and sharp tongue. They had agreed to meet in the afternoon, but she planned to go early so she could stop by the bank before it closed.

An uneventful cab ride brought Alexa to his shop. She pressed the buzzer three times with no response, then knocked hard on the metal door. The door squeaked open a crack, and thick cigar smoke billowed from the doorway.

Vincent's pointy nose peeked through the opening. Alexa couldn't help but think that everyone in Paris had a pointed nose and a pompous air. The thought brought a sense of humor to the situation that helped diffuse her fear, and the tension in her shoulders eased a bit.

"You have my money, eh?" he sneered.

She nodded. He opened the door further, and she followed him inside.

It seemed darker than she remembered. The curtain of cigar smoke stifled her. Someone else was in the room with them. A young girl wrapped in nothing but a white sheet sat quietly on a chair away from them. Concern pricked Alexa's conscience as a wave of goosebumps rippled over her flesh. But the girl didn't look afraid. In fact, she seemed calm, bored even.

"Don't mind the girl. She wants to be *model.*" He said the word with disgust. "Stupid girl, like stupid American." He gestured to Alexa, who glanced back at the girl. The girl managed a half-smile, as if she recognized the word *model.* Alexa frowned; she couldn't be over eighteen.

Vincent handed Alexa the faux passports. She flipped through the pages quickly. *They look genuine. But what does my opinion matter? Will the authorities and police inspectors believe they are authentic?*

She took a deep breath and, with a leap of faith, handed the money over to Vincent. He proceeded to count it, then gave another hand gesture to shoo her away. Alexa cast a final wary glance at the teenage girl as she exited the shop.

The air outside was cool and fresh. Alexa breathed it in heartily. She headed to an international bank she had passed a few weeks earlier. *Time to test the quality of Vincent's handiwork.* She knew if her passport didn't pass the bank's inspection, there would be consequences.

She planned to set up an account under her new identity, Elizabeth Fuguay. If successful, she would head to a second bank to transfer funds from her current account to the new account under the false identity. For the first time, Alexa realized embracing a new life meant condoning deception. She would be living a lie. *It's a necessary evil,* she told herself. But she suddenly felt very similar to the youth shrouded in sheets at Vincent's, who could be thinking the same thing.

Struggling with finding a way to accept the deception that came with her plan, she forced herself to remember that she came to Paris to forget Alexa DeBrow and to forget the pain of her former life so she could embrace a new life. After everything she had experienced, didn't she deserve that much? *It's not really a lie. More like, a transformation. Yes, a transformation!* She could endure that.

Perhaps Elizabeth Fuguay can be an improvement on Alexa DeBrow. She can embody the courage and composure that I lack. Elizabeth can retain strength where Alexa faltered. The transformation meant possibilities, and finally, Alexa felt optimistic. Hope spread across her face like a ray of summer sunshine.

She carried her new outlook into the International Bank of Paris. The security officer at the door directed her to an English-speaking accounts manager.

"Hi, I'm Adam. I see you are an American." A young college-aged kid with sandy-blond hair held out his hand.

He's American! His accent sounded like music to her ears.

"Yes. I'm Elizabeth. Elizabeth Fuguay. It's a pleasure." She reached for his extended hand. His constant eye contact and persistent smirking struck her as flirtatious. *Flirting is a good sign. If he likes me, he might be less likely to question my passport.*

They made small talk. They chatted about where they were from, what brought them to Paris, that kind of thing. Alexa rattled off a story about being from Ohio, going to London for college, then traveling to Paris and staying on a whim. She told him she'd finally gotten her own job and wanted a separate account from her parents'. He bought her untruth.

Alexa had just over the minimum amount of cash to open an account. The American man happily accepted her money and supporting documentation to open her foreign account. He stepped out of his little glass office to make copies of her identification. When he returned, she was all set to go.

"We appreciate your business." They shook hands again.

"Anytime. It's good to see another American, for a change."

They exchanged smiles, and Alexa walked out the door, giddy as a schoolgirl. "Thank you, Vincent," she whispered into thin air.

She left later than she had planned. She would have to save her second bank trip for another day, perhaps tomorrow morning. Friday morning. Friday night was the night of Castro's birthday extravaganza, the night she planned to kill him. Alexa stored her nerves in the pit of her stomach. She stopped by the drug store on the way back to her hotel to buy a nice big bottle of antacids. She spent the evening hours in her hotel room sprawled on the bed, plotting her attack.

Serge had told Alexa to meet him downstairs at ten p.m. His cab would arrive at her hotel, and they would make a few short stops to pick up other members of the entourage before arriving at the party. She didn't know when she would make her move. She would have to play it by ear. After slipping Castro the poison, she needed a quick getaway.

That's where it got tricky. She needed Serge to get into the party, but she didn't know how to flee the scene quickly and unnoticeably after slipping Castro the poison. How could she leave safely? With Serge or without him? She imagined the worst-case scenario: Castro dying in front of her eyes and everyone suspecting her, brutes circling her and shooting her on the spot.

"How can I keep them from suspecting me?" she pondered aloud. How could she fool them into thinking her closeness to him prior to his death was mere coincidence? *I will sip the poison first. Surely if they watch me drink from the same tainted glass, no one will suspect a thing.*

Her own idea made her uneasy. Putting that poison in her mouth seemed extreme. *It's not a suicide mission. I have the antidote.* But it was an intravenous antidote, and would require a venous puncture for its administration. Moreover, she would have to administer it immediately — and secretly, to prevent causing a scene. Worry lines spread over her face. *Maybe I won't have to drink the cyanide liquor mixture, but I should be prepared either way. I'll need needles and syringes from the pharmacy.*

Her hand went to the bottle of cyanide pills sitting on the pillow. Each pill was coated a pale yellow color. She hoped they would dissolve in liquor, but she didn't have a spare to test the theory. *So many unknowns make planning difficult.* She rubbed the spot between her brows with her knuckle to smooth the tension lines on her face. *Relax, Lex. If it becomes too difficult, bail.* But she didn't want to admit defeat. *Elizabeth Fuguay wouldn't bail.* The words echoed in her subconscious. *Doing this will prove that the world is a better place without Jamar Readings and Mohammed Ahmeds running around hurting innocent people. Their victims need justice. I have to do this.*

She didn't sleep that night, but she hadn't expected to. There was no use trying. Instead, she went over a list of items she would need from the pharmacy: IV needles, IV tubing, empty syringes, and a bag of normal saline. She would need to crush the cyanide pills, and she would need a saline-locked IV prior to administering the poison. She would need a vein that was covered by her gown, and tape to hold the IV in place. The list should be easy to acquire at the pharmacy. European guidelines were less stringent than U.S. guidelines.

She planned out her attire — a red gown with a lace bust halter-top and an exposed back and strappy heels. She wanted to rent nice jewelry for the occasion, but wasn't sure of her options. It would be something to investigate in the morning.

Lastly, she contemplated what she would say to Castro. She tried various opening lines, but nothing sounded right. Everything she thought of was either too cliché or too flirtatious. Her final decision was to go with the one tactic she knew to get any man's attention. Show him you are having a good time, make eye contact, and smile a provocative smile. If he didn't come to her, she would move closer and try again.

While rehearsing her plans, Alexa had an urge to call Charles MacDonald. She yearned for his approval — and perhaps, a few pointers. She didn't call Charlie, but she wanted a confidant. *I wish I wasn't doing this alone. I'm tired of being alone.* She closed her eyes and found herself in a state of semi-consciousness, not quite awake, not yet asleep, sitting on a porch in a wooden rocking chair, sipping morning coffee. The sun rose in the distance over hills of grape vines. A man sat next to her. In that perfectly serene moment, she felt content.

Her leg twitched. Her eyes popped open. The sun was still rising, but this time it was through her hotel window. The memory faded from her mind, the happy feeling with it. She couldn't help but think, *Maybe I'll find love again.*

She swallowed two antacids with a glass of milk and headed to the pharmacy to load up on supplies. It went quickly, like grocery shopping. She found everything she needed, including a mortar and pestle to grind the pills. Next, she went to the bank and deposited twenty thousand dollars into the Elizabeth Fuguay account. The transaction went seamlessly; the lady behind the counter merely nodded and accepted her deposit without question. Her remaining stops were only for beautification.

Alexa popped into a nail salon to get a quick manicure. A very petite young woman painted her nails dark gray while Alexa sipped a glass of rose-colored champagne. The bubbles turned her giddy, and she reminisced about other times in which she would spend a whole day primping for special occasions. Weddings. Every other time she had her nails done and they served champagne, she was a bridesmaid for a friend's wedding. She looked around the salon at the handful of other patrons and wished they were her closest friends, and she had a reason to celebrate today. Alexa left the idea next to the half full glass of champagne and a three-euro tip at the salon counter.

Remembering the swanky jewels layered atop the guests at the last soiree, she needed jewelry. *Now for some bling to impress the terrorist king.* She stopped by a consignment shop where she could purchase jewelry and later return it at a loss. She found an appealing ruby necklace she was able to purchase for eight thousand dollars, with a guaranteed return within one week of seventy-two hundred dollars. She accepted the offer and wore the necklace back to her hotel, in spite of it being too elaborate for her outfit.

CHAPTER 20

When Alexa reached her hotel room, she removed two of the cyanide pills from the bag and crushed them into a fine powder with tools she had purchased at the pharmacy. She poured the pale yellow powder into a tiny glass vial that she disguised in an empty lipstick container. *The poison is ready; now to prepare the antidote.* She mixed the antidote as directed in a fifty-milliliter bag of normal saline. She attached IV tubing to the bag and set it on the counter.

Her heart skipped a beat. *Time to get ready for the party.* She went to the bathroom vanity and pulled her hair back with a multitude of pins. Her golden locks brushed her shoulders in loose curls. She worked like an artist with a variety of brushes, painting her features different colors. She swept smoky dark shadows across her lids and painted her lips a bloodstained hue. She slipped into the red gown with the plunging V-neck and adjusted her cleavage appropriately. She needed the V-neck to distract away from her stomach. The fabric was heavy and gathered in layers just above the navel, which gave her space to hide the IV tubing.

Alexa pulled up the gown to expose her midsection. She saw a nice sized superficial vein coursing to the left of her umbilicus. *Perfect.* She grabbed a butterfly needle and pierced the vein carefully. She threaded the IV catheter over the needle and removed the needle. She drew back blood into the tubing and flushed it with saline before locking the IV with a plastic fastener and taping both to her skin. She poured herself a vodka tonic to calm her nerves while she waited to hear from Serge.

She watched herself in the mirror. The fierce makeup was striking, but was it enough? She needed to charm him, to entice him. She feared she was too old to pull off such things. From a distance, her reflection seemed flawless. But when she stepped closer, the lines on her face became the haphazard stokes of a Monet, and her features turned lackluster. She frowned at the flaws, and the scowl made the woman in the glass completely unbearable. *Confidence is beauty. Just be confident.* Alexa grabbed the IV bag containing the antidote/saline solution and taped the bag to her inner thigh. She taped the tubing to her stomach, but didn't connect it to the IV she'd placed. She wanted some freedom to move.

The hotel phone rang. "We're waiting, pet," Serge's voice whispered into the phone.

Alexa wanted to bring a handgun, but declined in fear of a bag search. So she stepped into her heels and grabbed her Louboutin studded clutch before heading out the door.

Serge had arranged for a private car tonight — a step up from the taxi the entourage had been using. Inside, a small mini bar sat on the floor by their feet. Serge had already picked up the blond man and the redhead from before, and they were making their way to pick up the other girl in the group.

The group exchanged kisses on the cheeks and hugs and laughs. Alexa feigned amusement and tried to hide her internal jitters. The blond man didn't appear happy to see her. She grinned widely when their eyes met and poured him a drink, trying to ease the tension.

He grabbed the glass of gin and took a swig. "You're too serious for us," he scoffed.

Alexa was surprised he was able to speak any English. In their last encounter, he didn't speak a word of it. She couldn't help but think he learned those words just to wound her after the cold shoulder she'd given him. She dropped the grin for only a moment. "I'll be more fun, then." *I need everyone to like me tonight.*

They arrived at an old, three-story brick mansion from the seventeenth-century. It stood in the middle of dark alley filled with deserted, boarded-up buildings. Cars came and went. Their black Mercedes lined up behind two black Bentleys. A long, black runner led guests from the street to the front door of the old mansion. A doorman with a turban opened car doors, and guests spilled out onto the runner. It wasn't a very polished scene. Old overweight men struggled to stand while their thin, clumsy, drunken wives stumbled about in their heels. Alexa found the spectacle amusing.

Serge's entourage scampered out of the car with ease but a lack of posture or poise. Alexa made sure to stand upright and leave the car with an attitude of sophistication. Serge escorted her into the party.

Inside, food and alcohol floated around on serving trays

while men with flutes, belly dancers, contortionists, and snake charmers moved about the room. A small empty stage in the front of the large ballroom had been decorated with white flowers. Serge's crew flocked to one of the small bars in the corner of the room. Alexa followed. The group had a round of vodka shots. It helped to calm her nerves. She reached into her clutch to grab a couple of antacids she had stored to quell the ulcer she continued to develop.

She searched the room for her target. With so many people crowding the space, she couldn't see much beyond the group just ahead of her. She looked for turbans, but the room was full of them. She would have to move about in order to find him. Serge caught Alexa's eye.

"I want to mingle," she said seductively.

"Me, too." His accent seemed thick. She headed to a small clearing in the center of the room. She recognized a few faces from the last French party, but she didn't recall their names or any specifics about them. She slithered through the crowd, scanning the passers-by. At the slow pace, it took a solid thirty minutes before she found Castro. He flirted with two young girls in the corner of the room to the left of the stage. His security men stood about three feet behind him on either side.

She walked toward him while trying to devise a plan. The two girls grabbed his arms and guided him toward the flute player, where the three started dancing. Alexa eased off. *Now is not the time.* She turned to her left and saw Serge flirting with a thin, twenty-something man with spiky brown hair. She watched their gestures and body language. Their motions were a type of foreplay, the way they jutted their pelvises toward one another. She had seen this with Serge before. He wanted to take another lover.

Her eyes diverted back to Castro and his companions. Their dancing had stopped. Castro walked back toward his security guards.

Alexa felt a hand on her arm, and her heart leaped in her chest. She turned to see Serge.

"You having fun, my pet?"

Alexa smiled. "It's great." Her pulse throbbed in her ears now and nearly drowned out his voice.

"Good. I think I leave you this time." He motioned to his male comrade.

Alexa hesitated. *No!* She wanted to be able to leave with Serge and his private car when all of this ended. She bit the inside of her lip hard, then glanced at the spike-haired man. *Something seems familiar about him. Something about his features, the hollow cheeks and temporal fossae. The prominent folds along the corners of his mouth.* It was a pattern all too familiar. *HIV-associated lipodystrophy.* She'd seen it frequently in the hospital. HIV patients were often sent to radiology to have their spinal fluid drawn, and Alexa had performed numerous spinal taps on such patients. She presumed the doctors on the floor did not want to risk a needle stick with an HIV patient. Her theory fit with the CYA "cover your ass" medical practices to which she had become accustomed.

Only, in the medical community HIV was distastefully referred to as *the hiv*, as in: he will be lucky to *live*. Alexa became familiar with the politically incorrect term as an intern, and it became more universal throughout the years.

Serge's soon-to-be next lover has the hiv. Seems awfully risky.

I can't let him go through with this! I could tell him, Serge has a right to know. But the idea didn't sit well with her. Sharing that fact with Serge was like disclosing someone's personal health information without his or her consent. *I can't go around discussing someone's HIV status.*

She grabbed Serge by the arm and led him away from his partner. He disputed, but she wouldn't release her grasp. When they were a safe distance away, Alexa turned to Serge with an air of jealousy and contempt, hoping for a tactful way to change his mind.

"Not tonight. Not like this. Don't leave me," she pleaded.

He looked baffled and amused by her anger at the same time. He laughed out loud.

"I don't have to leave you, pet. Come join us in the fun. No?"

"No. Not tonight." She had to convince him, even if it meant ruining her plans. She wanted to protect Serge. Even if it meant letting Castro run free. *I'll never forgive myself if I don't intervene.*

"Stay with me tonight. We can leave here. I want to see the Eiffel tower, now, tonight. Please." She began to sulk.

He laughed again.

"Tonight, tonight, you want to see the Eiffel tower. You live in Paris all this time, and now you want to see the Eiffel tower?"

"Yes."

"No, pet. Another night." He put a hand to her pouting chin. "You want me to stay? I stay. We dance tonight. There are other nights for lovers."

Alexa shook her head adamantly.

"No. Promise me, no. Not *him*." She motioned to Serge's proposed lover.

He frowned. "Fine," he said with a bit of hostility.

"Let's dance," she begged, grabbing his hands.

As they danced, she lost track of time. Her thoughts become muddled, and she had a hard time concentrating. All of the spinning on the dance floor with Serge didn't help matters. She had nearly forgotten about Mohammed. In between spins, Alexa tried to locate her prey. Too many people and too much motion confused her.

Her gaze landed on his security guards, and she scoured the ground near them. Castro stood about three feet in front of them. Predictable.

She took one last glance at Serge's face. She needed to be certain he wouldn't go back to his proposed lover. His eyes didn't lie. His countenance had changed drastically. He wasn't in the mood for romance any more. She needed to separate herself from him and move on to Castro. A few more twirls and a final dip, and the music came to a halt.

Serge headed to the bar. "You want a drink, pet?" He spoke kind words with a sharp tongue that failed to mask his irritation.

"No, thanks. Go ahead." She watched him walk away then turned back to Castro. He hadn't moved. She wanted to go to him, but something stopped her: rumbling nausea and acid in her throat. She rushed to the bathroom and vomited in the stall. On the way in, she passed one of the servers and grabbed a glass of scotch from his tray. She needed the drink for Castro's poison. Although Muslims rarely drank alcohol, Alexa had seen Castro sip scotch periodically. He was an odd

Arab, to like American women and alcohol.

The vomit burned her throat. Was it the nerves, the alcohol, or the spinning that got to her? She thought about what she was about to do, and her stomach churned violently. *Without a doubt, it's my nerves.* Before leaving the stall, she hiked her gown up to her bosom and looked down at the IV tubing. She'd nearly forgotten to connect the tubing together. *Get it together, Lex!* She scolded.

She attached the tubing from the bag containing the antidote and saline to the IV in her umbilical vein. A little blood seeped back into the tubing. Alexa tested the tubing by pressing her inner thighs together and squeezing the bag. The antidote passed through the tubing upward and into the IV. *It works.* She dropped her gown and opened the clutch that contained the empty lipstick container with the hidden vial of poison powder. She dumped the powder into the drink, stirred it with her quivering little finger, and watched the yellow dust dissolve into the liquid. She applied a veil of powder and a hint of rouge to her face before heading back to the party.

Castro held his position. She quickly glanced around for Serge. Nothing. She raised her eyelids wide and allowed the flush of the alcohol to warm her cheeks. She crept toward Castro, her footsteps keeping with the melody of the flute player's song.

He caught her gaze while she remained a few yards away. With his eyes locked on hers, he tilted his head to one side and two fingers went to his chin. She forced her lips into a coy smile. Even the music had a seductive quality to it. She floated nearer, and the last few steps were made by him to meet her.

"Hello, again." His accent mangled the English.

"Why, happy birthday." She hummed the words like a cherished lullaby. In the perfect moment, a server walked by with a glass of scotch for Castro. Alexa scooped the glass off the plate for herself, and handed the poisoned glass out for him.

"We should toast for your birthday." She whispered, stepping close enough to brush his arm with hers.

He reached for the glass, but hesitated. The security guards seemed stiff with trepidation. *He doesn't trust me.* Slyly, she pulled back the glass before his hand could touch it, and took a small drink herself. She pretended to swallow while holding the liquid in the back of her throat, knowing she may have to swallow eventually. She twisted a gold lock from her shoulder with her fingers and turned her glance away from him. It was enough. Fearing he would lose her attention, he grabbed the poison glass and drank heartily. Alexa now put the clean glass of scotch to her lips and carefully spat the poison back into the glass. Then she swallowed a sip of the watered down version of the poison she had spat into the untainted liquid.

"Jeers," said Castro.

"Yes, cheers!" she echoed.

Alexa pressed together her inner thighs, slowly squeezing the liquid antidote into her veins. *To your health.* Castro drank just over half the glass of poisoned scotch. She began a mental countdown.

The server passed by again, this time with a tray filled with champagne flutes. "Ooo, I love champagne." She sounded like a schoolgirl. "It goes straight to my head." The server took Castro's poisoned glass, and she placed her poison-spit glass on the tray also.

In the center of the room, a man started to give a birthday toast. The man was Castro's brother, and he called for Castro to come to the stage. The timing was impeccable. Castro abandoned Alexa, and she clapped for him as he approached the stage. She continued to press her thighs together, sending more of the antidote into her veins. Alexa's shaking legs backed away from the watchful guards, and she went to find the server with the poisoned glasses.

She only had moments now before it happened — until his cells began to suffocate, and he collapsed onto the floor. She meandered through the crowd and found the server. She scooped up the glasses and headed into the bathroom once more. Every time she let off pressure on the IV bag, it began to fill slowly with her venous blood due to gravity. She felt the warmth of the bloody liquid against her upper thigh.

Inside the bathroom stall, she poured the rest of her poisoned beverages into the toilet. She flushed and plunged both glasses into the toilet water to rinse away any residue. She used a wad of toilet paper to dry her hands and the outside of the glasses. She pressed her thighs together to force some of the blood out of the IV bag, then hiked up her dress to her bosom and made in a knot in the IV tubing to keep the bag from filling with any more blood. Beads of cold sweat covered her pale skin. She refrained from disconnecting the tubing, fearing blood would drip onto the floor and she couldn't clean it. *No need to leave a blood sample at the scene.*

She'd spent only a couple minutes in the bathroom, but

when she exited, she knew it had been too long. She entered a commotion of noise, screams, and people running out of the room. Strong shoulders bumped her trembling frame, and she stumbled forward, dropping both glasses. They shattered into a thousand pieces. The shuffling footsteps scattered them about the room.

Oh, that's perfect! I destroyed the evidence. She sighed in relief and followed the floundering crowd trying to flee the building. The swarm of people filed through the exit doors, in spite of the growing sounds of hostility that filled the air behind her.

She heard members of Castro's party threaten guests not to leave the room. They yelled their warnings in various languages. The bottleneck of people at the door thrust forward like a powerful creature. Outside, the crowd dispersed into their private cars. Alexa spotted Serge. He waved at her, and she ran to him. He waited by his car, holding the door for the rest of the group.

Gunshots fired into the air. People panicked. Some cars sped down the street; others were blocked by the surrounding traffic. More gunshots echoed in the night. Alexa scurried into the car, where she found the blond male and female from their entourage. The redhead was absent. Serge yelled at the driver. Their car raced away, unobstructed by the remaining cars still waiting for their owners.

Alexa questioned Serge, "What happened?"

He ignored her and spoke with the other man in the group. They started a heated discussion that she couldn't translate. They spoke for five or ten minutes before Serge finally acknowledged her. He still seemed angry with her. She was not his *pet* anymore. Her demands had crossed a line.

"Your proposed lover died tonight."

"What? Died? Died how?" Alexa feigned ignorance.

"Just died. Put his hand on his chest, gasped, and died. Heart attack, maybe."

"Heart attack? But I just saw him. He was fine."

"On stage, he spoke, then on the floor, dead."

Alexa painted a stunned look on her face, and imagined Castro dying on stage. Her fingertips tingled with excitement. She wished she could have seen the skin on his face develop the subtle cherry pink hue that comes with cyanide poisoning. She felt alive. She had succeeded. She turned her face to the window to conceal her look of satisfaction. She needed to tell someone. She needed to tell Charlie Mac. She would call him the moment she left the car.

The group remained silent the rest of the drive. Hers was the first stop. She let out a solemn "goodnight," and exited the car. When the car drove away, she ran to her room and dialed Charles' number. It rang and rang. She got his voicemail. She dialed again. No answer.

Alexa pulled up her gown and yanked the IV and blood-filled bag from her body. She pressed a wad of tissue against the wound. *Hold pressure.* The words could have come from a ghost. She dialed again. He finally answered.

"Who is this?" he growled, and cleared his throat.

"Charles. It's Alexa DeBrow. It's done. He's dead."

Silence.

CHAPTER 21

"**M**s. DeBrow, what have you done, exactly?" His voice sounded accusatory.

Alexa became fearful under the hostile air and stuttered, trying to maintain her composure. "I-I told you I was going to kill one of your most wanted criminals, and I did it. Tonight. Tonight I poisoned Mohammed Ahmed. I killed him at his birthday gala in Paris."

"When was this? How long ago?"

She checked her watch. It seemed like an eternity had passed.

"About twenty minutes ago." It was only an estimate.

"Give me the address, now."

"I don't know the address. The closest intersection is Rue Caude Warcoquier and Rue de la Coque, in the northern part of Paris. It's the only three story building near the crossroads."

Charlie rustled with papers.

"We will speak again, Miss DeBrow. Stay close to this number. I must handle this quickly." He hung up on her, but

Alexa kept the phone to her ear. A void washed over her, drowning out her earlier euphoria and replacing it with confusion.

Is he angry with me? Did I do the right thing? Should I run? She needed closure. She needed answers. Alexa clenched the receiver until the dial tone changed to a buzzing sound. Dismayed, she sat on her bed and waited for her phone to ring again. But it didn't. She tried to imagine what was going on in the northern part of Paris. *Are U.S. agents storming the building? Will there be a shoot-out? Will they surround the place and throw tear gas inside?*

She assumed Castro's body and his entourage were still in the building, though they could have just as easily taken the body and abandoned the premises by now. Perhaps the bodyguards had taken guests hostage for questioning. That thought made her stomach turn, and she pushed it from her mind. She refused to acknowledge that innocent people might be placed in danger because of her haphazard actions.

She lay in bed a long time letting questions swim around in her mind. Perhaps a local news station was reporting the event. She flipped through channels precariously. She watched multiple news channels, local and international. Nothing mentioned the night's proceedings. Alexa waited for a response until morning, and still none came. After hours of lying in a void, she settled for a cup of Joe and a hot shower to clear the fog from her head.

She yearned to wash away the night with scalding water and vigorous scrubbing. Lather pooled in the hollows of her supraclavicular fossae, and she watched the bubbles trickle down her body as the water washed them away. A bruise developed where she had started the IV in her umbilical vein. It looked like someone had punched her in the stomach. The area of ecchymosis was the size of her fist. It felt tender to the touch and sensitive in the hot water. After the shower, she placed a few cubes of ice on the area and rubbed them into the skin until they melted away.

Alexa pulled back her wet hair, put on a white tank, jeans, and black Roberto Cavalli pumps. She looked at herself in the mirror and saw a murderer looking back at her. A large pair of sunglasses hid the killer from view. Her reflection was as disheveled as her state of mind.

Charlie's questions repeated in her head like a worn out soundtrack, and her sleep-deprived state made her fearful. *What if Charlie's after me? What if Castro's men are after me? Get out, Lex! What are you waiting for? You need to disappear.* Paranoia crept in. On a whim, Alexa gathered her designer clothes and shiny little handgun and moved her belongings into a smaller hotel farther down the street. She checked into the new hotel under her alias, Elizabeth Fuguay.

It wasn't enough. She needed air. She walked the street in a daze, passing at least one or two cafés before she finally acknowledged one. It sat across from a Catholic cathedral with bells chiming the nine o'clock hour. She couldn't help but stare at the cathedral. They were scattered throughout Paris, but this was the first time she felt the urge to go inside. Something about those chiming bells drew her in like sirens to fishermen. They tempted her, even if they were a leading her to her doom; she gave in to the temptation.

Inside the cathedral, she felt more at ease. She and Britt had planned to marry in a similar Catholic cathedral in

Austin. A few tourists scattered inside snapped photos while others kneeled on pews. Alexa looked at the walls of the church lined with religious paraphernalia. She saw statues of saints and stained glass windows with engravings of the names of the donors. In the corner, at the back of the church, a group of candles sat beside an iron donation box. She walked over to the candles. She had to come to terms with what she had done. For the first time in a long time, Alexa acknowledged God's presence. She had put him aside since the incident. She didn't know how God felt about her actions, but she wanted to find out.

The last prayer to cross Alexa's lips was a prayer for the nightmares to stop. This time, she whispered aloud into the emptiness around her. "God, if I have angered you, punish me." She lit a new candle and stared into its flame. She watched the fire burn bright. *Levende lys.*

The rattling of beads startled her. A nun wearing a wooden rosary stood only a few feet behind her, eyeing her shrewdly. Alexa fumbled with a few coins and dropped them into the donation box, hoping to calm the nun's angry glances. When she turned back to the nun, the holy woman's scowl remained as bitter as ever.

Is she angry because my shoulders aren't covered or because she sees the darkness in my soul? Alexa wondered how many sins she had committed. She tried to comfort herself with an excerpt from Matthew: "An eye for an eye, a tooth for a tooth." *See, everything is justifiable.* Without finding solace, she dropped the senseless moral debate once she reentered the streets of Paris.

She crossed the street to go the café on the other side.

The aroma of espresso lured her in. Alexa ordered a double espresso and a brownie. She devoured the brownie and sipped the espresso for half an hour. She put down her cup and saw a man sporting a chic blue sweater and gray trousers staring at her from outside the store. She let her glance fall back to the beverage for a moment. Then her attention moved to the other patrons in the room. A happy American couple sat by the window and a nanny with two children hovered in the back of the room. The children played with a doll next to a door that led to the bathroom. Her gaze went back to the man outside. He had crossed the street and now leaned against a light post while talking on a cell phone. His eyes remained fixed on her. His stare turned her stomach sour. She stood and made her way to the back of the café. She felt the sudden need to escape. She intended to go to the bathroom and lock the door, but as she neared the bathroom she caught a glimpse of a back door opening through the kitchen at her left. One more look over her shoulder revealed that the man had entered the café and moved closer at a brisk pace.

Alexa darted into the kitchen area, passing by a barista and a pastry chef, then headed through the back door that led to daylight. She heard a ruckus behind her and knew he was following her. She needed to escape, but she couldn't outrun him. Once outside, she stood next to the heavy metal door and waited for him to follow. In a second or two, the door swung open. Alexa used all of her force to slam it back, hard. The heavy metal door hit him in the face before he had time to stop it. Alexa heard the thud of the door and the crunch of his nasal bones breaking.

She ran before she could see his face. She turned a street corner and looked back. The blue sweater, gray trousers, and bloody face pursued her.

She didn't get far before her left heel gave way. She stumbled as it broke under her weight, but she didn't fall to the ground. She lasted a few more steps before the other heel gave way. Again she didn't fall, but she became more handicapped trying to run in broken shoes. She could hear his steps close to hers as she leaped into traffic. She weaved in and out of cars, heading toward a river tour boat that was slowly pulling away from the shore about twenty yards ahead of her. She felt a bumper on the side of her thigh at one point, but it only nudged her. The bloody-faced man wasn't so lucky. He ran in front of a taxicab that didn't have time to stop. His body rolled across the front of the car and left a dent in the hood.

He had the agility of a stuntman, however, and the injury only stunned him. Alexa didn't stop to see him make it to his feet. She kept running toward the boat. She darted through grass, over a sidewalk, and onto a small pier. The boat had left the pier and started to take up speed. Alexa hoped her momentum would carry her aboard when she jumped. But she lost traction in her broken heels. Her feet missed and landed in the water, about a foot shy of the boat. Her face almost made contact with its rear. She lifted both hands to protect her nose from the impact. Her arms smashed hard into the bottom of the boat. Her feet slid underneath it. She became caught in an undercurrent. Taking advantage of it, she grabbed the back pontoon and managed to climb up the back of the boat one hand at a time.

Once the top half of her body was safely out of the water, she turned back toward the shore. The man with the bloody face didn't follow her into the water. The boat sped away from the shore, and they were already a good thirty yards out. He would never be able to catch them swimming. She hoisted her body onto the floor of the vessel. She lay quivering in a puddle of water for a moment. She'd boarded a tourist boat, but thankfully, no passengers sat near her and no one seemed to acknowledge her spectacle.

She took a few seconds to regain her composure. Then she stood and headed for a bathroom where she could clean up. In spite of everything that happened, her predominant thought was to get the stench of the river water off her body.

The bathroom odor paralleled that of the river. A commode resembling the toilets seen in planes sat against one wall. The other had a small sink, and a makeshift mirror composed of some sort of unbreakable glass. Alexa saw her pitiful reflection, with rivers of mascara streaming down her cheeks. *I have angered God, and he is punishing me.*

She plunged her hands into the cool running water and doused her face repeatedly. Undressing in the private bathroom, she washed herself and her clothes with the hand soap on the wall. She braided her wet hair down her back. She redressed in her freshly wrung clothes and stared at her left shoe with the broken heel. The right one had fallen off in the river when she hit the water. She buried the remaining shoe in the bottom of the small wastebasket next to the toilet then opened the door to face the world again.

The cruiser seemed peaceful, filled with happy tourists floating down the river. She sat near the back, hoping to catch a breeze and some sun to dry her dampness. No one seemed to notice her disheveled appearance. They were too distracted by the sights to pay any attention to the barefoot American in the wet clothes.

Alexa wasn't sure where the boat was going to stop, but she was sure by now the man with the bloody face knew where her boat would dock next. How quickly things had changed. Within twelve hours, she had gone from being the hunter to the hunted. *It isn't possible to run forever. Who is chasing me, and how long will I be pursued?* She didn't have any answers. *I need a way off this boat.*

In broken French, she managed to find out that the boat made two more stops. The first was near the national library of France in the eastern part of Paris. The second stop returned to where she had boarded, close to the Louvre. Alexa feared her pursuer was waiting for her at the library stop, but she was even more afraid of returning to the scene where she had seen him last. She shuddered and chose to disembark at the first stop. She wished she had a weapon to defend herself with. She yearned for the little handgun Smokey Joe had sold her back in Austin, but it was safely tucked away with the rest of her belongings in Elizabeth Fuguay's hotel room. At least with a gun, she'd have a fighting chance.

Maybe the man in the blue sweater isn't trying to kill me. He could be an undercover officer — Parisian or American. Maybe he wants to arrest me. Yep. That's the bright side — someone wants to arrest me. She let out a long sigh as the boat neared its next stop.

Her clothes were drier, and aside from being barefoot,

she blended in fairly well with the other departing passengers. She tried to bury herself in the middle of the small crowd as they scampered off the boat. Groups dispersed in different directions, while Alexa darted into a little tourist shop. Inside she found beach gear. She purchased a pair of flip-flops and a large floppy hat with the wad of wet Euros in her jean pocket. She used the hat to disguise her face.

She scanned the faces outside the store before going back into the street. She wanted a taxicab. She saw a youngster on a bike built for hauling tourists in a little cart. It would serve little as a means of cover, but perhaps it would get her to safer grounds. Alexa jumped into the cart and yelled at the boy, "Eiffel tower!" before he had a chance to acknowledge her presence.

The boy started pedaling, and they gained speed. She had no desire to go to the Eiffel tower; she just needed a landmark the boy would understand easily because she didn't have time to chitchat about any details or sort out French phrases.

She kept the brim of her floppy hat pulled snuggly against her cheeks and tried to mask as much of her face as possible. She continued that way for several blocks, and the number of streetwalkers quickly diminished as they left the waterfront. The boy stopped at a traffic light and turned back to Alexa.

"Eiffel tower eight kilometers." It was farther away than she wanted to go. Eyeing a café a few blocks down the street, she pointed at it. He nodded. He stopped at the café, and she paid the boy with more wet Euros and strode inside.

CHAPTER 22

Exhausted, she ordered a bowl of soup and a cup of hot tea and collapsed into a seat away from the door. She peered through windows clad in red and white print curtains that hung too short for the panes. She saw no one. Above the drapes, ceramic knick-knacks lined the walls on a ledge that circled the room. Little candles in red glass votives decorated the tables. *There is something familiar about this place. I've been here before.* She cocked her head toward the window and looked off into the distance, and she saw the Eiffel tower. This was the café where she and Britt had their fight. The night their funny little waiter pointed down to the candle and said *levende lys*. After all of this time hunting throughout Paris, she finally found it. If only she had the time to enjoy it. She pushed aside the urge to reminisce and concentrated on her next step.

The man chasing me has sandy-blond hair — not the type of character Mohammed Ahmed would associate with. She hoped Castro's party was not on her tail. *He could be American, and may work with Charlie. Or, perhaps, an undercover French officer, but that seems less likely.* If he works with Charlie, his motive could be to kill her, arrest her, or question her; she wasn't sure which was more plausible.

Her thoughts switched tracks, like a train derailing. *I'll flee Paris, using my alias!* Everyone who knew her in Paris knew her as Alexa DeBrow; only her hotel was booked under her new identity. She hoped that meant she could safely return and gather her things before leaving Paris. *I'll head south, to Nice. Perhaps I can absorb a few glorious days by the beach before deciding where to spend my life in hiding.*

Alexa took another sip of her tea, unaware of the man next to her until he put his hand on her shoulder. The touch sent a shock from her head to her heels. The hand gripped tightly. Another hand pulled back a tan blazer to reveal a handgun in a holster mounted to the man's side. Too distraught to look at his face, she sat unmoving, refusing to believe that she had been found. Her plan to escape would never materialize. She would never run away as Elizabeth Fuguay. *It can't happen this way. Not here. Not in our place, our café in Paris filled with beautiful and perfect memories of Britt!* Those memories were ruined now, forever tainted by the new memory of a man revealing his gun and filling her with fear.

"You'll want to stay where you are, Miss DeBrow."

She'd heard that voice before. She looked up at the man and saw a face she didn't recognize. *But that voice, I know that voice.*

"Charlie Mac." She said it casually, like two old acquaintances running into one another in a restaurant. Their eyes locked. She had thought of him as a confidant, but now he was giving her orders like a prisoner.

"We meet at last, Miss DeBrow. Funny, I didn't think it would happen this way." He softened his grasp on her shoulder and pulled up a chair with the other hand. He sat close to her. She looked at his pale gray eyes. Shallow crevices formed at the corners of his eyes and spread across his forehead.

"I'm afraid you broke the nose of one of my co-workers, Miss DeBrow." Alexa arched an eyebrow, satisfied in knowing she had broken the nose of her assailant.

"I trust you'll be more well-mannered in dealing with me." He paused for her response, but she said nothing. "All right, Miss DeBrow, gather your things. We are going to take a walk."

Suddenly terrified by his demeanor, she blurted out, "Why are you here?" *Are you going to take me somewhere private where you can make me disappear?* He was already standing, but her tone stirred the attention of onlookers. He pressed his gray houndstooth trousers flat and sat back down.

"Mohammed Ahmed is dead. This is old news to you. After your phone call to me, things happened rather quickly. My men went to the location you gave me and made several arrests. They found Mohammed's pretty pink body. He looked like a Muslim cherub, Miss DeBrow."

Alexa couldn't hide her faint smirk.

"His allies are being held for questioning. Most of them aren't talking. Some are." His stern look softened for only a moment. "All of this happened because you called me. Now I need to question you."

"I'm sure you know more than enough about me, Charles. There isn't much to begin with. You know my history, you told me so. I was a doctor. They tried me for murder. But they released me . . . and now I'm here." Her voice faded into nothingness, like she had somehow lost track of her life along the way.

"Why are you here, Miss DeBrow? Why did you decide to kill Mohammed Ahmed? Why did you call me? You involved me in this situation. I'm here because I couldn't ignore your phone call that day. So tell me, why did you call?"

She bit her lip while she hesitated. The difficult conversation required delicate word choices, and she never chose her words wisely enough. She stared at the well-dressed man in the Kenneth Cole wool-blend blazer across from her and felt like she was on trial all over again.

"Let's go for that walk, Charles. I don't want to taint the air of this place with this kind of talk."

He stood and took her arm in his. Charles dropped a couple of euros on the table, and they walked outside. Alexa didn't want to talk about it; the emotions she felt were too overwhelming to explain. But she didn't have a choice. She fought hard to find the words.

"Why did I kill Mohammed Ahmed?" She directed her speech into the empty space in front of her. "Because I believe the world is safer without him in it. I believe justice is the death of a man who is a murderer a hundred times over. I think it was the right thing for me to do — in spite of how wrong I know it sounds." Her words evaporated. She was still making sense of it herself, and she couldn't put her thoughts into words in a manner that formed a convincing argument.

When Charlie lit a cigarette, she saw the pale circle

around his left ring finger and wondered how long he had gone without his wedding band. *Are you married to the job, Charlie?* She reached down and rubbed her own bare ring finger.

"I'm not here to judge you, Miss DeBrow. The majority of my business doesn't involve doing what is right. My job is to benefit the cause. The cause for our country is determined by the minds of a few choice military and political authorities. I'm not to give my opinions or deem what is necessary. My job is to carry out the wishes of those above me." She avoided his glance, keeping her gaze on the pavement. "It just so happens that my superiors wanted Mohammed Ahmed dead, and his confidants captured. With your help, we were able to attain that goal." He tossed his cigarette on the pavement and snuffed out the fire with his Italian loafer. "That's why I'm here, Miss DeBrow — because your decision to kill Mohammed has summoned my appearance."

Summoned? Like a genie in a bottle? When do I get my three wishes, Charlie? I wish to disappear.

He continued, "Now that I'm here, I need to evaluate your character. I need to see if this delicate sort of information is safe with you, and I need to see if you can be of any additional service to me."

His words rang with casual threats. She feared a slip of the tongue now could cost her her life. *And if you decide you can't trust me? I'm sure you'll find a way to keep me quiet.* She feared his strategy would require the use of a bullet rather than a muzzle.

"What do you want from me?"

"I have a proposition for you, Miss DeBrow."

"What proposition of yours could interest me?" Her tone came off defiant.

"You have managed to impress a few of my colleagues. Not because you were sly enough to slip a drink into Mohammed Ahmed's willing hand. Not because you are lovely enough to capture his eye. And not because you were cunning enough to plan it so carefully and pull it off — but because you knew the risk involved and proceeded despite it. That's what makes for successful careers in my field — a willingness to put your life on the line for the cause. That's why I'm here. I need to know if you would be willing to put your life on the line for the cause, if such an opportunity arises in the future."

"What do you mean, exactly?" she pressed.

"Why don't you tell me how you convinced Mohammed to drink from that glass? Bodyguards surrounded him. Not one of them tried to stop him?"

She shrugged.

"I drank from the glass first. I had to convince him that it was safe."

"You drank the poison. How?" He sneered.

"I took the antidote. I attached it to an IV. I took the antidote right when swallowing the poison. It made him to trust me." She blinked.

"I see." Charles sighed a long, deep sigh. "That's enough."

"What do you mean?"

"I want to offer you a position, Miss DeBrow. I want you to consider a job with me. I realize you are a layperson. You would require training of sorts. Any training you require would be offered on a case by case basis."

Alexa interrupted. "I'm sorry, didn't we already have a business agreement? One million dollars for the death of Mohammed Ahmed?" She was more than a little disgruntled by the fact that he hadn't yet mentioned this.

"Yes. We have an agreement. All of that will be settled. I will need an account number. I'll have the money transferred to your account, tax-free. Everything will be arranged shortly. I have other matters to discuss with you. I want you to consider an indefinite position with my department. I think your skills and accomplishments thus far make you an ideal candidate for such a position. You assassinated one of our most wanted criminals, you averted capture by Agent Harrison, and even managed to break his nose. I'm convinced we can use you, Miss DeBrow."

Putting a name to the man with the broken nose suddenly made Alexa feel guilty, but she pushed the feelings aside, along with all of the other ones she'd buried. "You want me to work for you? As in, FBI or CIA or something of that nature?" He nodded in response. "I'm not sure. I don't know that I'm interested. I was ready to head to the south of France and relax for few days." She didn't care that she was digressing; his questions seemed unfathomable.

"Take a few days. I don't mind. We'll be in touch." He reached into his pocket and pulled out a cell phone. She figured he wanted to take her number to reach her. Instead, he handed her the phone. "Take this. I'll call you when I need you."

Alexa reached out, then stopped and shook her head vigorously.

"I don't want it."

"It's my way of getting a hold of you."

"No. It's your way of knowing where I am. I'll call you when I'm ready to talk."

He chuckled lightly. "All right, Miss DeBrow, have it your way. I admire your spirit. I'll be here when you're ready."

"What if I'm not interested?"

He shrugged. "Then you're not interested."

"There's no penalty for refusing?"

"None that I'm aware of. You should know, however, that you've gained the attention of my agency. It's unlikely you will lose their attention in the near future."

"You're telling me I'm being watched?" The idea disgusted her.

"Not watched, necessarily. Monitored. Your recent actions have made you a relatively high-risk individual. It's going to take some time for that kind of attention to die down."

Alexa sighed heavily.

"You are currently under surveillance. You should know, Miss DeBrow, I don't need a device to track your whereabouts."

Like you tracked Mohammed Ahmed? Alexa questioned with a hint of sarcasm.

"What do you suggest I do, Charles?"

"Do whatever you want. You're still free to decide — only your options are weighted on each end."

"What's it like to work for you?"

"You wouldn't be working for me. Let's clear that up

right away. You would be working with me. It's a kind of business I used to participate in. Frankly, it's not much different than what you did with Mohammed. You persuade people. You lie to people. You live a false identity. You gather information from those around you. Sometimes you kill, but you always avoid being killed, whatever the cost." He pursed his lips tightly.

"And you find satisfaction in that?"

"Didn't you find satisfaction in poisoning Mohammed?"

Alexa blushed. "Yes. I did. I'm not sure if I should have, but I did."

"Don't fret one moment for Mohammed's death. We both know he deserved far worse than what he got. Truth is, there are a lot more out there just like him. They deserve what they have coming to them, as well. I'll give you a few days. Take your money, go to the beach, and indulge in French wine. Just know I need to get in touch with you soon. I'll give you ten days. Then, you call me. That's the best I can offer you."

"And if I decline?"

"Suit yourself. But I suggest that you lay low for a while. Don't do anything to draw attention to yourself."

Like flee the country under a false identity?

"And if I accept?"

"I don't think you'll have any regrets. You're not the type to regret killing monsters, are you?"

Alexa shivered. She knew he was referring to Jamar now, not Mohammed.

"Goodbye, Charles."

He put out his hand and slipped her fifty euros.

"It's your cab money. Least I can do after what we put you through today."

He turned around and hopped into a black Mercedes idling just a few feet behind them in the street. Funny, she hadn't noticed the car while they were walking. She scolded herself for missing this important fact. *That's not the kind of thing an undercover agent would miss.*

CHAPTER 23

Alone on the street after Charles MacDonald's black Mercedes sped away, she wondered, *what now?* She'd spent the last several hours convincing herself that Alexa DeBrow would have to disappear indefinitely and let Elizabeth Fuguay step into the forefront. Now that idea seemed impossible. She wasn't sure if Charlie knew about her alias, but given the type of surveillance he spoke of, she knew assuming an alias would be frowned upon. *I'll have to remain Alexa a while longer.* She needed to check out of the boutique hotel where she'd registered under the alias. *I must keep Elizabeth Fuguay hidden as long as possible, and maybe someday I can safely assume my new identity.* She walked several blocks before she came across a cab to hail back to her hotel.

After a quick shower in her room, she gathered her things and discreetly checked out. She hauled her belongings to the nearby train station. *I'm going to the south of France, to Nice.* She didn't bother saying goodbye to Serge. They'd split on bad terms, and she wasn't ready to speak with him again. *I'll call him from Nice and invite him to stay the weekend, knowing he'll decline.* The friendship had ended, and the closing remarks were a mere formality.

She bought her train ticket and perched on a bench inside the station. She had an hour wait, so she curled into a ball and laid her head on one of her bags and latched her feet around another. Her purse fit snuggly under her arm, and she closed her eyes to rest.

A stench hung in the air that smelled like the river. *Is that remnants of the water in my hair or something else?* Her olfactory nerves detected ammonia — the smell of old urine. Someone had urinated on a nearby bench, and the smell permeated her nostrils. Trying to ignore it, she breathed through her mouth. She closed her eyes tighter and saw Britt.

Her mind drifted to the night of their first kiss. The happy memory found its way into her heart. Two days after they first met on that afternoon run, he invited her for tapas and mojitos. A simple first date. They shared chicken skewers, hummus, meatballs, and apples with Brie. Through smooth, lively talk he shared his novel ideas, opening himself up like a book. The words he spoke were the feelings she held silently inside herself and never confessed to another. Their similarities made her smile, and she became intoxicated with him.

Then the center tables of the restaurant were cleared away, and a small band and a dance floor appeared. The rhythms of their heartbeats and the music collided, and they found themselves holding one another while moving to the music. As their bodies moved in harmony, his chest brushed against her bosom. His chin hovered at the level of her brow. Britt sniffed her hair and nuzzled his lips up close to her forehead, while reaching down to place his hand on the small of her back. He pulled her close until their pelvises united. His arms fell to her waist while she wrapped hers around his neck. Strong arms eased her toes off the floor. Their lips met. She melted. Her heart stopped, as she fell into a serene oblivion. She loved him, and he let her.

The screech of train brakes roused her from her peaceful sleep. She took a moment to be thankful for the pleasant dream. They were few and far between, and she didn't want to take it for granted. Her train had arrived and was accepting passengers. She climbed aboard, looking forward to seeing Nice. As other passengers settled in, Alexa acknowledged the many single male faces and wondered if any of these men worked for Charles MacDonald as her surveillance team. She yearned for her freedom, so she forced the dismal thought out of her mind.

She remained uneasy until the train reached its destination. Then, the beauty of Nice drowned all other thoughts from her mind. The vibrant colors of the landscape were livelier than a Van Gogh. Deep blue skies, white washed buildings, terracotta roofs, vivid greens, and so many flowers. Alexa gathered her bags and stepped off the train, letting the sun pour onto her shoulders and warm her skin to her soul. She breathed a little easier for the moment. Nice was so much more colorful than Paris. She hadn't realized Paris was lacking anything while she was there. She had been too mesmerized by the city of lights to see beyond it. The small town on the coast had enchanting views of the sea and she wanted to find a hotel with an ocean view. *I owe myself that much.*

She found a small hotel that served breakfast daily. The cheap room had a twin bed and lacked enough wattage to run a blow dryer. Nothing glamorous enough to attract standard tourists, Alexa saw it as a hidden gem. She checked in under her old identity with a sigh: Alexa DeBrow. After everything she'd suffered, nothing had changed. She was still trying to run away from a past that haunted her.

The small room lacked a balcony, but she opened a large window to let in the sea breeze. It was enough. She made her faux invite to Serge via a voicemail she left on his phone. It took until late the next evening for him to return her call. Was he purposely avoiding her, or did he sleep in late after staying up into the early hours? She wasn't sure which. He countered her offer to come to Nice with an invitation to another Parisian party. She gave a dry response.

"I'm not sure I can handle another party of yours, Serge. Your last party was too much for me. I need some fresh air."

He seemed bored with her answer. "That's fair. Enjoy the sea views. Perhaps we meet again sometime." It was their last correspondence.

Alexa tried to find peace in Nice. She drank wine and swam in the ocean and napped on the beach. She ate hearty salads and fresh ocean fish. In the evenings, she melded into the serenity of the orange and pink and purple sunbeams setting into the sea. Her body felt rejuvenated, but her mind became stir-crazy. She carried on as such for five or six days before she lost count. More than once, she thought about calling Charlie Mac, but she shook the thought off each time. *Calling Charlie means giving up my freedom.*

With time, however, freedom settled into boredom. She

needed something to occupy herself. She needed a challenge, something thought provoking to stimulate her mind from this state of idleness. She needed obligations back in her life.

She didn't have to succumb to Charles MacDonald; he contacted her.

The call came directly to her hotel on a weekday afternoon while Alexa was lounging by the pool. The bartender who staffed both the pool bar and a small patio restaurant told her she had a phone call. She followed him to the hotel front desk, and he handed her the receiver.

She knew it was Charles. True to his word, he followed her every move.

Alexa put the phone to her ear. "Hello, Charles."

"Alexa." He dropped his degree of formality with her. Now, they communicated on a first name basis.

"You found me. I'm not surprised."

"I've known where you were every moment since we last spoke. I was waiting until you were ready to hear from me. Are you ready, Alexa? Are you done relaxing like a little Houston *celebutante*? Are you ready to do something meaningful with your life?"

His tone provoked her.

Ready to do something meaningful? I'm not sure your idea of "meaningful" equals my own. He continued without waiting for her response. "I have someone I want you to meet. Mike Shepard. I don't have any more time to wait for you, Alexa. He'll meet you by your hotel pool in an hour. Just listen to him. It's all I ask. The choice is yours to make." He hung up without another word. She stood there holding the receiver in silence. The man who gave her the phone took it away from her, and she wandered back toward the pool.

Skirting the desire to change into something more appropriate, she slumped back into her lounge chair by the pool and tried to contemplate what Charlie was planning for her. *Charlie MacDonald.* A chill swept over her, and she pulled at the sheer cover-up draped over her shoulders. *What do I do? I don't have enough information.* The hour flew by while her mind toiled recklessly, grasping for a clarity that lay beyond her reach.

CHAPTER 24

A big man, nearly seven feet tall, with a wide build and a powerful stance appeared at her side and interrupted her precarious train of thought. His large frame cast a shadow over her entire body. She felt small next to his intimidating stature. *Mike Shepard.* She tried to make out the details of his countenance, but the sun shone directly behind him, and the glare obscured his features. The rays emanated from his silhouette in a seemingly supernatural way.

Without a word, Alexa stood and tied the sheer cover-up at the waist to cloak her midsection. She pointed to a table where they could both sit. He was older than she'd expected, maybe in his late forties or early fifties. She spoke first.

"So you're Mike Shepard?"

He nodded. She bit the corner of her lip. His face was like stone.

"And what does Mike Shepard do?"

"I work with Charlie, Miss DeBrow." A deep and expressionless voice bellowed from his lips.

"Of course you do. But was does that mean? What does

Charlie want with me? Why did he send you to interrupt my little European holiday?" She stopped herself before she could ramble further. But he didn't answer any of her questions.

Her teeth sunk farther into the flesh of her lip.

"What is it that you do, exactly, Mr. Shepard?"

Silence.

Christ, he's an ogre of a man! Is his silence a game? Is he trying to intimidate me? She made her voice louder and firmer this time. "Tell me what you do, Mr. Shepard. I have to know what you do, *exactly*. This is not a game. This is my life. This is no easy decision. I need to know details. Tell me what you want from me." She scrutinized his expression through narrowed eyes.

"I take people *like you* and turn them into what Charlie needs them to be. I train them. I teach them. I instruct them. My job is to make you capable of succeeding in the tasks Charlie asks of you."

His words slipped through yellowed teeth — the color of chronic tobacco stains. She didn't smell smoke on his clothes; maybe he was a former smoker. *How many pack-years do you have under your belt, Mike?*

"I see. What is it Charlie wants from me, then?"

"It's not that easy. It's not a straightforward answer like you want it to be."

"Fine. Give me the long version. I have nowhere to be."

He pulled out manila folder that had been concealed under his jacket and handed her a photo of a thin blond man who looked near her age. Alexa eyed the photo.

"That's Ivan Verden. He's a Russian hit man. He's been targeting businessmen who've tried pocketing politicians.

Some high-roller businessmen bribe influential politicians to change tax laws. When things go awry, tempers flare, and threats become violence. Enter Ivan." He tapped the photo for emphasis. "Ivan kidnapped and killed the teen daughter of J.T. Global's CEO, Mark Phelps, after he bribed a member of the Federal Assembly of the Russian Federation. But the bribe didn't pay off, so Phelps threatened the politician. In return, the politician hired Ivan to kidnap and slay Phelps' only daughter."

He withdrew a series of photos from the envelope and spread them across the table. The graphic photos depicted the slain teen, her skin stained the rusty color of dried blood. Blood matted the once-blonde hair and splattered across the otherwise nude body. She scanned the photos before her eyes shot back to Mike.

"Okay. Russian man slays teenage girl for money. Now what?" she questioned him.

"After knocking off the daughter, Ivan demanded more money from the politician who hired him. When the man didn't pay, he lost his wife. We haven't recovered the body, but Ivan sent four of her fingers back in the mail."

"So you're trying to find the wife?"

Mike shook his head.

"No. Wife's dead."

"Dead? How do you know?"

"Coroner examined one of the fingers. He says she was dead before the fingers were removed."

"Two dead bodies. Sounds like it's over. What's left to contemplate?"

"Ivan managed to piss off the rest of the Assembly with

all of his threats. So, they want him dead. They put a bounty on his head. Shortly afterwards, a second member of the Assembly lost his father in a car explosion. No question it was Ivan's work. He has special training in explosives."

"So he's killing family members of the Assembly? Why? Doesn't he work for money? Why go to such lengths if there's no profit to gain?"

"Although many of the Assembly members are trying to pay him off, Ivan is no longer asking for money. He is a proud and arrogant man, not the kind of man you say *no* to, and not the kind of man you test. Now, he's making a point to prove his power. There's no telling how long his killing spree will last."

"And the Assembly —"

"They're afraid. They want Ivan dead. It's sort of a favor from our government to theirs. We've promised to take down Ivan."

She frowned.

"What do you want me to do?"

More photos spilled from the envelope, pictures of pretty, thin girls with blonde hair and perfect curves. Alexa couldn't help but realize the similarities she shared with them.

"Who are they?"

"Ivan is a womanizer. These girls are his former love interests."

Alexa shuffled through the stack of pictures. Their eyes were covered, their faces expressionless. She saw bruises and cuts on the women. She paused at a picture of a girl whose eyes were exposed. The photo looked like a mug shot, with a scowl across her lips and two black eyes.

"What happened to them?"

"He's a violent man. He has a temper."

She saw a photo of a cut on a woman's upper leg that made her shudder. She reached down and put a hand on the scar Jamar had left on her thigh. It was too much to bear. She stacked the photos neatly and handed them back to Mike.

"What makes you think I won't wind up like one of them?"

"You'll wind up a whole lot worse than that if he has any idea who you are."

"So you think I'll succeed?"

He shook his head.

"No. Not without a lot of help from me. He'll eat you alive. He'll see right through you —"

"And he'll kill me." She cut him off, coldly.

"No. He'll torture you. He'll torture you until your body has nothing left to give. Then, when it hurts too much to hold on, you'll let yourself die. That's how he operates."

She tried not to wince.

"And you think I should kill him?"

He shook his head again.

"No. I think he should be killed. Charles MacDonald thinks you can do it. That's why I'm here. Do *you* think you can kill him?"

She paused.

"I'm not sure."

"You've got to be sure if you are going to agree to this."

She found herself chewing on her lip again and felt a sore forming from all the biting. "Yes. I know. And the people he killed — they were innocent?"

Mike nodded.

"Yep. All innocent. I guarantee it."

"If he killed innocent people, I agree; he should be dead." Her own twisted sense of indemnification that somehow justified vigilante capital punishment disturbed her.

"You think you can kill him?"

His questions made her uneasy.

"Perhaps, with your help."

He jumped from his chair and stuffed the photos back into the manila envelope, his movements jerky and harsh.

"This isn't the kind of thing you go into half-hearted. You've got to know before you go." He turned away from her, cursing into the air. "God dammit, Charlie. What the hell are you doing?" She watched him prepare to walk away. She hadn't planned to stop him, yet she heard two words slip from her lips.

"Teach me." Her words shocked her. Mike's blank face turned back to hers.

"Teach me whatever it is that won't get me killed and allow me to kill Ivan Verden." She stared into Mike's face, taking in the details of the coarse features and hard expression. Several small, deep scars clustered together on his right cheek. They looked similar to scars she'd seen in her veteran patient population. She guessed they were from shrapnel, perhaps from an explosion. He also had a long scar down the left side of his scalp, maybe a knife wound. His features softened.

"All right," he stated. She waited for him to say more, sure he might change his mind at any moment. But he said nothing. She broke the silence first.

"What are you planning to teach me?"

She expected him to say, *how to kill*. Instead, he said, "How to conceal your emotions, to hide your fear, to attack without warning. You'll need to learn about Ivan. Know your target. Learn how to entice him. Reel him in. Learn what he wants from a woman. Those are the things that will allow you to kill him."

Her stomach churned. Something about all of this didn't set well with her. "Do you know where he is?"

Mike nodded.

"Then why all the secrecy? Why do you need me? Surely there's a simpler solution."

"It's complicated, Miss DeBrow. Ivan is a high-profile individual in some circles. Any political group that could be linked to his death could stir an even larger uprising."

"How's that possible?" *This is too much to absorb*. She felt in over her head.

"Ivan's client list is long. I'm not authorized to give you that information. Knowing the people on that list could be deadly."

So, it's too dangerous to give me details? She felt her frustration mounting and put her head in her hands with her eyes set on the ground. "Why me? Why do you need me?" she asked, looking up, her palms still cradling her head.

"Every kill has a signature, Miss. We can't have a U.S. government seal stamped on Ivan's corpse." He wiped the beading sweat from his bald head with one hand. His round scalp glistened like a polished brass knob. "I figure Charlie wants a novice — someone who can't be implicated politically, someone difficult to track. Frankly, you're not the assassin type."

Assassin? She frowned again. *Over your head, Lex.* Warning bells rang in her subconscious. She pretended not to hear them.

"Mike, do you think this is something I should do?"

He shrugged and propped a foot on the chair beside him, leaning closer to her.

"You fit the profile of what he likes. That's why I'm here."

"I see." A long sigh escaped her lips. "Now what?"

Shepard shuffled through the photos in the manila envelope one last time. He fished out the pictures of Ivan and handed them to her.

"Study these. Know his features. Tomorrow, you will meet with one of the girls Ivan has been with. She'll tell you how they met, his likes, his dislikes, what to expect. We'll talk again afterwards." She nodded. "Stay on your toes, Miss DeBrow. I'm not sure you're ready for this. I need to know you can handle yourself."

CHAPTER 25

Mike left Alexa sitting alone by the pool. She collected the pictures of Ivan and shoved them deep into her beach bag. Then she plunged her body into the saltwater pool and sat cross-legged on the bottom. She thought about what she had agreed to. The pictures flashed in her mind. There was Ivan, the sexy blond killer. Then faces of his victims flashed. She saw the teenage girl who resembled the love interests of Ivan, and Alexa feared what Ivan had done to the girl before he killed her. Then Alexa thought of the love interests — the girls with bruised cheeks and blackened eyes. Even if he didn't kill them, they were still victims. She thought of the girl with the cut on her leg that resembled the scar Jamar had given her. She thought about it until her chest hurt and her lungs felt like they would burst from lack of oxygen.

She jolted to the water's surface and gasped for air. *Yes. Ivan Verden must die.* She owed that justice to his victims. Otherwise, their sullen little faces would forever haunt her.

She swam to the pool's edge, pulled her emotionally

drained body from the water, and then gathered her bag and headed back to her hotel room. She recalled Mike's final words to her. *He warned me to stay on my toes. What can that mean? Is he planning to test me or challenge me in some way?* She wasn't ready for any additional challenges, and she hoped he'd go easy on her.

She figured the best way to "stay on her toes" was to finish the evening off with a long run. On the unusually warm spring evening, Alexa slipped into a sports top, gym shorts, and running shoes. She had grown accustomed to a laid-back life of ease the past few days, and her body craved a long workout. She carved out a ten-mile path through narrowed streets, out of the city and into some small hills on the outskirts of town. She used the time to give her mind a break from everything she had seen and heard that day.

Her thoughts drifted back to her college days and college friends — her party years. She thought about how their lives had changed since then. All of her close friends from those days were married long ago and had children starting grade school. She felt a huge disconnect from that group of individuals. They once had so much in common. Two girls had divorced and remarried already. Alexa attended both second weddings with Britt at her side. They were supposed to be the next happy couple. She was ready to settle down and join her peers for a quiet life in suburbia.

It could have been worse. A short marriage with a messy divorce would have been more difficult than no marriage. No. That's not true. Marriage and divorce are more acceptable in Austin than no marriage at all. That's why I left — too much explaining to do. She didn't want to have to make excuses for her life choices. She wanted only to answer to herself. She became lost in her thoughts, then became lost altogether. She stumbled onto a country road next to a small vineyard. Anywhere else, a vineyard would be a memorable landmark, but in France, there was always a vineyard a stone's throw away. The sun started to set at her back. *I must be heading east.* Her hotel on the coast was south of her location, but which direction on the road would take her there? East was downhill. West was uphill. She ran up the hill to get a better vantage. *This isn't right.* She turned around to head back the way she'd come.

When she spun around, she nearly ran into the car behind her. She hadn't noticed it until now. The silver SUV was an uncommon car to see in Europe. Most European cars were small compacts or luxury sedans. Alexa jogged past the car and felt an eerie chill as she shuffled by. She picked up her pace. *There's something odd about that vehicle.* She listened to its slow, quiet movements, and feared the driver was watching her.

She heard the sound of the tires on the gravel. The tires stopped turning, but the engine still hummed. She hastened her pace a bit more and scanned her surroundings. There was no one around to see or hear her. No building to run to, no place to escape, and no weapon to aid her. *You're all alone, Lex.* Gravel churned beneath the tires of the SUV once more. A brief pause was followed by another rustling of gravel. Alexa pictured the SUV performing a three-point turn. *It's changing directions. It's following me!*

Running faster won't help. You can't outrun a car. The wheels of the SUV spun faster and the engine roared louder as the vehicle approached. She looked for a place where she could go but the SUV couldn't. It was her only hope of escaping the car, but she feared she couldn't escape its driver.

Farther down the road she saw a little dry creek bed covered by a rock bridge lacking a sidewall. Gravel covered the top of the bridge, and tall grasses filled the creek bed. All of these factors helped to camouflage the bridge from the remainder of the road. Alexa listened to the loose gravel displaced by the SUV's tires as it landed on the ground behind her. *It's closer.*

She ignored the cramp forming in her side. *Faster.* She wanted to get to the little bridge, but it was still a distance ahead of her. Fueled by fear, she tore into a dead sprint as the vehicle neared. She reached the bridge and leaped off the side, aiming for the far bank of the dry creek bed. She fell to her knees on the uneven surface, but hurried to her feet and managed a few more steps before she heard the SUV dive off the bridge after her. The front of the SUV landed in the creek bed, but one of the back wheels remained perched on the bridge. The bottom of the creek bed lay a mere four feet from the height of the bridge, but it was enough to throw the slow-moving SUV into a nosedive.

Alexa took a quick glance at the scene. She tried to make out the face of the driver, but the airbag had deployed, and there was nothing to see from her angle. She considered confronting him, but she didn't have a weapon. Although strong-willed, she wasn't physically strong. If it came down to a battle of brute force with a man, she would lose every time. She dismissed the idea and fled the scene on foot.

She prayed he wouldn't come after her, but feared

otherwise. She ran back on the road for about three hundred yards before she reached another patch of grapevines. A glance behind her revealed nothing. She needed to take cover off the road. Cutting through the vines, she headed south. She moved toward the coast, hoping to reach civilization.

Beyond fatigued, she forced her body to persevere. She took a moment to survey the damage. Blood tricked down her left leg from the fall after she jumped, and her knees were scuffed with abrasions. Her feet ached, and she envisioned the blisters developing. Her lungs burned, and her throat was parched. *Keep moving.*

She ignored the pain and concentrated on listening. Her feet landed softly on the bare earth. She focused on the rhythm of her steps while trying to delineate if any additional sounds were present. Aside from an occasional gust of wind or bird chirp, she heard nothing.

The dirt beneath her feet turned to short grass as she neared the edge of the vineyard. The sound of her footsteps changed as the grass shuffled under her feet. Becoming fixated on the sound of her feet, she was slow to realize she *had* reached civilization. She approached the edge of the city and immediately recognized a café where she'd sipped espresso. *I'm near my hotel!*

She looked behind her and saw no one. Her feet stuttered trying to stop and her torso doubled over as her hands fell to her thighs. When her breath normalized, she started to hobble down the street, feeling her muscles tighten with every step. Her hotel sat at the end of the street. *Has the driver of the SUV been to my hotel?* She questioned the bellman in the lobby, "Has anyone asked for me?"

His eyes moved over her body, pausing at the bloody leg, and he shook his head.

"Can you bring me a glass of water?"

"Oui, mademoiselle." He brought her a glass of ice water, and she swallowed it in gulps on her way to her room. After unlocking the door, she kicked it open with her shoe. She stepped away from the doorway and leaned against the wall across the hall. *Is there someone inside? Is someone waiting for me?* Her mind fell into a state of disarray. The pounding of her heart rang in her ears. As her knees grew weak, she felt her body slump to the floor. *I'm afraid to go into my hotel room. Afraid of people chasing me. Always afraid. I'm so tired of being afraid!* Her face contorted into a pout, but her body couldn't spare the liquid to form tears.

At the end of the hallway, a young couple collected their bags. They cast perplexed glances her way. A maid popped in and out of a room two doors down. When she exited the last time, she pointed to the open door of Alexa's room and muttered something to her in French. Alexa blushed. *I'm being silly. Everything is fine. Just stand up and go in your room.* She coaxed herself inside.

Everything seems in place. The maid has come by, turned down the sheets, and replaced the towels. See? It's okay. The pep talk didn't calm her nerves, so she poured herself a hot bath and plunged her aching body into it. The water stung the abrasions on her legs, making it difficult to tolerate the bath, and she emerged before her muscles had a fair chance to recover. She settled for a vodka tonic from room service to take the edge off and help her sleep.

CHAPTER 26

On edge the whole night, every noise startled her. Around two a.m., a sound in the hallway made her jump to her feet. Her eyes scanned the room to make sure no one had ransacked the place while she slept. *Calm down, Lex. I have to put my mind at ease.* Her hands sifted through her luggage and found the handgun she'd purchased from Smokey Joe. She stuffed it under her pillow. *Jimmy was right. A gun buys peace of mind.*

Her fatigued body rested until mid-morning before she dragged herself to breakfast by the pool. This morning, she would meet with one of Ivan's former lovers. She'd just finished eating when the pool boy motioned her to the front desk for a phone call.

"Hello?" Alexa spoke into the receiver.

"Is she there?" It was Mike.

"Is *who* where?"

"Corbin. She's the woman you're meeting. Dammit. Just like a Swede. Stay put. I'll make sure she finds you." He hung up the phone.

Alexa ordered a glass of water, no ice, and sipped it slowly. She took out the manila envelope filled with pictures of Ivan and the girls. She wanted to memorize his face and features. One of the photos had a paragraph of descriptors attached to it. She read over the words that described Ivan.

Age: 38
Height: 6'4"

Here Alexa paused. *He will tower over my five-eight frame.*

Weight: 200 lbs
Hair: dark blond
Eyes: Brown
Race: Caucasian
Religion: n/a
Family: Estranged father, no siblings, mother deceased, no wife or children
Distinguishing features: tattoo right shoulder: Swastika, tattoo left forearm: Chinese symbol, tattoo right forearm: demon face, scar over left eyebrow

Alexa scanned through the collection of blonde pseudo lovers he'd acquired. They had similar features: long blonde hair, slender, pale skin. She examined their scars and bruises. One girl had a cut on her neck and a busted lip with abrasions on both wrists, as though she had been tied with a rope and had struggled to escape. Another girl had whip marks on her back. While a third had a broken forearm and cuts on both thighs. *Looks like the scar Jamar left on my leg.* Her hand covered it, reflexively. Of all the photos, only one girl didn't have her eyes covered with a black scarf. That face materialized at Alexa's side.

"Corbin, I assume," Alexa greeted. Corbin pulled up a chair and dropped an oversized Hermes bag on the table next to the manila envelope. The Swede's cat-like eyes seemed perturbed. Alexa fought feelings of intimidation.

The woman lit a long, skinny cigarette and sucked its fumes hungrily. She grabbed a photo off the table without saying a word. She'd picked Ivan's photo. Corbin's head turned from side to side as she viewed the image from different angles. Then she crinkled her nose, parted her lips, and with clenched teeth, hissed like a stray cat defending its territory.

She turned back to Alexa, straightening her neck and taking another drag from the cigarette. Alexa realized the parallels between Corbin's features and her own. *If this is the kind of girl Ivan is interested in, it shouldn't be hard to get his attention.*

"So you are looking for my Ivan, no?" Corbin let a wicked little giggle escape her crimson lips. "And what will you do with my Ivan — kill him? No?"

Alexa hesitated, unsure how to handle the unpredictable woman across the table.

"What do *you* want me to do with him?"

"Ha! Wouldn't you rather know what he is going to do with you?" Corbin sneered.

"Okay. Tell me what Ivan will do with me."

Corbin's sinister snicker twisted into a monstrous scowl.

"I met Ivan for business. I work as a professional escort

at —" She cut herself off, her eyes moving up and down Alexa's face. "It doesn't matter where I work. He called on a Monday night. We met around eight-thirty. I arrived wearing only my corset and coat. Son-of-a-bitch pulled me into the room by my hair. I kicked him. I don't do rough play. He pulled a fistful of hair from my head. He wasn't playing. It wasn't the S & M bullshit people talk about. He taped my mouth before I could scream. Taped me all the way around my head. When I finally got the tape off, I was half bald."

The Swede took a moment to reach a hand into her bag and pull out another cigarette. This one was bent in the middle, suggesting it didn't come from a carton; rather, it was loose amongst the other objects in the bag. She fumbled for a lighter. Corbin flicked the switch on the lighter repeatedly until a flame appeared. She took two long puffs from the new cigarette before she snuffed out the old one on the table and flung it onto the patio.

"Son-of a bitch tied my wrists to the bed posts. Ran his hands over my body. He pinched me so ferociously, bruises popped up all over. Bruises on my chest made some kind of symbol. He cut me and scraped me with a metal necklace he wore around his neck. He slapped me around, gave me two black eyes." She adjusted her cross-legged stance from left-over-right to right-over-left in a languid, orchestrated movement.

"Did he rape you?" Alexa interrupted.

The Swede shot Alexa a steaming glance.

"Not in the conventional sense. Metal things from a suitcase cut my insides. It hurt like hell, made me bleed. The pain aroused him. That's what turns him on, eliciting pain from others. He jerked himself off into a plastic bag in the corner." She shrugged and took a drag.

"And he whipped you?" Alexa continued.

"Yes, at the end. He cut my ankles free, flipped me over, and whipped his belt across my back. He left me for the hotel maid to find the next morning."

Corbin's story was gruesome, but Alexa wasn't alarmed. No shudder ran down her spine. Her stomach didn't turn. Years of medical training had hardened her heart. Too many heart-wrenching stories and painful events merged together into one coalescent story of grief. She'd seen everything from a quadriplegic woman suffering panic attacks while telling the story of how she was thrown from her horse the day before, to the man who watched his wife die beside him in the emergency room.

Alexa knew her part in the matter — she knew how to play the empathy card with her patients. No matter what their dilemma, when patients gave her the water works, her words were always the same: "I can't imagine what you're going through. This must be so hard." Then she would put her hand on their arm and offer them a box of tissue. "I'm so sorry for your (fill in the blank: pain, loss, etc.). Let me know if I can do anything to help."

In a way, she did know how they felt. The five stages of grief were the same for everyone: Denial, Anger, Bargaining, Depression, and Acceptance. Eventually, they all wound up in the same place: Acceptance. It wasn't a happy ending to the series of events; rather, it was the numb emotional state that resulted in a hardened heart.

But Corbin wasn't giving her the water works. She told

her story matter-of-factly, with cold words emanating through pursed lips. She didn't need empathy; her heart was hardened already. Corbin didn't feel sorry for herself; she still had a taste of hatred lingering on her tongue. She wanted revenge.

The Swede took another few puffs from her cigarette. "Are you ready for this? Ready for Ivan?" She raised her eyebrows into a high arch. Ivan's beating hadn't stolen her beauty.

Alexa shook her head. "No. I'm not ready. Not for any of this. But I think I could be. That is, I will be, when the time is right. . . ." Her voice trailed off. She wasn't convincing anyone, not even herself.

Corbin smeared another coat of red lipstick across her mouth, dumped the tube in her bag, and gathered her things. She rose from her chair.

"Good luck to you."

Alexa smiled. "Thanks."

Corbin scoffed. "You will need it."

CHAPTER 27

Alexa sat alone at the table. Her eyes glanced at the photos spread out before her. She sorted through them and placed them back into the manila envelope one by one. She paused at the picture of Corbin. *There's something different about her compared to the other girls, but I can't put my finger on it.*

A phone rang. Her phone still sat at the bottom of the Seine. Her head spun toward the sound. She turned to see Mike walking toward her with a cell phone in hand.

He silenced the ringing phone and handed it to her. "This is *your* new phone, my dear. This is the phone you will carry, and this is how you will reach me."

She glared at the phone, a much simpler model than the smartphone she was used to carrying. "Why?"

"I need to keep in touch with you, and this is a more secure device than the models you're accustomed to. It's encrypted. It doesn't store numbers. It doesn't have a memory. It doesn't have caller ID. It can't be traced. It's safer. Take it."

"Safer? You mean if something happens to *me*, right?"

"Yep. It's the nature of the job. Get used to it."

She took the phone reluctantly.

"How was Corbin?" He raised an eyebrow.

"Fine, I guess." Alexa fiddled with the phone in her hand.

"She didn't scare you away?"

She shook her head. "No. I guess not. I suppose it was all very expected — what she said, that is."

"Expected? All right." His lips pressed into a line. "I guess you're as screwed up as the rest of us."

She ignored his mockery. "Now what? Why are you here?"

"It's training time — for you."

"Oh. Okay. Do I need to change clothes or something?"

"I'm afraid you don't get that luxury. It's the nature of the job — no time to prepare. You can't prepare for the unexpected. In this line of work, it's all unexpected. Come with me." She followed him around the side of the hotel and into a parking lot. He led her to a black SUV that looked all too familiar. It was the same make and model as the one that tried to run her down the day before. He motioned her to the driver's side, and Alexa entered without questioning him. Inside the SUV, her hands naturally settled onto the steering wheel. Mike scooted into the passenger's seat. It only took a moment for him to whip out a pair of handcuffs and snap them on her wrists, attaching them to the steering wheel.

"What the hell are you doing?"

"Training." He jumped back out of the vehicle and wrestled with something in the back seat. Using a hook, he tossed a snake onto the floor of the front passenger's seat. She recognized the light brown snake as a viper by its coloring and the "X" on its head.

"What the fuck is this?" Alexa screamed, squirming toward the edge of the seat.

"Stay calm. I'm told they smell fear."

"Easy for you to say! You're outside the car."

Through slow, precise movements she manipulated the door handle with her left elbow, and the door popped open. The viper's tongue flickered rapidly as it slithered toward her. It raised its head high and displayed its fangs. Its head veered back and then darted forward, striking the seat next to her. As the snake recoiled, Alexa scooted her body out of the car door. Her left foot hit the ground. She stepped her right foot onto the door's armrest and flung her left leg onto the hood of the vehicle. She struggled to get more of her body onto the hood, but her wrists remained bound to the steering wheel.

The snake followed Alexa's movements to the driver's side of the vehicle and struck again at her dangling foot while she struggled to pull it away. When it saw its escape through the open door, it slithered out of the car and onto the pavement. Alexa exhaled and turned her frustration to Mike. His typically solemn face grinned from ear to ear. His unexpected grin somehow soothed her mounting fury. She hadn't known he was capable of it. He put his hands together and made a meager attempt at applause.

"You did good, girl." His head bobbed up and down. "That's two in a row for you. By the way, Charlie told me you broke a fella's nose. You must have a real knack for that. You broke that guy's nose yesterday, too. Broke it with the airbag, anyway." She writhed to keep her torso on the hood, given the contortion of her upper body.

"What are you telling me, Mike? That was *you* yesterday? The SUV that tried to run me down, that was *you?*" Her tone escalated.

"Not me, exactly. I used one of my men. I had to test you. I needed to see you think on your feet. It's for your own good. I can't send you out into all that shit without knowing you can handle yourself, that you at least stand a chance."

Her anger melted into understanding. She glanced over her shoulder. The snake was out of sight. "Am I done? Can you release me — or is this part of my test, too?"

He laughed. "No. I got the key. Give me a minute. I'll get you down, and we'll get lunch."

I'm not convinced these little mind games will prepare me to face Ivan. And I don't know how much more of this trickery my nerves can take. I'm still a wreck from the near hit-and-run yesterday. After this almost snake attack, I might not ever stop shaking. She watched her fingers tremble as Mike released the cuffs from her wrists. *I need wine. That will relax me.* She sighed as she shook her throbbing wrists. *I doubt Mike would allow wine.*

They walked to a restaurant adjacent to the hotel that she had frequented during her stay. She ordered a salad. He ordered pasta. They sat staring at each other in awkward silence. *How little I know about the man sitting across from me — the man constantly throwing obstacles at me. I need to know more. I need to trust him.*

"Tell me about yourself, Mike. I need to know who you

are." His guarded countenance told her sharing his life's details was not part of the job description.

"What do you want to know?" he asked, wiping sauce from his face with back of his hand.

"Something intimate; details about your family, your life before you started all of this."

He shoved a mouthful of pasta into his mouth and spoke around the food.

"I was married twice before I started working for Charlie. Neither relationship worked out. I don't know why I ever got married. I guess I liked the idea of having a family — it just wasn't right for me."

"Do you have children?"

"I have a daughter, from my first marriage. We had her young; it's why we got married. Hell, we were kids ourselves. That same year I joined the military and wasn't around much. Probably better off that way. Better for everyone, I think." His stare fixed on something off in the distance.

"Don't you miss her?"

He took another large bite.

"Your daughter, I mean?"

"I think about her, if that's what you're getting at. I think about her a lot. I keep up with her — but she doesn't know about that. She hasn't heard from me in a long time."

"*Keep up with her,* how?"

"It's not hard for me to find someone. Find out where they live. Where they work. Hell, I can check her credit history. I know she's doing all right that way. She bought herself a little condo in Atlanta last summer. I was proud of that. She saves her money. That means she's practical." He smiled to himself. "She's got a man in her life. He seems like a good guy, from a good family and all. He's a college professor. I looked into him; he checked out okay. Maybe they'll get married. I don't know." His voice trailed off. She could tell the small talk made him uncomfortable.

"You're a good girl, from a good family. You remind me a lot of her. Lily, that is, my daughter. You had a real nice life going for you. I did my homework on you, too. Then one bad turn of events, and you wind up here. Is this really where you want to be right now?"

His honesty was almost too much for her to bear. She tried to avoid such questions, but the words bubbled out of her like water from a mountain spring.

"You know I was a radiologist, Mike. Do you know what that is? The doctor who interprets MRIs and CTs and x-rays?" He nodded. "I was working overnight once in the ER. An internist came down to have me look at a head CT to evaluate for a bleed. We chatted. He asked me how many years of training it took to become a radiologist. I said my residency training was five years after med school, plus an additional fellowship year. I remember the way he rolled his eyes. Medicine is only three years, you see. He told me how he didn't understand why it took so long. He said radiology was easy — the answer was staring you in the face in black and white."

Alexa furrowed her brow. "He was naïve to think the job is easy. People tend to think things aren't difficult when they don't understand them. It's funny to me that what he saw was only black and white, when all I see are shades of gray. That's how I felt after the Jamar incident. Everyone around me judged my actions so harshly. All they saw was that I killed a man, and they condemned me because killing is wrong. It was different to me. I really saw some good in what I did. I thought taking one dangerous man out of the world would make it a safer place for the rest of us."

His eyes locked on hers. Soft eyes contrasted his harsh façade. A gnat buzzed around his ear; he didn't blink. She continued.

"Maybe it's different for those who see the world in black and white, wrong and right, bad and good. The whole thing is a little harder for me to swallow. For years, I devoted my efforts to trying to do what was right for those around me. I helped people, whether they deserved it or not. I'm not even sure *that* work ever really made a difference. Then, when Jamar died — I was proud for being responsible. I felt like I had changed the world, in spite of others' condemnation. Putting an end to something so evil seemed right. That's why I killed Mohammed Ahmed. He took so many innocent lives. He wasn't innocent; he was cruel. He needed to be stopped. I'm glad I stopped him. Now, I'll stop Ivan." She tried to sound confident, but her voice cracked with her last sentence.

Mike jumped up from the table and pushed away his plate. "You're not ready for this." He started to walk away.

Alarmed, she followed him.

"But I *will* be ready. With your help, I will be ready. Maybe I should meet with the other girls — the ones from the photos."

"Stop fooling yourself, kid." His back was toward her, and he kept walking.

"Talking with Corbin helped. The other girls could help

even more, help me to understand him —"

He cut her off. "Not possible."

"I'm not afraid, Mike. You need to know that."

He turned to face her.

"You should be afraid." His words cut through the air that separated them.

"But I'm not!"

"The other girls are dead. Ivan killed them. That's why their eyes were covered like that. He killed them all. They can't help you."

She paused mid-step and fought the lump forming in her throat. She scolded herself for not recognizing the post-mortem images on her own. His steps away from her grew longer. She hurried to catch up with him.

"I'm not afraid," she repeated.

"Why? Because you don't think you have anything to lose? You have a lot to lose, trust me. You have a lot to live for."

"I'm not afraid because I *can* do this."

"Bullshit!" He seemed more than angry; he was emotional. He'd been stone-faced. She didn't expect this. There was more to it than he was letting on. It was like he cared about her — but he didn't even know her, not really.

It hit her suddenly. *It's his daughter. He said I reminded him of his daughter. That's what this is about. Mike isn't trying to protect me; he is trying to protect Lily.*

Alexa focused all of her emotion and energy into sheer force and shoved Mike from behind with all her might. The ox of a man lost his balance for a moment and stumbled two steps forward. That's all she was capable of — shoving his three-hundred pounds two meager steps. He turned to face her once more. She gathered her balance and shoved him again. He was prepared this time; he didn't lose a step.

"I *can* do this!"

"No. Not you! We'll find someone else."

"I can *do* this!"

They were both yelling now. She reached out to shove him once more. This time, he grabbed both her wrists. His face had turned red, his eyes watery. Although shocked by his teary eyes, she held her ground. She spoke her next words slowly and firmly. "I *will* kill Ivan, Mike — with *your* help."

"Dammit, girl. Why do you want this so bad?"

"I don't know, Mike. But I need to do this."

He paused. His lips quivered, and he looked her straight in the eye. "All right. We'll give it a try."

"No. We are not giving it a try. This *is* going to work."

"Fine. It's going to be hard as hell, though."

The tension in her face softened. "That's why I have you. I need you. You can't give up on me."

CHAPTER 28

She led him back to the poolside patio. The usually deserted place would be a good spot to devise a plan. They settled at the table with the best view of the sea.

"Why do you think Ivan killed all of the other girls, but not Corbin?" she asked aloud.

He shook his head. "I don't know. She was lucky, I guess."

"I think it's because she stopped being afraid of him. I think she accepted death easier than the others. That's why he spared her. He lost interest when she stopped being afraid. It's not their pain that fuels him; it's their fear."

Mike nodded. "You may have a knack for this, after all. But I doubt that piece of information is going to help you very much."

He's right. That tidbit won't save me if things go awry. If Ivan gets the upper hand, no strategy will save me. He'll take my life without hesitation. She cringed.

They spent the rest of the afternoon discussing Ivan's history, distinguishing marks, and patterns of behavior.

Alexa took mental notes of the discussion. She even committed the benign details to memory, like the European brand of cigarette he smoked with a white carton and black letters. She saw the pattern of his attire; typically he wore neutral tones, shades of gray, black, or occasional navy. He wore turtlenecks and trousers. Never jeans. He donned dark aviator sunglasses throughout the day, wore his hair short, and appeared clean-shaven.

In one photo, he lacked a turtleneck, and his bare skinned neck revealed something interesting. She saw a scar on the left side of his neck that lie in a similar location to the place she stabbed Jamar. Alexa interrupted Mike's update on Ivan's recent travels. "What's this?"

He looked at the photo and shook his head. "Don't know." He dismissed the question and returned to his soliloquy.

She interjected again. "It looks like he has a scar on his neck." Alexa traced the scar on the blown-up image of Ivan's face. "It's right over — his carotid." *The resemblance is eerie.*

Mike had been mentioning details of Ivan's trek through Switzerland last week, but now stared at her blankly.

"Where is he now?" she asked.

"Versailles, outside Paris."

"How do you propose that I kill Ivan, Mike?"

"I assume you'll enter his hotel room just like all of those other girls, and shoot him. I'll give you a gun with a silencer and make sure you know how to use it. We'll work on that tomorrow."

"And if that doesn't work, is there a back-up plan?"

"No back-up plan. I'm your back-up. I'll be within ten

minutes of you the whole time."

Ten minutes is too long. I need a plan B — another weapon in case plan A falls apart. I can't wrestle Ivan, he'll ki — no. I can't wrestle Ivan. Alexa's finger still lay on the scar in the picture. She thought about using a knife. *I could stab him, just like Jamar.* She imagined her hand slicing through the air. *Seems risky. Doubt I can conceal a knife long enough to finish him off.*

What if I didn't use a knife? What if I used . . . a syringe . . . filled with air? Air embolism to the brain was a risk associated with numerous medical procedures. She had seen an air embolus once in a male carotid endarterectomy patient in his late seventies who had his vessels "cleaned out" from atherosclerotic plaque buildup. Air accidentally leaked into the artery that led to the brain, causing a stroke, and the patient coded on the table about twenty minutes into the procedure. Alexa had read the emergent CT scan of his head. A peculiar little collection of gas gathered in his Circle of Willis — the place where all of the arteries to the brain converge. Only a hyperbaric oxygen chamber could save him, but it was too late; he died on the scanner.

She couldn't shake the idea of injecting an air embolus from her mind. *If I put a sharp needle into the scar, he may not feel a thing.* Scar tissue often lacked sensation after the nerve endings were cut and regressed with healing. *I'd have to be very close to Ivan to pull that off, close enough to touch him.* She winced at the thought. If she let him get close enough to put his hands on her, she doubted she could escape his grasp. *I can't die like the other girls. It would be like letting Jamar win all over again.*

She scolded herself for the sudden feelings of weakness.

Jamar didn't win, she forced herself to remember. *Jamar will never win. And Ivan will die.* She repeated the words, letting them become her mantra.

Mike went over other details regarding Ivan's whereabouts and his thoughts of Ivan's upcoming agenda. She would meet Ivan in Versailles in three days to confront him. In the interim, Mike would critique her shooting skills and teach her some self-defense tactics.

As their discussion grew to a close, he reached a hand into his jacket and revealed a plastic bag filled with a couple of cards and documents. "I almost forgot. You'll be traveling under your alias. I guess this is something you and Charlie discussed. He said you had the passport already. I have a few additional things, including a credit card in your alias for expenses."

Alexa's eyes followed the card he slid across the table to her. She gasped when she read the name on the card: *Elizabeth Fuguay.* Her stomach flip-flopped. Her teeth gnawed into cheek, too afraid to speak. *If Charles MacDonald knows about Elizabeth Fuguay, he knows too much.* In spite of her agreement with Charlie, she had maintained the belief that she would one day escape all of the tragic events and start anew as Elizabeth Fuguay. But if Charles MacDonald knew of her proposed new identity, she would have to abandon it altogether. *He trapped me.*

Alexa reached out for the card and set both hands atop the documents he set before her. She traced the letters with her fingertips and whispered the name aloud. "Elizabeth Fuguay." *Not what I had planned at all.* Bitter irony burned in her gut. Instead of a new identity bringing her freedom, she had become a different kind of prisoner — one who answered to Charles MacDonald. Hot, salty tears pooled in her eyes, but she willed her body not to shed them. *Tears won't help.* She suppressed the feeling, placing it where she hid the rest of her pain. When she looked back up at Mike, her blank face proved her emotions were safely locked away. He stood.

"I'll see you in the morning. Get some rest."

She said nothing as he walked away.

She slipped into a state of confusion. *What are you planning, Charlie? You stole my future, my blank slate. Why? So I can be your pawn? Your sacrificial lamb?* Exasperated, she stretched her hands across the table and set her chin on her arms. *Why am I doing this?* She remembered Corbin's words and her bitterness. *For his victims. I kill him for his victims. Damn you, Charlie for getting me into this.* She forced a deep cleansing breath and told herself she was not a sacrificial lamb; but a wolf in sheep's clothing.

That night over a couple of vodka sodas, Alexa visualized meeting with Ivan and killing him. Mike had set her up with an escort service near Ivan, but she would have to wait for him to call the escort service. Based on his pattern of behavior, Mike thought he would most certainly call. Once he did, she would go to his hotel room. He'd open the door; she'd enter. The door had to be closed before she could carry out her plan. Mike was adamant about that part. The kill was supposed to be concealed and discreet. They didn't want to provoke any of Ivan's allies or cause a scene of any sort. He needed to disappear quietly.

Once the door closed, she would pull her handgun from her trench coat while pretending to undress, and shoot Ivan in the chest. No, she would shoot him in the heart, to be precise. She needed to be precise.

She visualized the events smoothly a couple of times. After the second vodka soda hit her, the details blurred in her mind, and Alexa lost her sharpness. Her imagination ran wild. She pictured herself entering Ivan's hotel room, and him shoving her to the ground. The gun tumbled out of her coat. They wrestled on the floor. Ivan got the gun. It was too late for Alexa; without a weapon, she didn't stand a chance.

She opened her eyes in a panic, shut them tight, and started again.

Once more, Ivan shoved her from behind and Alexa hit the ground, the gun tumbling from her coat. This time, she clasped a syringe in her hand and pierced Ivan's neck scar in the midst of the struggle. She imagined air bubbles winding through the segments of Ivan's internal carotid artery before swirling around in the Circle of Willis and depositing in his cerebral arteries.

In a moment of satisfaction, her eyes popped opened, and the corners of her lips turned upwards. Yes. *I will bring a syringe the day I meet Ivan. Maybe I should discuss it with Mike.*

A ring from the special phone Mike had given her interrupted her meditative state. The cheap little thing looked like a plastic toy from the bottom of a Crackerjack box.

"I need you dressed and downstairs in the lobby by seven a.m." Before he hung up, he added, "It's best you learn to lay off the booze."

What? How does he know that? I'm under a microscope for Mike and Charlie to scrutinize. She was like a teenage child being berated by an overprotective parent. *I should have another drink just to spite him.* Her mind danced in its tipsy state as she searched for the vodka bottle. *No.* She frowned. *He's right. I don't need anymore.*

She sulked on the bed, curling her knees into a fetal position while unanswered questions reverberated in her skull like laundry on the spin cycle. *Why did Charlie ask me to do this? Why do I have to be a female escort? Can't some man just shoot Ivan in the street? Do I really want to kill Ivan? Will it be satisfying?*

She focused her thoughts on what she knew was true and absolute. *Ivan is a horrible man, and the world will be a safer place without him. It's just like Jamar and Castro. Yes, Ivan's death will be satisfying. His death by my hand will be satisfying.* The swirling thoughts slowed, and she drifted to sleep.

CHAPTER 29

Mike picked her up in the morning at her hotel in his black SUV and drove her to a barn outside the city. He wanted to watch her shoot and teach her a few combat maneuvers. He confiscated her licensed handgun and replaced it with an unlicensed one. This gun was a larger model that came with a small silencer. He told her what it was called, but she quickly forgot the name of the fancy model. She learned to assemble and disassemble the gun, how to load and unload it. After dissecting its parts, it didn't seem as fancy.

He gave her tips on shooting targets while moving and strategies to conceal her weapon. He even taught her to shoot in reverse utilizing a hand mirror. Alexa thought her abilities would impress Mike, but he said very little. He had a lunch packed for them both, and they chatted some while they ate.

"I think you'll do all right after all, Poppy girl." It was the second time that day he had referred to her as *Poppy*. The first time Alexa dismissed the remark, assuming it was a slip up meant for someone else. The second time, she knew it was a new nickname he was trying out on her, and she couldn't help but wonder how it originated. *Is Poppy somehow related to Lily, his daughter's name? Mike must have a thing for flowers,* she mused.

"Mike, I couldn't help but realize your new nickname for me." He looked up at her, and their eyes met in an awkward moment. "Why *Poppy?*"

Mike spoke with his mouth full of food and bits of sandwich moved in and out of his teeth. "Poppy — just seems fittin', I guess. You're pretty, you know, like a flower."

Confused, she pressed, "Okay, why not Rose or Petunia?"

He smirked. "Poppies are different. Their seeds are used for opium, found in drugs like morphine and heroin. You're that kind of pretty. It's addictive to a man, like a drug. You're addictive, and dangerous — and, with my help, deadly. You're a poppy — a beautiful, deadly flower."

She appreciated the sentiment; she hoped the nickname stemmed from a growing confidence he had in her. His confidence was all she could ask for. In the back of her mind, however, she feared the nickname stemmed from the poppy flowers referenced in the poem "In Flanders Fields," where red poppies grew over the graves of the fallen soldiers. From those words, the flowers became memorial symbols for soldiers who had died in battle. Somehow, the remembrance poppy seemed more fitting for Alexa, seeing as how she had a very real chance of falling in her upcoming battle. A chill crept over her and lingered at the base of her neck.

Mike also went over various physical maneuvers, both offensive and defensive. In spite of the confidence her new nickname ensued, he focused mainly on defensive maneuvers, with both of them knowing if the fight turned physical, she would need a means of escape. He wrapped his thick arms around her neck and torso and instructed her how to escape. She became a contortionist, pushing or pulling to counteract Mike's forceful movements, fearing her bones would break under the pressure. Alexa held a constant grimace while writhing under her captor's hold. *Weaker sex, indeed. I don't stand a chance against Mike, and I won't stand a chance against Ivan if it comes to this.*

At the end of the long afternoon, they sat and drank water out of canteens. The cool liquid felt good on her lips, and Alexa let it drip from her mouth, down her chin and onto her chest. It left a wet spot on her white shirt right at the level of her cleavage. Alexa watched Mike avert his eyes. She fumbled with the canteen top, moving it between her fingers. She tried to suppress the one question that hovered in her mind. Just when she thought she had quelled her desire, the words tumbled from her lips.

"Do *you* think I'm ready, Mike? Ready for Ivan, that is." She needed his words of confidence to fill her ears.

He nodded a few times, as if he were answering himself before he answered her. "Yeah, Poppy. You're ready. We're all ready." He mustered a faint smirk, and his hand fell to her shoulder. She thought it would feel awkward, but it didn't. She felt comfortable. His presence seemed familiar.

"Will I see Charlie again — you know, before Ivan?"

His expression turned dry, and his eyes moved away from her.

"I don't think so." His voice became hollow. The words disappeared into the wind but continued to echo in Alexa's ears.

She wanted to ask him what he thought about the syringe idea. She had rehearsed what she wanted to say, but she wasn't sure Mike would understand her logic. She lacked the confidence to withstand his rebuttal. She opened her mouth to speak, but stopped herself because the words seemed silly. Yet, every time she closed her eyes, she saw the scar on Ivan's neck. *It seems like an easy enough target. If I were only close enough.* She shivered. She equated physical contact with Ivan with red poppies on her grave.

"All right, Poppy girl. This is where we part ways. Tomorrow is your well-earned day of rest. I suggest you spend an hour or so in the hot tub. You're gonna be sore. Give your mind and body a chance to heal." He spent the next few minutes going over the travel arrangements. Versailles lay just west of Paris. She would take a train tomorrow afternoon and arrive late that night. A private car would take her to her hotel.

Alexa nodded as he spoke, admiring the bruises developing on her forearms. "Mike, how do you know what day I will meet Ivan? Isn't he supposed to contact me via this escort service? How can you know when someone is planning to call an escort service?"

His look of consternation warned her he might be withholding information.

She repeated the question. "How do you know when he's going to call?"

He took a deep breath. "He's a predictable sort of man, that way. He behaves himself for a while, but he can't go for too long. He hits his max at about three weeks before he feels the urge again."

Urge to kill, you mean?

"We may have to wait a bit until Ivan makes the call. When he does, you gotta be ready. I'm heading to Versailles, as well. I'll be around in case any shit goes down. Don't worry yourself." He slapped her on the back before departing.

Back in her hotel room, Alexa poured a vodka soda to ease her nerves. She didn't drift off to sleep peacefully, though. She slipped into some kind of limbo where she wasn't fully asleep, but her mind started to dream anyway. She walked on a little brick path, surrounded by a field of red poppies, like in the Wizard of Oz. The field stretched as far as she could see. She hummed as she walked. A little ways ahead of her, she saw a bare mound of earth. A short line of people formed behind a stone next to the pile of dirt. She only saw the backs of the figures. They carried in their hands freshly unearthed poppy flowers, with clumps of dirt still entangled in their roots, and tossed them in a heap in front of the stone. The stone was a gravestone etched with her name.

The vision startled her, and her consciousness returned when she heard her own voice muttering peculiarities aloud. *Stupid vodka.* She had used it as a crutch to escape reality, but lately it was taking her to an uncomfortable place where she was neither awake nor asleep, nor in control. Mike's words resonated in her head. *Lay off the booze.* She couldn't ignore the practical advice. Alexa pressed her fingertips into her temples and massaged little circles into her skin. *Maybe I'll cut back a little.*

She wondered who the faceless figures in her hallucination could be. *Who would come to my funeral?* She created a list of potentials. In spite of their differences, her mother and father would attend. Britt's father would come. *What about Britt? He still loves me, like I love him. But I can't see him at my funeral. He wouldn't want to remember me like that. He would mourn in private. He would say goodbye while looking through a box of keepsakes, reliving cherished memories, imagining me in his arms, and indulging in a glass of wine — by candlelight.*

Britt's name brought a wave of warmth over her that stopped at her throat. She felt choked, trying to hold back the tears. Her airway tightened, and she fought the emotion. She continued that way until the moment passed, and she didn't cry. She slept.

CHAPTER 30

On her day of rest, she lounged by the pool skimming magazines until mid-afternoon, when she retired to her room to catch up on U.S. news. She listened intently to the anchorman while devouring the salad she had ordered from room service.

"Investigators continue the manhunt for the people responsible for the two bombs which exploded yesterday afternoon during the annual Boston marathon."

Her eyes glazed over as she absorbed the anchorman's words. *No. Boston? That's Britt's race.* The story seemed surreal. The newscaster spoke of two dead souls and hundreds of wounded individuals with lost limbs and embedded shrapnel.

Britt ran several marathons each year. The Boston marathon was his favorite; he had completed it the last two years. *Did he run Boston this year? Did he mention it at all?* She reran their conversations in her head. *Dammit. All of his words were encouragement for me.* She knew nothing of his plans.

Video of panicked faces flooded the TV screen. She saw the determination of those carrying the wounded and the agony of those injured. *I should feel sorry for them. Dr. DeBrow would feel sympathy and try to heal their pain.* But, instead of feeling sad or sorrowful, she felt a twinge of anger.

She picked up the Crackerjack phone and dialed Mike's number. The phone didn't save numbers; that was the point — anonymity. She had memorized his number. He picked up on the second ring.

"Alexa?" He must have expected her.

"Mike. Have you seen the news . . . the American news?"

"That shit in Boston? Yeah, I saw it."

She paused, waiting for the reason she called to percolate through all of the other thoughts swimming in her mind.

"Is this why we're here?" she blurted out. "Why we do these things that are . . . *so difficult* to comprehend? Is it to *prevent* things like Boston from happening? To keep those who are responsible from doing it again?" She started rambling, but she didn't have time to analyze the thoughts before they fled her lips.

She imagined Mike nodding on the other end. "Yep. Poppy girl. That's *exactly* why we are here, and why we do the incomprehensible things that we do. It sure ain't pretty. *Jesus.* The things I've seen. . . ."

Alexa nodded, too, accepting her fate. *Fuck me,* she thought. *Fuck me for choosing this.* Never would she have guessed such things would be in her future. *Who is Alexa DeBrow? Valedictorian? Yes. Accomplished physician? Yes. Former swimsuit model? Yes. Trained assassin?* She frowned to herself. It didn't make sense. She turned her eyes back to the television.

Who am I kidding? Alexa DeBrow is no trained assassin —

but Elizabeth Fuguay may be. She still held the receiver. She could hear Mike's heavy breathing. "Goodbye, Mike." She hung up and forced herself to absorb the gruesomeness depicted before her. When the news switched to another topic, she flipped to another station searching for more details. She continued such late into the evening, until she realized there was no new information to report. Frustrated, she turned off the television. "Whoever did that . . . I hope they pay." She tried to harness the anger that Boston elicited and focus it on Ivan.

The departure from Nice the next morning was uneventful. She packed in silence and caught a train to Paris, eventually arriving in Versailles. Mike drove separately in the black SUV and wouldn't arrive until the next day.

Alexa reached her destination late that evening and settled into a small, slightly run-down hotel in a rather shady part of the small city. Both the hotel in Nice and this one were charged to her government-issued credit card. She checked into Versailles as Elizabeth Fuguay. Although she had chosen the pseudonym, she was uncomfortable using it.

Charlie had instructed her to remain in the hotel until he called her on the Crackerjack. She busied herself with yoga, Pilates, and stretching on the floor of her small hotel room, ordering her meals from room service, and people-watching from the only window that faced the street. A quiet city of less than one hundred thousand people, it seemed like an ideal place for Ivan to disappear.

Charlie didn't call until late afternoon the next day. She jumped for the phone, eager with anticipation.

"Elizabeth?" She rolled her eyes to the sound of him saying *that name*. Elizabeth Fuguay was supposed to be her secret name. It represented her retreat to safety, her escape to freedom. He had stolen that from her. "Ivan checked into a hotel nearby. It should be soon — tonight, perhaps. Be ready. I'll call you when we have a time and location. That's all, Elizabeth." Charlie's somber attitude irritated her. After so much build-up, she needed excitement, not this melancholy that crushed her vigor.

Alexa arched an eyebrow. Her initial impression of Charlie had been generous. These days, his personality came off rather lackluster and dry. Moreover, she doubted whether she could trust him after the Elizabeth Fuguay incident. Charlie had told her she was free to decide whether or not she wanted to be on his team, but the gesture seemed to say, "Remember, Miss DeBrow, I have the upper hand."

She continued various exercises while confined to her room. Growing weary of the lock-down state, she was almost happy to receive Charlie's call on her second night in Versailles.

"It's time, Elizabeth." Charlie hissed into the speaker. "Ivan's in Hostel Rouge two blocks away. Get dressed. He's expecting you at eleven o'clock."

Alexa glared at the Crackerjack in her hand. *Malicious bastard. Why do I trust you?* She rolled her eyes. "Yes, Charlie. I'll be ready." The obedient tone she conveyed contradicted the scowl on her face.

"Good luck, Miss." His tone softened, as did her expression. She dropped the phone on the bed.

Alexa prepped herself in a little corseted lingerie outfit Mike had provided. She topped the ensemble with a plain tan trench coat, also part of her "uniform." She slipped into her stiletto heels and grabbed the fancy little handgun whose name she had forgotten. The gun fit securely into a little holster fixed to the corset that wrapped around her torso and held the gun just under her left shoulder. This way Alexa could reach across her body with her right hand and grab the gun while feigning she was merely removing her coat.

Ivan had chosen a cheap hostel two blocks up the street; his room number was 201. They were scheduled to meet at eleven p.m. It was only ten-fifteen, and Alexa paced the small room anxiously. *How do I spend the next 45 minutes?* The waiting was almost as unbearable as the act itself.

She twisted her fingers into a relentless knot before untangling them and reaching for the minibar. *I need a drink.* Despite her self-proclamation to cut back on the booze, she turned to vodka to calm her nerves.

She savored slow sips of vodka over ice while making adjustments in her outfit, hair, and makeup in the bathroom mirror. She layered thick coats of eyeliner and mascara. *Too much eyeliner always has a way of making a girl look cheap.* In the end, the girl looking back at her was unrecognizable. *I look like a hooker!* Alexa scolded herself when she remembered that was the point.

She adjusted her gun placement and made a few attempts to quickly grab it and take aim. On the third try, she remembered to take the safety off. *Wow. That would have been a stupendous failure. Alexa DeBrow, trained assassin forgets to take the safety off before she shoots.*

The mishap reminded her that she wasn't prepared for what she was about to face — not in the least. She took a larger sip of the vodka. She waited for the sting to hit her mouth and burn her tongue before she allowed herself to swallow. She needed to feel something — something to replace her jitters and confused stupor. She needed to stir up some confidence, and fast. Alcohol always had a way of helping muster up the confidence she needed. The night she decided to lose her virginity to Britt, she needed Champagne and tequila to give her the courage to proceed.

God, why must I think about Britt now? After his name entered her mind, it was hard to push away. She wanted to peruse his soft brown hair with her fingertips and feel his warm lips dance across her skin. *If I could have one more night of love in his arms, I would die happy.*

If I don't succeed tonight, I will die. She shook her head, and her teased blonde mess of hair tossed about recklessly. *Don't think of dying. Think of Ivan.* Fueled by a bit of liquid courage, she remembered the horrible things he had done. She harnessed her hatred for Ivan, Jamar, Castro, and those sons-of-bitches from Boston — every evil scoundrel she could imagine. Rage would become her power against him. She whispered to her reflection, "Tonight, Elizabeth Fuguay will kill Ivan Verden." *She has to.*

The alarm she set on the Crackerjack beeped quietly, and Alexa trembled in her stilettos. *Oh God, it's time.*

She glanced into the mirror one last time. The girl staring back at her looked more confident than she remembered. Somewhere deep within, she heard her subconscious whisper *you've got this.* In response, Alexa muttered aloud, "Yeah, now that the safety's off." She slammed the door behind her and headed down the street.

CHAPTER 31

The alarm had been set five minutes to show time. She took slow, forceful steps, with no intent of arriving on time. She couldn't imagine a hooker being prompt and figured it was better to be a few minutes late.

She entered the hostel lobby. The place was empty — no wonder Ivan liked it. He didn't seem to be the social butterfly type. She didn't see an elevator, only stairs. She climbed them leisurely. The click-clack of her stilettos thankfully drowned out the sound of her heart reverberating in her chest. *So much for liquor taking the edge off.*

Alexa used the second flight to go over her simple plan in her head. *Knock. Walk in. Shut the door. Pull the gun and pull the trigger.* The last step was supposed to be fast — one fluid step. *Aim for his heart*, she told herself. But her nerves threatened her abilities even with a large target at a short distance. *Damn! I forgot the syringe. So much for plan B.* Her teeth sank into her lower lip as she finished the stairs. She eyed a hallway of numbered doors lining dirty white walls.

Lingering smells of alcohol and vomit hung in the air.

Alexa observed the numbers as she walked and quickly became aware of the paper-thin walls of the building. One couple argued loudly in room 213. She heard a French sitcom on the TV in room 207. A raunchy fuck session shook the door of room 204. A chill crept down her spine as she tiptoed past. *I bet that's what Ivan has in store for me.*

His room was at the far end of the hall, somewhat reserved from the other rooms. Alexa hoped the seclusion would aid in her ability to be discreet. After witnessing the paper-thin walls, she feared the shot would be heard in spite of the silencer.

It's too late to contemplate such things now. She stood outside his door with her incisor still embedded in her lip, afraid to breathe. She closed her eyes and remembered the bitterness that would fuel her to victory against Ivan. It tasted like the sour blood that seeped from the tiny wound in her mouth. She let feelings of anger and vindication fill her, and when she reopened her eyes, her plan was clear.

Her knuckles rapped haphazardly on the door. She pasted a coy but indifferent expression on her face and watched the door swing open. Alexa stared at a beast of a man who stood a good eight inches taller than her in stilettos. Her eyes went to the scruffy red hair that covered his neck. She searched for the comfort of the scar that lay over Ivan's carotid — but it wasn't there. A quick look at the man's features revealed the obvious — this red headed man wasn't Ivan.

It's not Ivan! Alexa couldn't hide the blankness that swept over her as her plan abandoned her.

The man in the doorway eyed her voraciously. As her

heart thumped in her ears, she forced a demure smirk across her lips. She had to maintain her façade while she forced her brain to process the situation. She begged her neurons to construct a means of escape, as she cast provocative glances at the red headed brute before her.

He doesn't look surprised. He was expecting me. He was expecting a prostitute. She slowly opened her trench coat to reveal the delicate and decadent lacy goods that clung tightly to her curves. A wave of nerves sent chills rippling from her toes to her tits. Her nipples rose to attention and gathered the awareness of the man before her.

In her peripheral vision, she spied the doorway to the bathroom. She could see a portion of the toilet and a tiny open window with a curtain moving slowly in the breeze. *An escape route!*

The brute reached out for her ferociously. She grabbed his wrists and inched her face toward his. She nuzzled her nose against his left ear, and then flicked her tongue against his earlobe. She tugged at his ear with her teeth, the way Serge used to do, and let her tongue slide down the side of his cheek.

"Are you ready for your little she-devil?" Alexa whinnied like a little pony. His hands moved toward her body, and she inched her hips away from him, hoping he wouldn't brush against the gun she carried. He lurched his mouth toward her breasts.

"Not yet," she stammered. She shoved his hands away and let go of his wrists.

He let out a snort that turned into a growl. He narrowed his beady green eyes at her and furrowed his brow. Alexa tried to tame his developing anger.

"I'm not ready. Almost." She motioned to the bathroom. "I need a moment, then I'll be at your service." She gave him her best "she-devil" grin. Backing away, she maintained eye contact until she reached the bathroom door. She pursed her lips together, traced her upper lip with her tongue, and then bit down hard on her lower lip. The brute started to unzip his pants and expose his erection. Alexa held up a finger to restrain him while she slipped into the bathroom and pulled the door shut.

Her quivering hands fumbled with the doorknob as she searched for the lock. *No lock.* She'd have to be quick. Her chills became tremors racing up and down her body. Her torso convulsed, and her breathing staggered. *Get it together, Lex!* her subconscious screamed at her.

She scurried toward the little open window in the shower, flushing the toilet as she passed it. The window was about the width of her shoulders. It would be a tight fit.

She grabbed the window frame above her. It was at the level of her head. She hoisted herself up and squeezed through the opening. On the second floor, there was a drop of nearly twenty feet to the ground. She held the windowsill and lowered her body as close to the ground as she could get. She took a breath and let go of the windowsill.

She landed on the balls of her stilettos. Her heels hit next; something gave way, then she fell to her left hip and rolled onto her flank. The gun remained secured in its holster over her left side, and it dug into her skin when she rolled. Alexa scrunched her eyes together, fearing the impact would make the gun fire. It did not. She reached around and clicked the safety back into place.

Above her, the brute cursed through the bathroom window. His voice scared her to her feet and sent her scampering off down the street. She assessed her injuries as she fled. Only mild injuries, scrapes and bruises, no broken bones — nothing serious. *Where's the hotel?* Before she gained her bearings, a black van swooped around the corner and stopped in front of her. The side door thrust open, and Mike's face appeared in the darkness. He reached out his arm and scooped Alexa into the vehicle. The dark interior was sprinkled with a myriad of lights, monitors, and switches along the opposite wall. Mike sat on the bench seat at the back of the van, a laptop and headphones lying next to him.

A pale-faced young male crouched on his knees next to the technical equipment. With his short blond crew-cut and his fitted red sweater, he looked like a young Captain Kirk sitting in front of the Enterprise control panel. He and Mike both stared at Alexa. She could only see the dark hair of the driver in the front seat.

Alexa broke the awkward silence. "It wasn't Ivan," she stammered. She pointed toward the building she'd jumped from. "He — he wasn't Ivan."

Captain Kirk sat motionless while Mike nodded in her direction. "Yeah, Poppy. We know."

"What? How do you know?" Then she realized the TV monitors were displaying pictures of the red headed brute shouting from the window of the room she had just escaped. She soaked in the details as her glance moved from one monitor to the next.

"You sent me there, and it wasn't Ivan. Why?" Her voice

was smaller than she could have imagined.

Mike shrugged. "I was as surprised as you. We didn't have a visual when we sent you in there. Didn't get a look at him 'til you showed up. Don't know where the mix up happened." He reached up with one hand and rubbed his chin.

She blinked and turned to Captain Kirk. He had a wicked smile on his face. "Maybe it was a test — to see if you could handle it." Kirk snickered.

She swiveled to face Mike. "A test?" she questioned.

He kept rubbing his chin, deep in thought. "He wasn't one of our guys. Wouldn't make sense to test you like that, could be dangerous."

Captain Kirk laughed out loud. "Dangerous? Sounds like one hell of a good time to me."

His words stung to the core. Already on edge, she couldn't ignore them. She turned to him accusingly.

"What the fuck do you mean by that? That son-of-a-bitch could have raped me. That's a sick idea of a good time." She fumed with anger.

"Jeez, Mike, call off your bitch!" Kirk shouted across the car.

It was a poor choice of words. Mike's eyes hardened, and his right fist smashed against the kid's chin. It made an impressive smacking sound. The impact sent the kid into a sideways spin, and he fell to his shoulder. Alexa's eyes widened in disbelief.

The authoritative sound of Charles MacDonald's voice over an unseen speaker system interrupted the action. "That's enough." His speech brought calm to the chaos in the van. The kid rubbed his already swollen jaw. Alexa couldn't tell if it was broken or dislocated, but his face looked deformed. Surprisingly, he didn't even wince in pain.

Charles took control of the situation. "Elizabeth, you acted on the information we were given. The information we were *all* given." His use of her pseudonym sent another set of chills coursing over her flesh. "It shouldn't matter to any of you if this is a test or not. No matter the circumstances, this is your job. You follow your orders. Your orders are from me and are handed down from my superiors. We all follow orders." Alexa's head drooped like a dog being disciplined by its master.

"Elizabeth, Ivan is in Versailles. You will meet with him soon. Another night. Be prepared. At this point, you should all go back to your quarters and reconvene when I contact you next." The speaker cracked and went silent. Alexa looked at Mike, then the floor, purposely avoiding the eyes of Captain Kirk. The van came to a halt; she hadn't realized they'd been moving. Mike reached behind her and opened the car door. She stumbled out of the van, favoring her sore leg as she limped into the building. She didn't even say goodbye to Mike.

The car sped away into the night. Alexa hurriedly closed her trench coat and tied the belt tight around her waist. She must've left it open after the great reveal to the redhead. She climbed the stairs and settled into her room.

It wasn't until she was alone and her door was locked that the heart-wrenching emotion of the night's escapade fully rose to a conscious level. A whirlwind of feelings coursed through her veins. Fury. She had put so much trust in her team tonight — her team led by Charles MacDonald.

But they failed her. This was the same team that couldn't find Ahmed, one of their most-wanted men. Her eyes narrowed as she noticed the trend. Had Charlie Mac purposefully led her astray? *Did Charlie betray me?* She had trusted him to lead her to Ivan. She had a plan for Ivan.

Other emotions simmered to the surface more slowly. Fear. Alexa had mentally prepared for tonight's events with the understanding that she would follow a plan established by her teammates. The red headed giant was a kink she hadn't prepared for. She couldn't handle that kind of uncertainty. Fear could cost her her life.

She swallowed hard at the thought. Her subconscious tried to push it back down, but it was useless. She hobbled toward the bathroom. The fear billowed from her stomach into her throat and presented itself as a chunky-green vomit she spewed into the toilet. She slumped onto the bathroom floor, her mind becoming clearer after vomiting.

She would not succumb to the fear. Instead, she reminded herself that she had survived the night's precarious turn of events. In spite of the incidents that transpired, in spite of the chaos, she had escaped with her life, and she didn't even have to shoot the brute. That had been her first thought when she realized the man wasn't Ivan. *Who the fuck cares if he's not Ivan? Shoot the bastard and get out, fool.* But she had restrained herself. She managed self-control and maintained her senses. *Yes. I can do this.*

After her nerves settled, Alexa realized she was more confident than before. Maybe this was a test. Maybe Charlie Mac was making a point. She stood in front of the full-length mirror in the corner of her tiny room and watched herself undress. She watched herself pull off the layers of her high-dollar hooker costume piece by piece. Her appearance was an odd combination of eroticism and humor. On one hand, she felt like she was on her way to a Halloween party. On the other hand, she found the way her skin peeked through the lace allowing all the sensuous areas to show alluring. Her delicately tapered upper thighs, buttocks, lower abs, and cleavage were in full view. *I look like Lady Gaga!* She laughed out loud and shed the ensemble. *Tomorrow, I'll buy something else. I need something I feel confident wearing when I meet Ivan.*

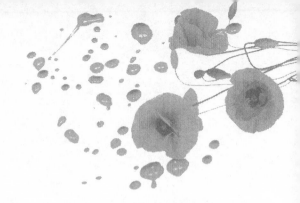

CHAPTER 32

She woke that night from a convoluted nightmare. She didn't remember it fully, something about Ivan trying to suffocate her. She fought back, but he was too strong. She pulled something from a belt or pocket. Yes, the syringe. She aimed for his carotid — and woke in a flurry.

"Dammit!" she cried aloud. *I'm so tired of nightmares.* She wanted to say a little prayer to ask them to stop, but she didn't let herself. She doubted God would answer any of her prayers anytime soon. She shook off the idea. *I'll handle my own nightmares.* She rustled under the covers until the sunrise beckoned her to her feet.

She ignored Charlie's orders to remain in her room. It looked beautiful outside, and she yearned for sunshine and fresh air. Feeling more confident today, she decided to go for a run through town. She put on a sports bra and loose tank over a pair of spandex running shorts.

She stepped into a crisp, clean morning. The chill that hung in the air meant she could run without overheating. She tucked both her work-issued credit card and her hotel room card key into her sport top. As her sneakers skipped across the sidewalk, her thoughts became jumbled as her mind darted haphazardly from one topic to the next.

It feels so good to disobey Charlie Mac after last night's spectacle. She could have giggled. Then her mind turned to Britt. *Barbados.* She remembered their hang-gliding experience offered to them by one of the locals. They had dared to fly tandem on the same glider. She remembered the beautiful view of the trees, flowers, and beaches below them. Britt's face beamed with an adventurous smirk. They were supposed to land on a large open area of beach, but a gust of wind took them through bushes and brambles that scraped across their legs before depositing them about fifty yards out into the ocean. Britt's strong arms caressed her frame as they scrambled to disembark from their glider and make their way to the shore.

Never a strong swimmer, she would have drowned in the ocean waves if it weren't for Britt. *I should have been scared. But Britt's grasp had been so reassuring, and when his eyes sparkled like that, I forgot to be afraid. He gave me courage and strength I didn't know I needed.* Without him, she was incomplete.

Alexa shoved the feelings from her mind, and a new topic bobbed to the surface: Jimmy Thornton. *What is Jimmy Thornton doing now that I am gone? Has he found some other young, naïve female doctor to make unwanted advances upon? Why did he ever go to those dreadful hearings? He was so eager to help me by giving Appleby that list of names. The list I never thanked him for. . . .* An audible sigh escaped her lips. *Maybe Jimmy had genuine feelings for me — something more than the lust he portrayed. I'll never figure him out. Trying to do so will make me crazy.* The last day she saw Jimmy was also the day she ran into Britt's father.

Ugh, back to Britt. She couldn't help but worry about his father. His health was only so-so when she left. Even though he pretended he was as strong as an ox, he'd suffered a small heart attack a few years back, and his cardiac function was dwindling. Alexa always thought she would be around to help out Dale Anderson in his old age. She shook her head from side to side as if to physically clear the thoughts from her brain.

The syringe from her dream popped into her mind. She recalled the image, and for a moment she felt powerful — invincible, even. She needed to carry that syringe with her the day she met Ivan. Just in case. Delivering direct oxygen into the brain's bloodstream wasn't a fast death, but it was death, nonetheless.

She stopped, and then glanced in both directions trying to figure out what caused her subconscious to halt her. Her eyes went to an adult store on the other side of the street. Their storefront contained many black leather, dominatrix-looking pieces. If she were meeting Ivan dressed as a prostitute, she wanted something that made her feel *dominant.* Alexa jogged across the street and entered the store.

A teenage girl manned the counter, and the store was otherwise empty. The girl's green eyes peered at Alexa mischievously. The store shelves were filled with toys and racks of clothes that ranged from pearl string panties to leather chaps, whips, feathered brassieres, and stiletto platform heels with dice embedded in the heels. Alexa perused the women's section and came across a faux-leather three-piece outfit that looked promising.

She grabbed a brassiere with mesh panels built in the sides that came with a matching bottom. *Not much left to the imagination.* Nylon stockings with a garter belt completed the look. She sneered at the costume. *At least it's opaque. That's an improvement from the red lace outfit.* Alexa took the garment to the checkout counter, where she found the store girl making pouty expressions into a hand mirror. *What a peculiar girl,* Alexa thought as she headed back to her hotel.

She entered her hotel room elated from her secret rendezvous. As she tossed her bag onto the bed, she heard the ring of the Crackerjack phone. *Dammit! I forgot about that silly phone.* She raced to pick it up.

"Where the hell have you been?" Mike hissed at her.

"Sorry. I just now heard the phone," she lied. "Have you been trying to get a hold of me for a while?"

"Only the last two hours. Dammit, Poppy! You gotta keep that phone with you at all times. That's the deal. Where the hell have you been?"

"Out," she half-whispered.

"Don't give me that bullshit. I know you went for a run. You're not hiding anything from me. Look, I don't care if you run, just try to lay low. Okay?"

"Fine." She seared, hating that he had caught her and was disciplining her like a child. She changed the subject. "Mike, why did you call? Has there been a new development?" Her tone quickly changed from aggravated to eager.

"Yeah. We need you to be ready. Ivan's checked into the same hostel you visited last night. Expect a call from me later this evening. Lay off the booze today, and for Christ's sake, keep that phone on you at all times. Got it?"

"Got it," Alexa murmured.

Oh, fuck! Attempt to kill Ivan — round two. She frowned; she knew a stiff drink would be needed to walk into that situation again. She hated to go against Mike, especially after he went out of his way to stand up for her against Captain Kirk the other day. But she wanted to steady her nerves.

Alexa poured herself a strong vodka soda, plopped on the bed, and rummaged through photos of Ivan. She concentrated hard on the details of his face, the tone of his arms, his tattoos, and that scar on his neck. She laid out the new ensemble she had bought, a pair of black heels and red lipstick. She chose a pair of cheap heels with an ankle strap that would help hold them in place if she needed to run. She ran her fingers over the thin strap of leather. *Who am I kidding? Running in heels is a losing battle. It's as hopeless as hand-to-hand combat with a man.*

Nervous, she found herself pacing the floor waiting for Mike's call. Through narrowed eyes, she willed the Crackerjack to ring. After an eternity of silence, Alexa turned the television on. Her fingers flipped through various news stations until she found one covering U.S. news. She wanted a follow up on the Boston marathon bombings.

The faces of two young, accused men flashed across the screen. Next came glimpses of a shootout scene that ended in the death of one of the men, and a reporter spoke of a manhunt for the second man. Alexa remembered her conversation with Mike the other day. "It's okay," she said out loud. "You're doing the unfathomable to protect the innocent — like those poor people in Boston." The garbled quality of her voice made her even more choked up. *Don't be sad now, Lex. Be angry. Let the story fuel your fury and boil your blood. Let anger replace the fear and give you the strength and adrenaline you need to overcome Ivan. Kill the son-of-a-bitch.* Rage swept over her like a fever.

The news channel switched to cover another story, so she turned the TV off. Grabbing her iPod, she played a Limp Bizkit song. Soon, she found herself jumping about while lip-syncing to "f— this" and "f— that" lyrics, to help her maintain the blood boiling state. She felt invincible. *Bring it on, Ivan. You've met your match.* Alexa swallowed another shot of liquor and began shuffling through photos of Ivan's victims.

She carried on such for another hour or so — until the Crackerjack phone rang. *Oh no! Mike!* Alexa jumped to her feet, and a pang of nausea spread from her stomach to her head. *Damn vodka. Don't vomit.* She adjusted her footing, and the nausea subsided. The phone rang again, and a sobering adrenaline surge replaced the nauseous wave.

"Hel-lo?" Her voice cracked.

"You ready for this?" His tone was a mixture of excitement and anticipation.

"Yes. I'm ready. Tell me what you know." She tried to enunciate her words clearly; she didn't want him to know she had defied him by drinking alcohol. He paused. *God, he's analyzing my speech.* She felt his urge to interrogate her, but the moment passed. Instead, he went over the details of the night's plan.

"Same hostel, room 318. He's expecting you in half an

hour. I'll be watching you through surveillance cameras. I'm no more than five minutes away."

Five minutes! Dueling voices clamored in her head. A timid voice shouted, *A lot can happen in five minutes! I'll be a gutted carcass in five minutes.* A more confident voice yelled, *That's plenty of time to kill that SOB!*

As if aware of her mental debate, Mike added a reassuring, "Relax; you don't need me."

"You're sure it's Ivan?"'

"Yeah. Looking at the surveillance footage now. Got a visual this time. It's Ivan."

Still hesitant to hang up the phone, she deliberated over discussing the syringe, but her argument seemed senseless. Again, she decided against telling him, and they said their goodbyes. "Poppy, you got this."

Alexa nodded. "I know, Mike. I know."

It's show time, better get dressed. She took a big gulp of her drink and gargled the alcohol till her throat burned before swallowing. Piece by piece, she donned the dominatrix garb. She lined her lips with a crimson stain, her mouth forming a perfect "O" in the dresser mirror. Alexa pressed her red lips together tight and forced them open, making a delectable smacking sound. She grabbed the syringe leftover from the Castro operation and screwed an eighteen-gauge needle on the tip. *Oh, and the handgun!* She disassembled and reassembled the gun while humming to herself before placing it in its holster. *Safety off, Lex.*

She took a few moments to visualize the event, same as before, only the images were clearer this time after having been inside the building. She reminded herself to wait until she was inside the room and the door was closed. After a couple quick run-throughs, she opened her eyes and grabbed the syringe. She wrapped the trench coat around her scantily clad physique and stepped out the door.

CHAPTER 33

As she marched toward Ivan's building, Alexa repeated a mantra to herself. *I will kill you, Ivan Verden.* She repeated the words until she reached the hall to Ivan's room. Perhaps less aware of her surroundings tonight, she didn't hear the background noises of the patrons in the other rooms as she walked down the hall.

Room 318. Ivan's room. Alexa's knuckles rapped on the door. Then with her right hand, she smoothed the fabric of the coat where it covered the gun. Her left hand held the syringe buried in her palm.

The door swung open wide. His face was unmistakable; the brown eyes, the scar over the brow; it was Ivan Verden. Alexa felt her breath escape her. He wore a tight-fitting white tank, nothing like the outfits in his photos. His tattooed arms were exposed, as well as the scar over his carotid. *I will kill you, Ivan Verden.* She managed a wild-eyed smirk and entered the room without invitation. Ivan leaned his frame against the open door while his gaze followed Alexa's steps. He held a stone face, but his eyes twinkled with anticipation. Alexa slowly untied her belt and revealed her dominatrix ensemble. A furrow developed on his brow for a moment. *He dislikes my outfit.* But his countenance changed, and a devilish look entered his eyes. Alexa watched the open door with hesitation. *Shut the goddamn door!* Instead he placed one hand on the doorframe and motioned with the other for her to spin around. She winced at the thought of waiting another moment to shoot him, but he wouldn't close the goddamn door. She opened the front of the trench further and pulled the top of the coat down to her shoulders. She couldn't lower the coat anymore, or it would show the handgun concealed over her left flank. She turned halfway, making a seductive pose with her head still facing Ivan. She turned her head to the other side to look over the opposite shoulder.

When her head turned, the door slammed shut, and Ivan made a swift move toward her. *Fuck!* In that disoriented second, he grabbed her from behind. His left arm wrapped around her neck, and his right hand cinched her upper arm. His tongue moved along the side of her cheek. Alexa squirmed to get away. She didn't scream. He didn't say a word. They struggled in silence. He swiftly lifted her off the ground and carried her toward the bed. He held her right arm too tight for her to grab the concealed gun. Somehow, Ivan hadn't noticed it pressed between their bodies. His mouth moved down to her left shoulder, and he sank his teeth into her flesh. She saw his actions in a mirror that faced the bed.

His right hand reached across her torso toward her left arm. He hadn't yet trapped the hand that clasped the syringe. She maneuvered the device in her palm and shoved the needle into Ivan's thigh. She withdrew and tried to stab again. Her hand cut through the air, but he avoided her aim. He smashed her head into the footboard of the bed frame. The flimsy particleboard cracked under the force. He released her body, and she fell limp to the floor.

In the moment of freedom, still on her knees, she fumbled for the gun, pulling it from its holster. But she was too slow; Ivan smacked the gun from her hand and it flew across the room, rattled against the floor, and slid into the wall without firing. No weapon — it was what she had feared from the beginning. Ivan's face broke into a monstrous scowl. *He is enjoying this, and he's ready to beat the crap out of me.*

He lurched toward her and picked her up off the ground by her throat. Her feet kicked the air; her body dangled wildly like a puppet on a string. His stare burned into her skull as though he were trying to read her thoughts. Alexa dug the nails of her right hand into the arm that held her. He reached up and secured her hand.

As the veins in his neck popped out, she eyed the scar over his carotid. Alexa pulled the plunger of the syringe back with her left thumb, and air filled the empty chamber. In a single swift movement, she aimed the needle and plunged the syringe into Ivan's neck. His face flinched slightly. Just as she presumed, the scar tissue had little sensation, and he probably thought it was her fingernails at his throat. Ivan tightened his vice grip on her. She grew weak, and her feet stopped kicking. She strained to breathe as black spots danced across her vision. She fumbled with the plunger in her hand, struggling to push the air from the syringe. The room started to fade from view. The pain at her throat was numbing, the lack of oxygen debilitating. Ivan's face turned black.

A sound emanated through the darkness. The struggle with Ivan seemed like a distant memory. Alexa's mother called to her. *Alexa! Alexa!*

Mom? Mom. There's something I need to say. Something I forgot to say. . . . The thought escaped her.

And then there were waves of pain. She couldn't pinpoint where they came from. Sound returned. She heard yelling and heavy breathing. The pain was followed by dizziness and nausea. A warm, wet sensation rolled down her cheek.

I'm crying. I'm not dead. No — Ivan is having his way with me. He's torturing me!

Her mother's voice continued to echo in her head. As it became louder, it took an eerie twist. It was her name she heard, but the voice was not her mother's. It was the gruff voice of a male. *Ivan!* Alexa forced her eyes to open, although the rest of her body refused to respond to her commands. The light stung her retinas, amplifying the nausea, and she closed her eyes again tightly. *I'm going to vomit. But I can't move.*

She heard her name again, and this time she recognized the voice. It wasn't Ivan — *Mike!* She made another meager attempt to open her eyes. She tolerated the light better this time, and she started to make out some of what she was seeing. She was moving. Mike was carrying her. The combination of motion and light was too much to bear; she convulsed, and then vomited. Mike managed to turn her just in time for the vomit to land on the street.

"There you go, Poppy girl. You're gonna be all right. Everything's gonna be just fine. You did good. I'm proud of you."

He continued murmuring such things, but the words slurred together in her mind. She couldn't process anything clearly. The sensation was like being severely hungover and drunk at the same time, and it left her feeling as though she'd had a stroke. Yes. She felt like she'd suffered brain damage. *Oh, fuck! What did that son-of-a-bitch do to me?* She feared the worst and contemplated scenarios in which Ivan had managed to beat her senseless. All the while, her senses slowly regained function. She could move her extremities. She became more alert. Mike's words became clearer, and she could see well enough to know where she was.

He had put her into the van from the previous night. Mike, the dark-haired driver, and a new man who sat in Captain Kirk's seat were with her. At the back of the van next to Mike lay a large black bag. *A body bag — an empty body bag.*

"Mi — " Alexa's voice broke off. *Damn, it hurts to talk.* She couldn't ask the questions plaguing her mind.

Mike interrupted. "He's dead, Poppy. You did it. Hell if I know how. You didn't leave a mark on the man, but you did it."

She frowned. She didn't remember killing Ivan, and the body bag was empty. She tried again to ask, but she couldn't form the words. Her throat burned something fierce. It wasn't the only place that hurt.

Mike continued. "He strangled you. I thought you were a goner. But you came through after all. As far as I can tell, he took a bite from your shoulder, broke your collarbone, and bruised your forehead. That's all."

That's all? Alexa looked down to her collarbone. Her frown deepened. Clearly, her left clavicle was broken and deformed. She closed her eyes and imagined what her x-ray would look like and what her dictation of the exam would read. *Fracture of the junction of the middle and distal thirds of the left clavicle with angulation and inferior displacement of the distal fracture fragment.*

Alexa tried to move her left arm. Excruciating pain ran over her, but she was glad to pinpoint the source of the agony. Her head ached, too. Worse than a migraine, her head hurt inside and out, and she could feel the bruise developing on her forehead. *I'm exhausted. There's something about losing consciousness that really wears a body down. And it's still hard to breathe.* Her throat was swollen, and it felt as though her airway was half of its normal size. She used the majority of her energy to breathe.

With some difficulty, she managed to put her fingers on the source of the pain in her throat. She traced the mid portion of her neck with her right index and middle fingers. She came across a sharp jutting bone in the middle of her neck. Another shockwave of pain ran through her. *Another broken bone — my hyoid bone. That son-of-a-bitch broke my hyoid bone trying to strangle me.*

During her first year of radiology training, Alexa had encountered a case of a hyoid bone fracture on a CT of the cervical spine. The physician ordering the study had asked her about the clinical relevance of a hyoid bone fracture, and she informed him that hyoid bone fractures are infrequently seen motor vehicle accidents, blunt trauma to the neck, and strangulation attempts. The associated soft tissue swelling could lead to airway constriction and asphyxia.

Alexa concentrated hard on her breathing. She pushed

each breath in and out of the small airway as if breathing through a straw. *Asphyxia.* The process was labor intensive. She wasn't sure how much longer she could keep it up. Her airway was too swollen to provide adequate oxygenation.

Mike shook Alexa's shoulder. The movement made her broken clavicle throb. "Poppy. Open your eyes. I need to see your eyes. You're not out of the woods yet."

Asphyxia. Alexa opened her eyes. *I can't breathe!* She reached a panicked arm toward Mike. Her hand flailed about.

"Shit!" He yelled as her world turned dark once more.

Fuck you, Ivan Verden. I hope you rot in Hell. . . . Her thoughts blurred, and her world fell silent.

CHAPTER 34

During the prolonged silence, she didn't open her eyes. She didn't talk. She didn't dream. She didn't breathe. Mike was at her bedside when she awoke. Her neurons began firing all at once; the sensation was jarring. *I'm supposed to be dead.* She couldn't remember the details of the preceding events. She looked around with hesitation. She saw Mike's face, but it took a long, thorough gaze before she found his features familiar. She didn't recognize anything else.

A current of air moved in and out of an orifice in the center of her throat, startling her. She reached up to investigate the phenomenon. One of her fingers passed into the orifice, shocking her to the core. Alexa's bottom lip quivered spasmodically, and her eyes instantly filled with tears.

Mike grabbed her shaking hand and forced it down to the bed. "None of that, now. You hear me?" His voice was authoritative and patriarchal.

She frowned at his tone. She didn't allow the pools of saltwater to roll down her cheeks. He watched her fight back the tears, and slowly her vision cleared.

He continued. "You stopped breathing on me. I had no choice but to take you here."

Here meant the hospital.

"After a couple of failed intubation attempts, a surgeon cut that hole in your neck and put a tube down your throat to help you breathe. A ventilator kept you alive the last two days. I came by a few times. You just mumbled in you sleep, mostly. They pulled that tube about an hour ago, once you could breathe on your own again." He released her hand.

"Ivan beat you up pretty bad — worse than I thought. But you got the best of him." He winked and grinned down at her.

Ivan. She remembered now. She remembered struggling to breathe in the van. She remembered the empty body bag in the back of the vehicle. *Empty body bag* — Alexa perseverated on the words. *Ivan was dead, but the bag was empty.* A thought suddenly occurred to her: *The bag wasn't meant for Ivan. It was meant for me!*

"You've been here two days, Alexa," he murmured. "Can you talk?"

She was afraid to speak. She couldn't get used to the feeling of her breath moving in and out of the hole in her neck. She ignored his question and looked down at her left clavicle. *Still deformed. Wow. I'm unconscious for two days, and they can't even fix my deformed collarbone?* She rolled her eyes to herself.

"I need to hear you try to talk. Doc said your voice should be okay. You broke some little bone in your neck, but he put a pin in it. Can you try to talk?"

No. Ivan broke a bone in my neck — my hyoid bone. He broke my hyoid bone. Her eyes made another exaggerated roll. The situation irritated her. She sighed deeply, but the air coming out the tracheostomy in her neck made an even more irritating whistling sound as it passed. *Wow. This is sexy. I have a deformed shoulder and a hole in my throat.*

With those thoughts of vanity, Alexa realized she still cared greatly for her own well-being. She cared for her appearance and her safety. *What the fuck was I thinking by getting myself into this mess?*

"Poppy, please say something. . . ."

Alexa sighed again. *Damn that whistling.* She scolded herself for forgetting so quickly. She looked up at Mike and opened her mouth with hesitation. "Mi-ke." Her voice cracked, and didn't sound like her own. The words resonated low in her throat rather than her nasopharynx, and exited both her mouth and the tracheostomy. The sensation was even more peculiar than merely breathing through the tracheostomy. Beyond that, it was painful; not excruciatingly painful, but there was a dull soreness that accompanied her attempt.

"All right, that's more like it." He grinned.

She forced a meager smile. "Wh-er-e's Iv-a-n?" She tried to make the words come out her mouth only, but it was useless trying to stop the air from flowing out of her neck. This time the "s" sound made little droplets of saliva spray out of the tracheostomy hole. She stared at Mike, willing him to answer her and ignore her spitting.

He looked puzzled by her question. "He's dead," he whispered.

279

She waited to hear more. But it was all he said. "His b-o-dy?" she asked. It hurt to get the words out, but she needed to know where they put him.

Mike dropped his voice even lower and neared her ear. "We needed to leave Ivan in the hostel. He has to be found dead in his room. I know that might not make a lot of sense to you, but it's the message we needed to make. We needed to kill him quietly, remember, without a signature, and let him be found by his cohorts. We took pictures of his body, sent them to our allies. His body may not be found for a couple of days. It's probably better that way." His focus turned to a window in the corner of the room.

Alexa nodded to herself. *The body bag was indeed for me. They never planned on moving Ivan's body from the hostel.* She wanted to sigh, but she stopped herself this time.

His face turned back to her. "You remember it all?"

The events flashed through her head, and she nodded. *Yes.* She remembered the second night she almost let a man kill her, and she remembered struggling to push the plunger on the syringe. *Yes. I did push the plunger, and that syringe saved my life.* For a moment, she felt proud of herself. Her plan B succeeded when their plan failed.

As if reading her mind, Mike scratched his head and asked, "Can you tell me how you killed him? Looks like you stabbed him. I grabbed a syringe from the floor. I had the lab run it for tests. They didn't find any poison."

She took pleasure in his confusion. Bursting with pride at this point, she muttered, "Air em-bol-ism."

His forehead became a maze of wrinkles, resulting in an even more dumbfounded expression. She swallowed hard, saliva gurgling out of her tracheostomy site. She tried again, this time covering the hole with her hand. "I in-ject-ed air in-to the blood to his br-ain."

"That's what killed him?"

She nodded. "Slow-ly," she stammered. She imagined what Ivan was doing to her as he was dying. She pictured his arms wrapped around her neck, her bones breaking under the pressure. *He could have broken my neck. I could be paralyzed. Or I could be in that body bag.*

"Gotcha. Hell, whatever works. I could have sworn you poisoned the bastard." Mike turned to her accusingly. "You know, that wasn't part of the plan." He raised an eyebrow.

"I kno-w," she murmured. She didn't feel up to a lecture from him right now. "I want to wa-lk." Her body needed to move. She tried to sit up. Moving felt exhausting and liberating all at once. She felt the catheter tubing that led to her bladder shuffle against her legs, and she peered at the compression devices attached to her legs to prevent blood clots. Mike reached over to help her just as a nurse walked into the room. She helped Alexa sit up.

"I best let you be now," Mike said. "I'll swing by tomorrow and check in on you."

Alexa nodded as the nurse helped her to her feet. Disoriented, Alexa shuffle-stepped down the hall like the old lady from the apothecary shop. Her gait improved on the return to her room, and at the end of the walk, the nurse offered to remove the urinary catheter. *A step toward freedom.*

An hour later, the surgeon who had performed the emergent tracheostomy dropped by to inspect her airway. The doctor was an older American gentleman. "Glad to see you're awake. We should be able to close this up in a day or two."

Her head bounced up and down excitedly. "To-morrow," she stammered.

He narrowed his eyes in contemplation. "I suppose we can arrange, that Miss." She pointed to the clavicle. "That one will have to wait for another day; I'm afraid I can't intubate you until your throat is fully healed."

She sensed judgment in his narrowed glance. Realizing this man must have seen her in her dominatrix outfit, he probably thought she was a hooker. *Oh no! Everyone at the hospital probably thinks I'm a prostitute, half-strangled by my pimp.* It was a rerun of the bouncer from the club the night Jamar died. The nurse probably felt sorry for her. She imagined how embarrassed Mike must have felt visiting.

After a couple more days of recovery, Alexa could walk, talk, and eat without assistance. Her clavicle remained deformed, and it still hurt to talk and swallow. On the morning of her fifth hospital day, the nurse pulled her IV, and she was discharged by noon. Mike met her at the hospital with a bouquet of flowers — poppy flowers. *How fitting.*

He drove her to an upscale hotel in Paris, where she settled in for the night. Her stuff was already inside the extensive suite when she arrived. She put the poppy bouquet on a side table and sprawled out on the sofa in the living area. She had a prescription for pain pills and an antibiotic to prevent infection in her neck. She took the antibiotic and ripped the pain pill script into pieces.

She spent her first evening out of the hospital in a daze,

which continued into the next morning. She felt lost. She forgot to eat, and her sleep was inconsistent throughout the night. She needed direction, but she wasn't sure where she would find it.

The ring of the Crackerjack phone interrupted her prolonged meditation. She had forgotten about it altogether, and the sound surprised her. She tried ignoring its cruel ring, but the caller was persistent, and Alexa was forced to locate it if she ever wanted the ringing to stop.

She found it plugged into a charger perched on the bedroom nightstand. She stared at it with hesitation, knowing it was either Charles or Mike. She groaned internally and answered the phone.

"Elizabeth?"

Damn. She shuddered. "Hello, Charles." Her voice quivered. Her throat still ached.

"I'm glad to hear you're recuperating." His voice was unrightfully cheery.

"I should congratulate you on your work with Ivan. Not what I expected, but whatever works, Miss Fuguay."

His determination to use her alias made her skin crawl. She lost her patience with him. "Do you need something, Charles, or is this your futile attempt to cheer me up?"

"Do you need cheering, Miss Fuguay?"

What an antagonizing tone!

Charles continued without waiting for a response. "I need to meet with you. We need to discuss your future and new possibilities for you."

Alexa's throat itched, a side effect of healing. She needed to clear her throat to speak comfortably, but she couldn't do that without pain. She forced a few short, dry coughs.

"When do you plan to meet, Charles?"

"This evening. I'll send a car for you. It will be there at six. I'll see you then."

He hung up without waiting for her reply. Her shoulders slumped. She was expected to attend; the invitation wasn't optional. A glance at the clock on the wall told her she had three hours of freedom until the fated meeting. She decided to drag her carcass off the couch and attempt a run.

CHAPTER 35

The run didn't last long. Her body gave out after a paltry half mile. The tightness in her throat made tedious work trying to suck air in and out. She settled for a walk in the fashion district. Paris had lost a degree of its luster. Yet, her hotel was in one of the more luxurious neighborhoods, and each esteemed step was surrounded by grandeur. The buildings were glorious, the architecture and history lining the street surreal. Alexa slowly inhaled the beautiful scenery; it was intoxicating. She wandered past designer clothing boutiques. Exquisite leather handbags and pristine wool jackets filled the windows. *Perfect little pieces of art.* Her fingers traced the outline of a jacket she admired. *Why can't my hands create such things?*

She became distracted by a glimpse of her own reflection in the store window. The juxtaposition of the beautiful accessories hanging in the storefront and her own dreadful reflection disturbed her. She frowned at the sight. Her eyes fell to her hands on the glass. *Instruments of death.* She shuddered without understanding why. Regret? Remorse?

Her ability to discern right from wrong was fading. Every act she had performed within the past year seemed muddled in a sea of gray somewhere on a spectrum in between right and wrong. She evaluated her actions, her decisions, every move, and found herself in a quandary. She wrung her hands, tangling her fingers in knots. *The things I've done. Why?* She couldn't remember. Did she ever really know? How could she move forward if she wasn't sure she'd chosen correctly in the past?

In the store window, Alexa could distinguish the beauty of the fashionable art from the ugly appearance of her sallow countenance. She looked at the deformity of her clavicle, the healing scar on her neck, and the hollow look in her eyes and cheeks. She felt ugly inside and out. She sighed out loud, causing a tickle in her throat where the whistle used to be. *I want to be beautiful again. I want to bring beauty into the world, since I failed to bring good into it.*

A clock chimed above her, and her digression was interrupted by a sudden awareness of the time. *Oh no! I have to meet Charlie soon.* Although apprehensive about the meeting, she didn't have a choice. *Mr. MacDonald cannot be stood up.* If he wanted to meet her, he would find her. Alexa knew better than to piss him off. She tore her eyes away from the store window and headed back to her hotel.

She had no desire to pretty herself up for Charlie. She felt ugly, and she made no attempt to hide it from him. She wore her workout attire and sneakers, her hair pulled back into a ponytail. She stepped out of the hotel and found a private car waiting outside. It took her to another hotel about eight blocks away, where she was guided to an empty conference room in the back. He sat alone at a dark mahogany-stained table.

"Hello, Charles." She spoke first. He stood and motioned for her to sit.

Charlie was dressed casually compared with their first meeting. He wore a gray knit sweater and khaki pants, while Alexa sported spandex capri pants and a tank top.

"You look well, Miss Fuguay," he bluffed.

Alexa squirmed in her seat when he said that name. She diverted her glance from his just long enough to manage an eye roll.

"It's good to see you, too," she jeered. Her hand reached up and rubbed the healing scar on her throat, a nervous habit she'd acquired.

"We should talk about your recovery and — um, when we can get you started on the next project. I have plans for you —" His words cut off abruptly, as though he had lost his train of thought. He looked older than she remembered. She saw the age in the creases around his eyes and the discoloration of his teeth. His hair seemed grayer and duller than before. It was as if the life had been washed out of it long ago. He looked weary, and for a moment, she wanted to feel sorry for him. She fought the emotion and tried to remain stone-faced.

"What plans do you have, Charles?" she asked, trying to speed up the conversation.

"We have another opportunity coming up. Given the success of your last assignment, I'm considering you for the position. Of course, we have to make some adjustments before you can proceed." He waved his hand in the direction of

Alexa's clavicle. "We need to get that fixed. It's unsightly."

She narrowed her eyes. *You don't like my battle scars, Charlie? Imagine how I feel.*

"We can have that taken care of for you — if you're interested in continuing this line of work." He paused and his gaze burned into Alexa's eyes, as if he were trying to look past them and peer directly into her thoughts. She almost broke under the pressure. She tried to contain her emotions, but a lump rose in her throat, which brought her attention back to it, and she found herself rubbing the scar again. *Is he giving me a choice? Is he offering a way out?* She was too timid to ask Charles these questions aloud. She could only hope he knew what she was thinking.

"Do you want to continue this line of work?" His soft tone and slow speech disarmed her.

She diverted the question. "I want to have this fixed . . . first." She forced herself to move her hand from her throat to her broken collarbone.

Charles nodded in agreement. "Of course. We can't have you running around with that hump sticking out." He frowned when he pointed his long skinny finger at Alexa's deformity. She realized how self-conscious the deformity had made her. "And we'll have that other scar fixed, as well." He motioned to her neck, and her hand reflexively covered the area he spoke of. "For the task we have at hand, you must look your absolute best, Miss Fuguay. You see, it is a similar assignment to your last, and like Ivan, this man has very specific standards." She bit her lip and shifted in her seat.

"Are you interested in another assignment, Miss Fuguay?" he continued.

Alexa's head shook back and forth. Her subconscious answered *no* for her, but all she was capable of saying was, "I need some time to think about it — time to recover."

The corners of his lips sank in dismay. "I had high hopes for you, Miss Fuguay." He leaned forward and raised an eyebrow, and Alexa knew she was about to get a patriarchal lecture. "I want you to remember you came to me. This was your idea. No one has asked anything more of you than you were willing to commit on your own behalf."

She nodded reluctantly. He was right, after all.

"Do you wish to tell me what has changed your mind, then?" His tone turned overly charismatic, as if he were trying to cajole a secret from a small child. She didn't answer. *Of course I don't want to tell you. I'm afraid of the potential repercussions.*

"I'll remind you of your remarkable success with your last assignment. You should be very proud. With this recent victory comes strength. You are more prepared now than before. You will continue to grow stronger the longer you work with me, Miss Fuguay. I suggest you rethink your decision. You can become something remarkable."

"Or I can wind up in a body bag." The words slipped out, and she couldn't take them back. Not that she cared. She stared him down. His jaw dropped, but only by a small margin. The moment passed, and he was his composed self again.

He started to speak, but Alexa interrupted him. "That body bag in the back of the car — it was for *me*. I thought it was for Ivan. But I was wrong. You were expecting me to fail — expecting me to die." Her shoulders rose in an exaggerated shrug. "Sorry, Charlie; as it turns out, I have a lot to live for." She stole Mike's words. He had been right; it just took a while for the message to sink in. Hot tears gathered in her eyes. The salt water burned. It was a good burn; it complimented the anger coursing through her veins.

Charles stood. He held out his hand for Alexa to shake. Surprising. She didn't expect to part on good terms. She stood as well.

"It was a pleasure, Miss —" His words cut off.

He didn't know how to address her anymore. The two shook hands before he continued. "You've had a desire to change your identity for some time now. You should have that privilege after everything you have undergone. I know your choice was Elizabeth Fuguay. I'm afraid that won't be an option for you anymore. That name has been associated with too much in our agency." He reached up with one hand and stroked his chin. He looked Alexa in the eye. "You're sure you want out?"

She nodded weakly.

"All right, then. I'll need you to tell me what name you want now. It's up to you. You have the freedom to be anyone you want, go anywhere you want. This is your chance to start over — if that *is* what you want. We'll set you up with a new bank account and put your money into it."

Alexa contemplated the words Charlie spoke. *Freedom to be anyone you want.* It was all she had ever asked for, and now he was handing it to her, just like that. This was her opportunity to wholly embrace fugue state and adopt her new identity. She analyzed the events of the past year in her mind. *I don't want to run from the past anymore.* She didn't want to condemn those events. They happened; over and done with. She wanted to embrace the future — her future. After all, she had a lot to live for. *What kind of life do I want?*

Charlie passed a blank sheet of paper and a ballpoint pen across the table. "Do you know who you want to be?" Deep wrinkles formed as he raised an eyebrow. "Just write it down for me. I'll take care of the details. Make it a pretty name. A pretty girl like you deserves something pretty."

Her mind was in a tizzy. An unsteady hand reached out and grabbed the pen and paper. The other hand went to the scar on her neck. *Who do I want to be?* She stared hard at the paper. *It's a blank slate — an empty canvas, waiting to be transformed.* She felt a flutter of anticipation run through her, and then calmness as she wrote on the paper:

Alexa DeBrow.

Charles stared at the words. He scratched his chin, and after a pause, he looked up at her. "It is a beautiful name; it suits you."

Charles mustered a weak hug, both unexpected and rather awkward.

"Good luck to you. I wish you success in all your future endeavors," he mumbled.

Alexa half-smiled, and they parted ways.

CHAPTER 36

The next couple of days were a blur. Within forty-eight hours, she gathered her things, settled her affairs with Charlie Mac, and booked a flight back to the States. She was going to New York, where she'd arranged for an orthopedic surgeon in New York City, Jeff Huggins, to fix her clavicle deformity. Charlie would cover the bill.

Jeff had attended medical school with her. He graduated in the top of their class, right behind her. She knew he might mention the trial, but she was ready to answer any questions he had. Accepting the past was part of being Alexa DeBrow. She couldn't shy away from the pain any longer if she wanted to move on.

Before leaving Europe, however, she had to meet with Mike one last time. They met for an early lunch, around eleven before she embarked for her flight back to the States. They met at a casual restaurant near the airport. It was a small place, with only a half a dozen tables. Mike wore a collared shirt and a light wool jacket over light gray slacks, finer attire than his norm. He had a great big goofy grin on his face, the kind a shy teenage boy would give to a teacher he had a crush on. Something about Mike reminded her of Smokey Joe. In a sense, they were the same for her — two separate people playing very similar roles in her life, but in very different ways.

She returned his expression when their eyes met. He greeted her with a hug, which seemed a little over-the-top for him. Usually, he was reluctant to give a handshake. She avoided Mike's eyes as his gaze shifted from her clavicle deformity to the scar on her throat. Neither commented on her lingering battle wounds.

The two splurged with pasta dishes and red wine. Both the conversation and the meal were slow and savory. "What have you got planned in the States?" he asked between fork loads.

She shrugged. "Just my surgery in New York."

"Did Charlie take care of you?" he asked with an air of authority. He couldn't break away from his patriarchal demeanor.

"Yes. He set me up an account with all my funds. And he's taking care of the surgery." Her account contained nearly two million dollars. One million was the reward for Mohammed's death. Her work with Ivan accounted to a slightly smaller financial retribution. Alexa wasn't in a good position for contention, however, and she accepted the settlement on Charlie's terms.

"Gonna miss you, Poppy girl," Mike said with a nod and a wink. "You gotta know, I'm gonna keep track of you after we part ways."

She nodded. "I expect nothing less from you, Mike."

"I'm interested to see what you do with yourself."

His voice sounded less gruff than she was accustomed to. She nodded to herself. She couldn't agree more with Mike's words. He was the one who told her, "You have a lot to live for." She was ready to figure out what that meant.

He paid the bill and escorted her to the airport. "Anything I can do for you before you go?" he questioned.

Without hesitation, Alexa answered solemnly, "Yes. Tell Corbin Ivan's dead. And burn that damn body bag from the car that night."

The two locked eyes. He nodded. They shared a final, quick hug. "Thanks for taking care of me, Mike," she whispered through watery eyes.

Mike frowned. "You took care of yourself, like you always do. Now, go conquer the world — if that's what you've got planned." He placed a hand under her chin and lifted it slightly. She imagined him saying, *Raise your head high and go face the world.*

"I'll miss you, friend," she whispered.

During the long flight back to the states, Alexa drifted in and out of sleep. Nightmares haunted her, as usual. She found herself stumbling through a crowd of people. The crowd passed, and she saw the field of red poppy flowers again. This time, atop a mound of fresh dirt lay the black zippered body bag she remembered. But it wasn't empty. Alexa could make out the figure of a body. Dead and wilted plucked poppy flowers were strewn over the corpse-filled bag.

Alexa awoke, mildly shaken. She tried to remember the words from the poem "In Flanders Fields," but she could only recall a few short verses of the poem. She recited the lines in her head.

In Flanders fields the poppies blow
Between the crosses, row on row . . .

We are the Dead. Short days ago
We lived, felt dawn, saw sunset glow,
Loved and were loved, and now we lie
In Flanders fields.

Within moments, she was back asleep. The next time she woke, she grabbed a vodka soda from the stewardess. Charlie had splurged, upgrading her to first class, where the alcohol flowed easily. Alexa deplaned a little tipsy and grabbed a taxi to the Waldorf Astoria. She had already sent her x-rays to Dr. Huggins and underwent a phone consult, so she was scheduled for surgery the next day. She was anxious for Jeff to make her look whole again.

He met her in pre-op the next morning. She had already changed into her hospital gown when he strolled into the room in black scrubs and sneakers. He had put on a few pounds since med school, and his hair was thinner than she remembered.

"Hey! It's been too long, Lex." He smirked as he wrapped one arm around her shoulder and squeezed her tight. A Texan at heart, he still spoke with that alluring cowboy drawl.

"Hi, Jeff. It's good to see you." She smiled coyly at him.

"Damn! You haven't changed a bit." She blushed. She

suddenly remembered she would likely be stripped down in the operating room, and it was possible Jeff was going to see her naked in the next hour. Perhaps she should have chosen an orthopod she didn't know personally. *Too late to change plans now.*

"How's work?" he questioned.

"I'm taking a break." She lost the gumption to go into any details. Her hand went to the scar on her neck. His questioning made her nervous.

"Yeah, I heard you had a bad go of things. Sorry to hear that, Lex."

God, it's soothing to have someone show a little sympathy. That's why she liked Jeff. Not only was he a smart guy; he also had a heart. She waited for him to ask, "What are your plans now?" But he didn't. He stepped out and let the anesthesiologist put her to sleep.

She awakened in recovery a mere half hour after receiving the anesthesia and was discharged the same day. She went to recover in her hotel. The anesthesia made her nauseous, and Alexa vomited every hour on the hour, like clockwork. Unfortunately, the post-operative pain equaled the pain of the fracture Ivan caused. This was because Jeff had to re-break the healing fracture site in order to set the bones in proper alignment before fastening them together with a surgical plate and screws. He offered her different types of oral pain meds to soothe her through the first few postoperative days, but she declined vehemently. She already overindulged in cocktails. She didn't want to add narcotics to the list.

She slept easily after her surgery, but awoke the next

morning with pain shooting down her arm and toward her back. After twelve hours in bed, she needed to stretch her limbs and move around. She needed fresh air and a change of scenery. She paired the sling on her arm with leggings and sneakers and started walking the streets of New York City. She walked most of the day. Her clavicle throbbed rhythmically, and she paced her steps to the sensation, like timing her feet to music. Her mind drifted. *I'll be recovered in a few days. Then what? Where do I go?* She wasn't ready to face her family. She didn't want to return to medicine.

The questions lingered as she made her way through Central Park, grabbed a quick lunch, and went to explore Fifth Avenue. Done with nature's beauty, Alexa wanted something man-made. She wandered in and out of designer stores, admiring shoes and bags and jackets. She was captivated by the construction and the details.

An idea emerged. *I can do this. I want to do this. My hands can create beauty . . . not bring death.* The word made her shudder. *No regrets*, she scolded. She didn't regret her actions, exactly, but she was conflicted over them. It would take time, and possibly a great deal of alcohol, to make a fresh start. She hailed a cab back to her hotel with the goal of finding a way to follow her new aspiration. A two-day Internet search and a few phone calls brought Alexa an answer.

She had a destination: Savannah, Georgia.

CHAPTER 37

Alexa packed up her things and headed to the Savannah College of Art and Design for two four-week introductory fashion design and sewing classes. She wanted to become like the designers she admired, sculpting beauty out of fabric. These short classes allowed open admissions, but she would have to apply with a portfolio in order to attend the full semester classes if she wanted to pursue things further.

She traveled light, and the transition was as simple as a one-way flight and a short-term lease agreement that were both settled the week before her first class started.

The sudden change of pace intimidated her. Returning to school was a bizarre concept. She would need new training if she wanted a different life. *I can stay Alexa DeBrow and have a new start*, she thought, happy with the compromise. She was moving forward without running away from the past.

She rented a converted old carriage house near downtown Savannah. Just one bedroom and one bathroom. It was small but private, and all she wanted. She hoped the historic setting with cobblestone alleyways and converted gas lanterns would be inspiring.

She recovered enough to set the sling aside for her first day of class. Her fifty-something feminine sophisticate instructor gathered information about the students and showed basic draping techniques. After class, Alexa stopped by to ask the teacher a few questions.

"Mrs. McAlister, would you mind giving me a list of materials that I need to purchase for working at home? The recommendations on the website were so vague, and I'm new to this." She blushed.

"Of course you are new, my dear." The instructor spoke with perfect enunciation and poise, her decorum equal to that of royalty. "This is a transition for you, no doubt. Was it a divorce that spurred the change? Or perhaps the children are school-aged now and you need a new hobby? I see it all of the time. It's not a problem. I hope you get whatever it is you are looking for out of my classes. I can email you a list of the necessities. It is a pleasure to have you with us."

Alexa invested in a brand name sewing machine, a serger machine, and a dress form. She acquired other accessories as time progressed. She learned darting and French seams, draping and bias cuts. She even got to know her classmates. Everyone was either younger or older than she was. Several were fresh out of high school or college dropouts of less than twenty. A handful of others were in their fifties, perhaps struggling through a mid-life crisis. She spent a few evenings at happy hours around town with a shy younger girl, Emily, and a fifty-something dynamic divorcee named Bernice. Neither woman knew Alexa's former life, and she was content maintaining her anonymity.

One night out with the girls, a drunken sailor recognized Alexa. She overheard him talking about her with his friends. The overgrown, barrel-chested man spoke with a brash tone.

"That woman over there." He pointed a stubby finger at Alexa's face, a mere ten feet away. "She's that man-killer doctor I saw on TV last year. Damned if they didn't let her out to walk the streets with the rest of us." His words cut like knives. The eyes at the sailor's table turned in her direction.

Anonymity was short-lived. Rage inside Alexa made her want to lash out at this man. Her fingers itched for a gun. She stood to approach him, but stopped herself. *Wow. I really want to hurt him.* Acts of violence from her past tried to weave their way into the present. It was sobering to re-face her nightmares. *No regrets. Don't forget.* She regained her composure and sat down. *I will not hurt this man. I cannot hurt anyone else.* Alexa wasn't sure she believed her own weak promises.

"Is everything okay, Lex?" Bernice questioned, reaching a hand out for Alexa's arm. Alexa eyed her friends with trepidation and watched the gang of sailors pile out the door into the street. The three women sat in uncomfortable silence.

Alexa took a deep breath and gathered her courage. *Time to face the ghosts.* "About a year ago, I was out with my girlfriends, like this. When I left, a man assaulted me on the way to my car. He tried to rape me; I fought back. I killed him." She paused. "I stood trial for his death, but I was released." There. She'd said it. Now they could judge her. She waited for a response.

Bernice spoke first.

"I was raped at sixteen, and once more at twenty-three. I only wish I'd had the nerve to kill just one of the bastards." She lifted her glass and took a long swig of the bourbon she was drinking.

Alexa sighed in relief and turned toward Emily. She was certain the timid and quirky girl would disagree with her actions. Emily crumpled in her chair and put a hand to her face to cover her teary eyes. She looked up at Alexa and nodded her head repeatedly. With her chin quivering, she let out a mousy response. "I'm glad he didn't hurt you."

Emily pushed her bony hand across the table and wrapped her childlike fingers around Alexa's. Emily didn't condemn her. *See. That wasn't so bad,* a boisterous voice inside her head claimed with pride.

"Next round's on me," Bernice offered, waving a hand at the waitress. The drinks accompanied more light-hearted story swapping, and it was early morning when the three parted ways.

Alexa slurped her liquor heartily following the moment of weakness until a warm alcohol blanket soothed the pain. She walked home in a drunken tizzy, stumbling into the trashcan on her way to the back door of the carriage house. The can toppled over with a bang. The sound was followed by another noise, the tiny mew of a small kitten curled up next to the building. Alexa could barely make out its shape in the shadows. She struggled not to see double. She reached down and scooped the little thing into her hands. It was so small and helpless — it needed saving. *Saving a life — what a nice concept.*

She took the tiny kitten inside. He was nothing but a small gray ball of fur. He spent his first night huddled up close to her in the bed. His body nestled along her healing clavicle, his little kitten paws stretched out over the scar on her neck. It was as if the animal knew where her injuries lay and was snuggling up next to them to soothe her. Indeed, the warm little body and kitten purrs were soothing. She drifted off to peaceful dreams.

Alexa spent most of her days at her sewing machine crafting new creations. When the four-week courses ended, she applied for a full term class in the fall. Each free moment, she spent painstakingly developing her own clothing collection. Using the techniques she learned in her classes, she created jackets, skirts, shift dresses, and an evening gown. Photographs of these pieces and a few additional sketches became the portfolio she submitted to Mrs. McAlister for acceptance into the fall courses.

As it turned out, the newly adopted kitten was partial to the operations of the sewing machine and sat at her side through most of her daily work. "You little gray ball of fluff, I'll call you Gray. My Gray muse. My Gray mystery. Gray for a world that lacks black or white," she whispered aloud. Her fingers nuzzled the soft fur on his chin as she wondered to herself. *Was I a martyr for something I believed in, or did I stumble into that world of loathsomeness by my want of revenge?* She buried her head into her furry friend's side. *Forever lost in my sea of gray.*

CHAPTER 38

She used her muse for inspiration when she couldn't find it on her own. His sleek physique inspired form-fitting attire, while his soft fur tempted Alexa to use fabrics that were equally pleasant to the touch. Her collection consisted of soft cashmere and wool blends, delicate silks, leathers, and lace she had purchased in France. She had created twenty-seven pieces thus far that were acceptable for daily wear. She wore an outfit from her collection to the coffee shop a few blocks away from her house. It was a black satin caplet over a billowing white silk top, and fitted, white-on-white textured pants. Alexa enjoyed a vanilla latte sitting alone at a table next to the window where she could admire the transparent reflection of her outfit. While sketching a design for a new white gown, someone approached her table.

"Lex."

Oh, God. That voice. Her head turned in the direction of the familiar sound and her eyes instantly locked with the man next to her. *Britt.* Her heart jumped into her throat. She recognized the longing in Britt's eyes, but there was something more that she couldn't quite place. *I'm dreaming. This is a dream.* She blinked hard twice. The image didn't change. Reality sank in, and for a second, the world stopped.

"I needed to find you, Lex. It's been so long since I've seen you — I just couldn't bear it anymore." His lips quivered as he spoke. *Britt!* Her heart sang out, afraid to speak or move in fear of bursting the miraculous moment. Her pulse quickened, and her breaths became erratic. He wrapped one hand around her entwined fingers on the table. Alexa's face contorted into an anguished pose, as the agony of his absence finally materialized in her expression. Hot tears streamed from her eyes. His grip tightened, and he moved closer to her.

Something about the way he moved caught her attention; it was unnatural. He glided toward her rather than shifting his body in his seat. Alexa furrowed her brow. *Something's wrong.* His fingers reached up and wiped the liquid from her face. She pulled away and looked for an answer to Britt's peculiar movements.

Britt is in a wheelchair. This is a nightmare. She blinked again. Alexa gasped when she didn't wake up. "Britt —" she lost her words trying to make sense of the situation.

"Lex, you look amazing." She got lost in his eyes once more. His eyes were wet, too, with tiny pools of saltwater forming in the corners. He pulled her closer, grasping her arms at the elbows. He was so close that she could feel his breath on her.

She spoiled the magic. "Britt, what happened?" They were the only words she could muster. She needed answers.

Britt's face turned cold and empty. His voice became apathetic. "I ran in Boston, Lex. I ran the marathon. My time was great, but there was a bomb. . . ." His words evaporated.

Alexa understood the emotions she saw in Britt's face. She recognized his loss and longing. *How cruel.* Something had changed Britt the way Jamar had changed her. "You were hurt?" She pressed.

He flinched at her words and his forehead wrinkled, revealing the lines of an older man. "I lost my leg, Lex." He scooted away from the table. Lonely, shapeless fabric hung down where Britt's left lower leg should be.

Somehow, I've pulled Britt into my nightmare. She fought to pull her stare away from the terrible thing and looked up to realize tears fell from his eyes, too. *Oh, God.* Her soul deflated. This was more than physically damaging. Britt was broken inside. He had been victimized. His personal freedom violated — like when Jamar attacked her. *There's something demoralizing about knowing someone has successfully destroyed your life. Oh, God. To be made so vulnerable — he must be very angry.*

She remembered her need for vindication and shuddered. She couldn't bear to talk about it any longer. She couldn't stand to see the pain on his face. "How did you find me, Britt?" She regained some composure by turning the conversation back to their reunion.

"Jeff Huggins. He texted me that he saw you in New York. He said he operated on you. I was worried." The old-man lines spread over his face once more. "I made him tell me where to find you, Lex. I needed to see you. I had to know you were okay." He tried to turn the worried look into a smile, but his face looked twisted and irregular. His expression reflected his broken demeanor. "What are you doing here, Lex?"

Unprepared for the question, she stammered, "I — I'm taking some classes at a fashion school here. I don't want to work in medicine, Britt."

A faint nod confirmed his understanding. "I'm done with politics," he offered.

No! Because of me? He didn't win the election. No. His dull eyes said it was more than that.

"I can't. Not like this, Lex." Hands motioned to the chair beneath him.

"Oh, Britt! There's so much to say. Can't we go somewhere more private?"

"I'm staying at little bed and breakfast nearby."

She cast her eyes around the café and shrank away from the strangers' glances. "Can we go there? I want to be alone with you." A lustful twinge arose in her bosom with the thought of being alone with Britt, and a pink hue settled on her cheeks. She watched him fumble to scoot away from the table and out the door.

He rolled awkwardly down the street. They moved together in silence. Never would Alexa have imagined seeing Britt again and saying so little to him. There was something very solemn about their stroll, as if they were departing a funeral. A few more tears slid down her face. She mourned Britt's missing leg and his lost pride.

He was so confident and boisterous, but now he hasn't any passion for life. His head hung lower than she remembered. *He seems apathetic. It's heart-wrenching.*

They waited until they were safe in Britt's room to say anything to one another. Alexa watched him struggle to move from the chair to the bed. She reached out a hand, but pulled it back, knowing the independent man she remembered wouldn't want help.

Once he was situated, she sat close to him and reached for whatever she could touch. Her hands caressed his thigh and shoulder.

Britt deflected her intimate touch. "Why did Jeff have to operate on you? Are you okay?" His eyes moved up and down her frame, looking for clues.

She lifted a hand to the scar on her neck. "It was nothing, really. A broken bone, that's all." She grew tense with emotion. Her face burned, and she cried in full force. "Oh, Britt. The things that have happened, the things I've done, you'd never believe. I can't imagine how to explain it to you." She'd never considered disclosing her actions, trying to justify it all to another human being. *It's incomprehensible.*

He leaned over and silenced her by pressing his lips against hers. She melted. Her heart settled on a feeling that was neither love nor lust. She desired a change — to alter the course of her life in a way that would once more coincide with Britt's. She couldn't risk losing him again. She needed to find a way to make this work.

Their kiss ended. He pressed his forehead to hers and looked into her eyes. "I never stopped loving you, Lex."

Her heart devoured his words, while her head toiled with the concern that he had returned to her only after having fallen from his pillar. He was a shell of the man he had been. Now a broken creature, he shared her wounded soul.

The change in Britt was more than she could swallow. She yearned for the man she once knew. Worse than her life falling apart was watching Britt's life shatter before her. "I've always loved you, Britt. I always will."

He kissed her again. Each time their lips met, it felt more natural. Resisting every urge coursing through her body, Alexa diverted her attention to Britt's missing leg. It was too early, too soon, but the doctor within her pushed forward. "I need to see your leg. Please."

The grimace he wore conveyed his dismay.

"Please," she repeated.

Reluctantly, he pulled up the leg of his left trouser and displayed his healing stump. *A below-the-knee amputation.* She crouched down and scrutinized the scar. *It's healing well.* Her glance returned to Britt's agitated face.

"We're getting you a prosthesis. You're ready for it. The scar is healed enough now —"

He stopped her with a finger to her lips. "Lex, not now. Please." He pulled her face close to his once more. This time she let herself fall into his embrace, and the two found themselves tangled in one another's arms. Lips, hands, and fingers moved across skin as they rediscovered one another. Alexa's body came to life, with tingles erupting throughout her sensitive places as Britt suckled her flesh until she moaned. Their reunion sparked a new energy within her. She longed to feel him inside her again — to be touched there. She gave into him instantly, and they made love on Britt's bed. It was different than before, in part because of Britt's new challenges. But there was more. Every touch felt more intense. He was more aggressive than she remembered. He had been so tender, his kisses so gentle.

Now, Britt moved with animal instinct. His lips pressed

hard with purpose, and his teeth nipped her skin impulsively. It was a confusing mix of pleasure and pain. Alexa felt herself behave more direct and forceful as well, her inhibitions unrestrained.

After ravaging one another, they collapsed on the bed. Britt drifted into sleep. Alexa lay there wondering. This intensity was so different than what they had known, but somehow it seemed right. *We share a core of pent-up aggression now. The hostility that allowed me to kill Jamar, the hostility that I embraced and allowed me to kill the others — Britt shares that with me now.*

Her lungs let out a long, deflated sigh. *How twisted we have become. He harbors the same internal hatred, but Britt never had his revenge.* Alexa contemplated their differences. *Maybe it's better if Britt never has the opportunity for vindication. Succumbing to that urge makes the dark inside even darker. I did things I never would have thought possible.*

She rolled over and admired Britt sleeping. He looked beautiful and peaceful and immaculate. As much as she loved him, and loved the opportunity to have him back in her life, she would easily forfeit their glorious reunion if it would make him whole again. She examined the rumpled sheets piled on the bed where Britt's leg should have been. *God, I would have given him up forever if I could have saved his leg. If I could save his soul from the darkness of revenge, I would give my own life.* Instead, he was broken just like her, and once more they understood each other.

Too tired to mourn another moment, she closed her weary eyes, and they both slept.

CHAPTER 39

Britt made the bed and breakfast his temporary residence, while Alexa stayed at her carriage house. They spent several hours together each day. She scheduled an appointment for him with a prosthetics specialist. In a stubborn moment of self-loathing, Britt canceled the appointment. He had no desire to recover.

She found his diffidence intolerable. Not only had Britt suffered physically and emotionally after the incident, his business began to suffer financially. It was another sore subject he didn't speak to her about, but she caught subtle details in his phone conversations before he slipped out of the room.

Determined to pluck him from his dismal state, she tricked him into attending a second appointment with the prosthetist. The clinic was on the path they strolled regularly, and she stopped him at the door. "It's time, Britt. You have to start walking again. It's ridiculous that you roll about in that chair all day like you're helpless, when you could be walking and running and independent again."

He winced as she broached the subject, wounded by her words. He never spoke of his leg. "You brought me here on purpose? Knowing I wasn't ready?" His expression contorted from a look of hurt to the wide-eyed fear of a child on his first day of school.

"You're here because you are ready," she pressed, grabbing the handles on the back of his chair and pushing him into the office before he had the opportunity to counter. "I push you because I love you."

In spite of his initial hostility, Britt tried multiple prosthetics, including sports models for running and more standard models for everyday life. Once upright, the muscles in his thighs flexed, and she recognized the chiseled physique of the athlete she remembered. When he was able to take a few steps on his own, she saw the life return to his eyes.

He spent hours each day in physical therapy while she put her time into her clothing collection. It took half of the fall semester for Alexa to design and finish thirty-seven separate pieces that she combined to form fifteen distinct outfits. Now, she wanted to show them to the world.

She began with a phone call to Jeff Huggins. His sister worked as a buyer for a national department store in New York City. She had worked with designers for years. Moreover, she knew several of them on a personal level. Jeff gladly gave Alexa his sister's contact information. He asked her about Britt. His tone seemed overly inquisitive, and Alexa tried her best to move past the subject politely.

"Thank you so much, Jeff, for bringing Britt and me back together. I never would have thought it was possible."

Jeff chuckled. "I figured you were still stuck on the guy.

I tried all my best moves on you, and you just shied away from me. I guess some guys have all the luck."

He was flirting with me the day of my surgery! She had suspected as much. "What can I say, Jeff? It was never really over for Britt and me. It never will be." It felt good to finally admit the truth after struggling a whole year to push him out of her heart.

"I understand, Lex. Best of luck to you both. I couldn't be happier for you."

Jeff's sister proved an invaluable resource. She had enough connections in the city that after four phone calls, Alexa had a meeting with a coordinator for a prominent winter fashion show featuring upcoming designers when a last minute spot opened up. Most of the designers were from New York fashion schools, and they were first-timers all around; however, the show was known for attracting a small crowd of celebutantes, well-known designers, and buyers alike.

Alexa became ecstatic as her new life materialized. She had only four weeks to prepare. The time lapsed in fast forward, consisting of romantic trysts coupled with Britt and moments of solitude toiling behind her sewing machine. She worked hard to keep some distance between them. She needed breaks of reality to maintain her senses and ease the transition. While she worked dutifully, Britt managed his company via teleconference. She kept her work out of his sight, waiting for a final reveal. He went solo to his physical therapy sessions working with the prosthesis, not allowing her to see his progress until she had to leave for New York, three days before the show.

She invited him to the carriage house to meet Gray. He eyed the cat sitting on the couch when he first entered the room. Britt set down the cane he had been using and walked across the room on his casual prosthetic without falter and scooped Gray into his arms.

"Oh, Britt! You walked perfectly! How could you keep your progress from me like that?"

He flashed a grin and gestured to the numerous garment bags lined up across the room. "I guess we all have our secrets, Lex."

She hadn't realized before the resemblance the garment bags bore with the body bag in the back of the van in Versailles. Her shoulders slumped. *Yes, Britt. We all have our secrets.* She licked her lips. *I have to tell him.* But she lost her courage and diverted her attention to the clothes inside the bags. "Will you help me load the bags into boxes for shipping?"

His eyes stayed on the cat. "My friend here and I don't get a peek first?"

She waved her finger in his face, interrupting his glance. "No, sir. Not until the show."

His fingers stroked Gray's ears. "All right. Looks like Gray and I are headed to New York."

While loading her boxes to be shipped, Alexa received a call on the relatively new cell phone tucked into her Fendi clutch. The screen read: number unavailable. It wasn't the Crackerjack phone, but she wondered if the unlisted number could be Mike. Both bewildered and excited, she answered.

"Hello?" Her voice quivered in trepidation. She heard heavy breathing on the other end of the receiver, but no response.

"Hello?" she repeated, this time with a sense of eagerness in her voice.

"Hey, Poppy girl."

"Mike!" she gasped. Her heart flooded with emotion as her eyes filled with tears.

"Had to check on you — make sure you were doing okay."

"Yes. Yes, Mike, I'm doing fine. How are you? Are you well?"

"I'm all right. They've kept me pretty busy since you left. Got me working with a couple of young'uns, still wet behind the ears. One of 'em didn't last too long. . . ." His voice trailed off.

Her mind veered back to the body bag, suspecting that was what Mike was referencing. Her insides shuddered momentarily, followed by instant relief that it wasn't her body in the bag.

"You have a new man in your life," he continued.

"No, Mike. He's not new — he just found his way back to me, that's all." The joy contained within each word was tremendous, and she knew Mike could appreciate it.

"Good. I needed to know that things went right for you, Poppy girl."

Alexa pictured Mike's watery eyes, his face warm and red with sentiment. It was the same emotional state he developed when he talked about Lily. *Lily.*

"Mike, how's Lily?" she had to ask. She knew he had a tendency to equate her with his daughter.

He paused before he answered. "I'm here to see her,

Poppy. I took some time away, and I'm in Atlanta to see Lily. She's gonna be married soon, and I just wanted a chance to see her before the wedding. I'm not sure how it's gonna go. . . ."

"It'll be fine, Mike. It will be joyful and sorrowful all at once. It will be emotional; you both will cry. But in the end, it will all be fine. Trust me. I'm someone who just had my lost love return. It's all I could have ever hoped for. She wants to see you. I'm glad you're going."

"Yeah, I'm glad, too. It's about time." He let out a long, drawn out sigh. Then his tone became serious. "I want you to know something, Poppy . . . the two sons-of-bitches that took your man's leg got what was coming to them. I guarantee you that. I know a couple of the guys who worked that case. . . . Anyway, I just thought you should know. That's all."

Alexa hesitated. *Yes. Of course he knows everything.* She rolled her eyes to herself and smiled into the receiver. *If only I could let Britt know, but that would mean telling him everything.* Her throat tightened. *We're so close now. Telling him could change that.*

"Thanks, Mike. I appreciate it. I'd like to see you again, when the time is right. You could meet Britt."

"I'd like that." His voice became anxious again.

"Mike, go see Lily. See Lily now. And thanks for calling."

"Bye, Poppy."

After dropping off her boxes, she headed to the airport to catch her evening flight. She left two days early to fit the models and finish any last minute details. Britt would arrive the day of the show. She used the flight to New York to hash out a plan to confess her European escapades to Britt in a manner he might find palatable.

After a half hour of reliving the horror of it all, she feared it was a worthless venture. *After Jamar, how could I discuss Castro or Ivan in a way he would ever find acceptable? How can I expect Britt to understand everything I've done? I'm not sure I understand it myself.* Distraught, she ordered a vodka soda. Although the vodka compelled her to keep the truth hidden from him forever, she resolved to tell him. No amount of planning in the world could make *those words* bearable.

CHAPTER 40

Her two-day prep time was a flurry of activity. Several models had been switched due to schedule changes and nothing fit properly on the replacements. She spent hours measuring and performing alterations. In spite of the incidents thrown her way, everything came together the afternoon before the show. Britt called from the airport as Alexa grabbed a cab back to her hotel. He came earlier than she expected.

She arrived in her room to find that Britt had beaten her there, and Gray was with him. They both sat sprawled out on the bed.

"Surprise, Babe." Britt's voice was calm and coy. He seethed confidence.

That's the Britt I remember. She bit her lip as she undressed him with her eyes. Her hands went to Gray, prolonging her desire for Britt. She plopped onto the bed and pressed her face into his belly. The cat purred loudly. *Mmm, so soothing.*

Britt reached his arms around her stomach and tugged

her toward him.

"I'm glad you're here," she whispered.

"I thought we could have a romantic dinner tonight to celebrate your big day."

"You mean celebrate *before* the big day? Isn't that a little supercilious?"

"No. Not in the least." He smiled his *come hither* smile that had won her over years ago. It was nice to see him playful and seductive. It had been too long. She had feared he lost that part of himself.

"When's dinner?" she asked, sliding her hand under his shirt.

He pulled her close, pressed his lips to hers, and then whispered into her ear, "After we shower."

She followed him to the shower, where they peeled each other's clothes off and slipped inside. There was a bench that allowed Britt to sit comfortably. Alexa straddled him and began moving up and down rhythmically. She shifted to turn backwards but Britt stopped her, clutching her toward his chest.

He pulled her forehead into his and vertical crevices formed between his eyes. "It has to be like this, forever, Lex. You can't just leave me like you did before. You said it was best for me, like you were trying to save me, or something. You have no idea. I needed you. I won't let you push me away again." He held her so tightly that his arms stifled her breath.

She nodded repeatedly until her whole body was moving up and down, her hips gyrating against his pelvis until they climaxed in unison. Afterward, Alexa dressed in a red silk, one-shoulder dress with an uneven hemline. The shoulder fabric covered the scar on her collarbone perfectly.

Britt put on a handsome gray suit. The two headed to dinner across the street at a pricey French restaurant for a five-course meal. Indulging in French champagne, Alexa was tipsy before they got to course four.

Everything was so familiar between them again. She felt whole and safe. She stared at the candlelight flickering on the table and reached out with both hands to feel its warmth. *Levende lys.* Just like their night together in Paris.

Britt stood and reached for something from his jacket pocket. It was a jewelry box. He fumbled with the lid. He was reciting something to her about love lost and love regained, but the candle warmth distracted her, and she pulled back her hands before she burned them. Beyond tipsy, she had slipped into a state of drunkenness and strained to make sense of his words. She cocked her head to one side.

Britt leaned toward her and opened the box. A beautiful gold and ruby necklace lay inside. She reached out with one hand to touch it. The other hand rubbed the scar on her neck nervously. *Oh, Britt you can't afford this.* Her mind swam as she tried to decipher what was happening.

"I'm so happy, Lex. I'm happy for you and me and — just happy. You're getting back on your feet. I'm getting back on mine. I just wanted to celebrate things right. I wanted to give you something beautiful." He took the necklace from the box and unfastened the clasp. "It's a choker, to cover your scar," he mumbled. "You're always touching it. I know you're self-conscious about it. I know what that's like." Britt motioned to his prosthesis. "Now when you reach up to touch it, you'll touch this necklace instead. Something beautiful and

323

happy." He smiled briefly.

Unsure how to respond, Alexa pulled up her hair and let him put the necklace on her neck. He sat down at the table and beamed at her. He was right. The necklace covered the scar perfectly. She loved it, but it made her uneasy. Covering her scars, her battle wounds, felt like covering up the truth. Her stomach churned. She was hiding so much from Britt. She had to tell him the truth *now*. She gulped down what was left of the champagne in her glass as the fourth course made it to the table. "Britt, the necklace is beautiful. I love it. I love you. Nothing is more important than having you back in my life." She paused and sank her teeth into her lip. "But I need to tell you what happened during the time we were apart."

He reached out a hand across the table. She touched it reluctantly.

"You're not going to like what you hear, Britt."

"Then don't tell me, Lex." His voice was suddenly stern.

"I have to."

"No, you don't. I don't want to know. You pushed me away before. Not this time." His eyes cut through her.

"Britt, you deserve to know the truth. So you can decide for yourself. . . ."

"I don't want us to be apart anymore." His hands clung to hers. "After Jamar, you wouldn't let me touch you. I tried to comfort you and you pulled away from me, like I was that monster. I stopped touching you because I was afraid of hurting you. I thought I had to leave you. But you're better now. We're better. Nothing can ruin this."

"I don't want us to be apart, either. But I want you to know the truth. You should hear it from me. If you can accept me for who I am —"

"What are you going to tell me? There was another guy? I don't care."

"No. There was no other guy."

"Did you commit a crime? I don't care." His gaze remained firm.

"Yes. Something like that." Her voice turned quiet.

"You killed someone?" His volume matched hers.

"Yes." She didn't shrink from his gaze. She would not be ashamed of her actions.

"Like you killed Jamar?" His face was blank, unreadable.

"Sort of."

"You killed someone who deserved it?"

She nodded. "Yes. I think so."

He blinked. "Then I don't care."

His reaction didn't make sense to her. She tried again. "You don't understand, Britt. I did it willingly. Not in self-defense. I willingly chose to take their lives."

"Their lives?"

"Yes. There were two of them. I killed two men."

His face remained blank.

"Why did you do it, Lex?"

"They were dangerous men. They killed innocent people." She couldn't believe she wasn't crying.

"Well, Lex. It sounds to me like you did the right thing." He took a long sip from his glass of wine. "Just like killing Jamar was the right thing. I understand that now." He finished off the rest of his wine and set down the empty glass firmly enough to jostle the table. "If I could have killed the bastards in Boston who set off those bombs, I would have done it."

His words shocked her. *Oh God, he is broken like me.* Alexa took a deep breath and massaged his hands with her fingers until his grasp softened. "Don't say that, Britt. Please. It's not as easy as you think. I don't know what's right anymore. I know that I did it. But I wouldn't say that I'm proud of it. Killing someone is not something to be proud of. If you can accept the things I've done, let's move on. Okay?"

"I can accept it." His face contorted like a sulking child, and resentment hung on his brow. She couldn't look at him like that. She lowered her glance and talked into the table.

"The bombers did pay, Britt. I was assured that. They paid, and you never had to dirty your hands in the matter. Please, take comfort in that. Okay?"

When she looked back at him, the lines on his forehead had relaxed. "Okay." A glimmer of warmth returned to his eye. "Do you really like the necklace?"

"Of course. It's beautiful!" She changed her tone to help change the subject.

"Then don't think of those horrible things when you wear it. Don't think of your scars and what happened. Think of me."

Just like with the nightmares, Britt was giving her a strategy to try to overcome the pain of what had happened. He was her pillar of strength once more.

"Then I'll wear it every day." She smiled, and so did he.

CHAPTER 41

The rest of the dinner was a romantic blur that ended at the hotel room with another moment of passion before Alexa fell asleep entwined in Britt's arms. Her slumber was interrupted by the sound of her early morning alarm. It was the day of her runway show, and she wanted plenty of time to prepare.

She stood in front of an oversized full-length mirror in the nineteen-forties Hollywood-style hotel suite and admired her outfit. She had opted for a white silk dress of her own design. The one-shoulder neckline concealed the scar on her clavicle, and she complemented the dress with the ruby red choker Britt had given her and a pair of sky-high gold, strappy sandals.

Alexa pressed her lips to her sleeping Britt and patted Gray on the head, and then grabbed a large red leather satchel full of supplies and a cup of coffee before heading out of the door. Although still dark outside, she didn't have to wait long for a taxi. With minimal traffic, she made it to the museum where the show would be held long before the majority of the designers and earlier than any of her models. She spent her time steaming garments and attacking them one by one with a lint roller.

The building slowly filled with people, and Alexa felt a hustle in the air around her. A middle-aged woman appeared in the masses, shouting Alexa's name.

"Miss DeBrow? Miss Alexa DeBrow?"

Alexa turned toward the sound.

"Yes. I'm Alexa DeBrow."

The woman pushed a clipboard into Alexa's hands. "I'll need you to sign for your flowers, Miss."

Alexa's initial thought was Britt, but when she eyed the bouquet interspersed with red poppies, she knew otherwise. She grasped the flowers and searched expectantly for the card. There it was.

Gonna walk my daughter down the aisle. I wanted you to know.

Warmth spread across her face as she read Mike's news. She put her face against the bouquet and inhaled the floral scent. *Thanks, Mike.*

Alexa set the flowers aside as her first model arrived and she directed her to the makeup artist. The rest of the morning consisted of hair and makeup adjustments and some last-minute alterations.

The announcer called her name, and her models began lining up. She was second to last of twelve designers. Alexa peeked out from behind curtain and made eye contact with Britt. Finally, her turn. She stepped out to make a brief introduction. "Hi, I'm Alexa DeBrow."

Her words immediately brought forth murmurs from the

crowd. She continued despite their whispers. "The title of my collection is Metamorphosis. It reflects my experiences over the past two years, serving as visual allegory of my struggles and fears, as well as the sense of clarity and purity I wish to gain. Enjoy!"

Members of the crowd were still exchanging glances with one another when Alexa turned and walked back behind the curtain. *They haven't forgotten. My name engenders distrust and fear in the minds of strangers. I could have chosen a different name. Charlie offered me an out.* She could have embraced fugue state and gained her indemnity; instead, she chose to resolve her past. *I'll make them forget. I'll replace that memory with something else, something beautiful. Just like Britt did with my scar and the necklace.*

She held her breath as the first model stepped onto the runway. She was a tall thin blonde with layers of structured black fabric wrapped around her body like armor. Selective cutaway elements revealed bare skin on the upper thigh and clavicle, the slashes in the fabric simulating Alexa's battle wounds. Her model's red lips were painted into pressed lines with upturned corners, like smiles on dolls; they bore the look of complacency.

Another blonde decked out in similar structured black armor followed this model. With each tramp down the catwalk, the color palate slowly turned to charcoal gray with more relaxed hemlines. One model wore a gray suit with a double cold shoulder, revealing bare skin on both sides. Alexa picked this tone of gray to match the fur of her Gray muse.

In time, both the color and the style became lighter, with the last couple of pieces being pure white. A two-piece, tiered white skirt and blouse floated down the runway. The upper tiers were more fitted, while the lower layers flowed easily. Her final piece was an extravagant white gown with a fitted torso and heavily layered skirt that combined different textures and fabrics. A high, wide slit cut through the center of the skirt and a medium-length train followed the model down the runway. Her lips were bright red, and she was the only model whose smile was genuine.

Alexa had made the dress to resemble an emerging butterfly. The upper half of the dress was a tightly wound cocoon, and the lower half spread like wings taking flight. Beautiful and opulent, it could be a wedding gown. It was the epitome of her Metamorphosis.

A chill cut through her core when she watched the dress move. She wanted to wrap herself in the white fabric until its purity rubbed off on her. With each piece, she tried to physically separate from the darkness within her and move to a state of virtue and truth. It was a complicated transition, and she felt lost somewhere in between. The dark armored pieces had been easier to construct. Their subject matter felt more familiar. The pieces designed to represent purity were more difficult; their creation seemed unlikely at times.

Alexa followed her final model down the runway and waited for the audience's scrutiny to present itself. Their applause was haphazard at first, with only a few members electing to participate. In time, however, the applause grew, and at least a dozen audience members rose to their feet. It was all Alexa could have hoped for.

She exited the runway and joined Britt, and they watched the final show together. It was an Asian twenty-something man with a very colorful collection.

A bony little finger tapped Alexa firmly on the shoulder. She turned to face the culprit. A middle-aged, black-haired woman with a long nose and close set eyes that gave her a certain haughtiness stood beside them.

"Hello, Miss DeBrow. I'm Marcia Douglas. I'm a buyer for a couple of department stores here in town. I'm interested in some of your pieces, if you're thinking of going commercial. Your clothes have an edginess to them that I find appealing, and the whole black and white thing is very marketable. That one at the end, however . . . you really should have gone with the over-the-top wedding gown approach. You know, given her a bouquet,. or a veil, or something. Well, now I'm just rambling. What do you think?"

Alexa was too flustered to respond. The audience's murmuring had left her guarded, and she had braced herself for verbal backlash and abuse, not compliments. The terms "marketable" and "commercial" were incomprehensible. Her jaw hung open slightly.

"Lex?" Britt's hand reached for her shoulder.

She turned to him. "Yes?"

"Lex, do you understand what she's asking you?"

Alexa turned to the black-haired lady. "Yes. I say yes." Her head bobbed up and down as she nodded to herself. "I would like to sell whatever you want to buy."

"All right, Miss DeBrow. Here's my card. I'll get your phone number, and I'll give you a call later this week to sort out the details. We may need a few more pieces than just those, so I suggest you keep working. I'll give you a rough idea of what we're looking for over the phone. Do you have a label?"

The nasal quality in her voice became more prominent when she asked a question, and Alexa found herself fixated by it. "Pardon?" she stuttered.

"Your label, your brand, does it have a *name*?"

A name? Like Elizabeth Fuguay or Alexa DeBrow? It always comes down to a name. After all this wedding gown talk, the name "Mrs. Britt Anderson" sounds pretty good to me.

"Yes. I call it *Levende Lys*," Alexa stated.

"I see. You'll have to include the name in an email if I'm going to get the spelling right. Well, Miss DeBrow, congratulations to you. You were my only pick today, which makes you very fortunate. I'll talk to you later this week. Are you from the city?"

Alexa blushed. "No. I've been staying in Savannah lately. I've moved around some. . ." She became distracted thinking of the places she'd been.

"I see. All right, have a safe trip back, then. Enjoy the rest of your time in New York. It is an *amazing* place. Good meeting you, Miss DeBrow." She smiled and gave a little wave as she hustled away.

Britt turned to Alexa, his face beaming. "This is great, Lex. I'm so impressed by the way everything is coming together for you. This is what you do now: Alexa DeBrow, designer. Absolutely amazing!"

She smiled back at him half-heartedly. "Yes, Britt. This is what I do, *for now.*"

"Relax, Babe. You're really great. If this is what you want, you'll be fabulous."

"This is what I do, *for now,*" she repeated. Nothing in her future seemed clear. "*For now* is different than forever. I don't know what forever holds. I thought I would be a doctor forever. Things change, Britt. I can't pretend this will last any longer than anything else has."

"We'll last forever, Lex. I promise." He smiled his characteristically seductive smile and squeezed her hand.

She melted into the warmth of his touch. *God, I hope so.*

The last runway show had ended, and a moderately noteworthy local designer gave a finale speech. Confetti erupted from containers in the ceiling. Loud popping sounds echoed in the room. Alexa instantly dropped her head and shielded herself with her arms, fearing a bomb detonated. A quick glance at Britt showed him also cowering. He lost his balance, his prosthesis faltered, and he crumpled to the floor.

Alexa knelt to the ground and grabbed Britt's torso in attempt to ease his fall. His frame was a little lighter after the amputation, and she found his weight more manageable. With their combined efforts, he was quickly upright on his prosthesis again.

It wasn't a bomb, or an explosion. The thunderclap sound was the confetti erupting from the containers that held it. When she looked into Britt's pale, frightened face, her eyes overflowed with tears. Their arms wrapped around one another in a unifying embrace. She felt his heart pounding against her chest haphazardly. *Oh, God. He thought they were bombs, too.* Her heart sank. They were equally broken and clung to one another as if holding onto life itself.

She tumbled out of the long dark tunnel.
And, as it turns out, at the end of that
hellish tunnel, there was a light.

For Alexa DeBrow, it was a candlelight.

Levende Lys

ABOUT THE AUTHOR

M.C. Adams is a practicing physician on the gulf coast of Florida. She spends her time battling her left brain, right brain tendencies. Medicine feeds her logical and analytical prowess, while writing, painting, and design projects fuel her creative desires. She also makes traveling with her husband a top priority, favoring beautiful places with rich history and high educational value. *Fugue State* is her first published novel, with a second piece in the works for your reading pleasure. She loves her readers' feedback! Please check out her website mcadamsauthor.wix.com/authorpage to leave comments. Also, feel free to join the mailing list at this link eepurl.com/boaY7X for an update on her next novel.

Made in the USA
San Bernardino, CA
16 October 2015